A STAR CALLED LUCKY

SEQUEL TO THE INTERNATIONAL BESTSELLER *LUCKY EVERYDAY*

BAPSY JAIN

is a best-selling author, educator and entrepreneur, noted for the international success of her debut novel, *Lucky Everyday*.

www.astarcalledlucky.com

www.astarcalledlucky.com

A Star Called Lucky

BAPSY JAIN

www.astarcalledlucky.com

Published by VOOK and MZI Global®

Vook Inc., Register office a Delaware corporation:
151 West 25th Street 6thFl, New York, NY
MZI Global® (DBA) Register office in New York, NY 55 west 14 Street #14D,
New York, NY 10011
Copyright © Bapsy Jain 2013 (1-1048653042)

Author and Publisher's Disclaimer

This is a work of fiction. Names, characters, places, organizations and agencies, and incidents
are either the product of the author's imagination or are used fictitiously, and any resemblance to
actual persons, living or dead, organizations and agencies, business establishments, events or
locales is entirely coincidental.

A LIBRARY OF CONGRESS CATALOGING IN PUBLICATION DATA
Jain, Bapsy
A Star Called Lucky
Sequel to the International Bestseller Lucky Everyday
PCN 2014945672
ISBN 9781632954244

Printed in the United States of America

ISBN 978-1632958075

Disclaimer

This is a work of fiction. Names, characters, places, organizations and agencies, and incidents
are either the product of the author's imagination or are used fictitiously, and any resemblance to
actual persons, living or dead, organizations and agencies, business establishments, events, or
locales is entirely coincidental.

DEDICATED
TO PEACE
AND
COMPASSION
AND OUR
COLLECTIVE
QUEST TO
REFLECT
THE BEST
IN HUMAN
NATURE

www.astarcalledlucky.com

www.astarcalledlucky.com

ACKNOWLEDGMENTS

Special love to my late parents Dina and Manek Medhora and my husband, Nitish, sons, Sammy and Gaurav, and my dear father-in-law, Dr Shashi, and mother-in-law, Neera Jain.

My sister, Ava Suntoke, and Priya Phadnis, who have worked patiently on editing this novel. All my family and friends who have encouraged me through my many years of writing.

My publisher and marketing team led by Ms Mira Zikovich.

And my sincere thanks to all of you who have traveled with me on this enjoyable journey, and the members of the S P Jain Global School of Management.

www.astarcalledlucky.com

www.astarcalledlucky.com

TABLE OF CONTENTS

www.astarcalledlucky.com

THE PLAYERS

The Realist

Vaala, Finland. September 16th, 1980. 6 a.m. The first heavy snow blanketed the woods, smothering shrubs and bending branches on the evergreens, turning the ground into a pillow-soft, featureless blur. It fell hard all night, just as the weatherman predicted, and it was still showering in light little balls of hard powder at dawn. The boy tumbled out of bed at the creak of the door of the old, cast iron Jøtul stove. In the unseen dark downstairs, his father stuffed a log into the coals, the door creaked and closed, and the latch snapped shut. The little loft grew hazy with wood smoke. The boy hurriedly pulled on his long johns and wool trousers, a flannel shirt, scarf, parka, gloves, and knit cap and laced up his boots. His father waited silently by the front door, a rifle cradled in his left arm. With his other hand, he held out a rifle to the boy. The boy silently took it and rubbed the long, smooth barrel with his gloved hand. The metal gleamed dully in the dim light. The rifle had been lovingly cleaned the night before, swabbed, oiled and inspected. The scope mounted and dialed in. The boy checked the magazine as he had been taught and secured the safety, then slung the gun over his shoulder and followed his father into the half-light of dawn. Outside, they trod a path so familiar they could walk it without a misstep, even under a six-inch blanket of snow. The path led into the woods, climbing a steep rise and then following a curving ridge line until it ended abruptly at the bluff overlooking a creek and a meadow and the endless wilds of Finland that ran in unbroken undulations from Vaala, on Lake Oulujarvi, until far beyond the Arctic Circle. The trees grew smaller and smaller as one travelled north, until there was just stunted, windswept brush and shrub, and finally just tundra. Along the way, they munched on butter sandwiches and salted boiled eggs. At the top of the ridge they grew quiet, moving stealthily. They crawled the final meters to the lip of the bluff. The boy tried to still his heartbeat and his breath, breathing through his mouth and down into the snow so that he would not raise a telltale cloud of steam.

They waited. A half hour passed and then the deer appeared on the far side of the clearing. The does came first, hesitant and alert, ears twitching. When they had moved halfway across the open space, the buck appeared—a magnificent, muscular beast with a twelve-point rack of a crown.

No words passed between father and son. All that needed to be said had been said in the lazy and long summer evenings when they lay in the lush grass amid clouds of mosquitoes and the father—once a national biathlon champion—drilled the boy on sighting, breathing, focusing on the target, and anticipating the recoil as the boy gently nudged the trigger home.

"You must shoot to kill," he said at last. "A clean shot causes no pain."

But it was one thing to shatter bottles at 250 meters—it was another to bring down his first trophy buck. The boy's hands trembled with cold and excitement. A cough welled up in his throat, a tickle no amount of will could force down. It was going to burst. In his mind, the boy saw the great deer cross the clearing in a single, blurry bound. It would disappear into the wood and that would be that. An instant before the cough his father said, in a voice barely audible, "Steady," but it was too late. The finger clenched of its own volition, the shot cracked, the boy coughed, and the buck bolted into the wood, leaving behind a trail of bright red blood in the snow. The does, too, vanished.

2

The father stood up and surveyed the scene. "He's throat shot," he said. "You'll have to track him down and finish the job."

"But it's cold," the boy said.

"And that buck suffers because of you."

"He'll die soon."

"Maybe, maybe not. Either way, you can't leave him in pain. You have to finish the job."

The boy looked around. It was ten degrees below zero centigrade, and the snow, like the temperature, was falling fast. "Go on," the father said. "It's your penance for rushing the shot. If you're going to shoot something, take it down with one bullet. And if you suffer, good. A lesson learned with a little pain ever after will remain. Now go on. Track him down. It won't be hard with all that blood. Kill him proper, then pack him home." The father turned and trudged back down the trail toward the cabin, the fire, and a hot breakfast.

The boy would track the bleeding buck, eventually walking in knee-deep snow until his feet were blue from cold. Three times he unlimbered his rifle only to have the buck rise and stagger off deeper into the wood. How much blood could one creature spill and live? How much cold could one boy endure? The hunt became a test of wills. It was afternoon when the boy found the buck collapsed and panting, exhausted in a mound of bloody snow. It looked at the boy with something like relief, or contempt, he couldn't tell. The boy sighted down the scope. The hole through the neck was so small, yet the buck was soaked in frozen blood all the way down to his front hooves. And as the boy aimed, the buck made a sound the boy would never forget—a short bark-like noise, followed by a high-pitched scream.

He gutted the buck in darkness. The blood froze to his hands. He wrapped the carcass in a sheet of canvas and bound it tightly with a long rope, leaving two long loops hanging from each end. These he took up like a harness, and walking until late evening, the boy dragged the deer home.

THE MASTER PLANNER

Seattle. March 4, 1973. 10:14 a.m. It wasn't that the Kingdome was ugly (for it certainly was ugly), but for the boy from Kalispell, Montana, it was the biggest building he had ever seen, much less walked around inside. He had seen it before on television, but television could not capture the enormity—the machine-generated breeze, the echoing roar of the crowd, the cavernous emptiness he felt inside, and now he stood on the field, a little bit behind where second base ought to have been, and gazed up at the lighting console and the catwalk that marked the very center of the gray, concrete dome. He had been three days in Seattle, escorted by his step father to all the proper sights—the Pacific Science Center, the University of Washington, the Burke Museum, and the Woodland Park Zoo; they'd even dined at the Space Needle, but the real reason for his coming had been this, not a baseball game, not the crowded stadium, but the National Science Fair, and at stake was a wealth of scholarships and internship opportunities at places like Berkeley and Stanford and Harvard and MIT, and for a boy growing up in a poor family and a rodeo town, there was a lot on the line. That, and he had put his whole heart into the trip.

His stepfather, a strapping, die-hard cowboy wannabe in jeans, a checkered shirt, a white Stetson hat, and black, alligator skin, Tony Lama boots, had never been proud of his smaller stepson—the boy who favored his mother's slight build and fair complexion. There was an older stepbrother playing linebacker at Idaho, and two younger half-brothers already taller and heavier than this boy, but what he lacked in brawn he had made up for in brain—even the father had to admit this—and so, reluctantly, on the boy's mother's insistence, the father drove the boy to Seattle, with all the fragile and necessary equipment loaded into the back of a 1967 Ford F-150 pickup. They had looked so shabby on arrival that the parking lot attendants first directed them to the rear of the building, the place where the hired help clocked in. But no, the boy insisted, he was here by invitation, the winner of the Montana State Science Fair.

From the front entry, the boy watched the others arrive, RVs and panel vans and delivery vehicles, even a Mayflower truck—the equipment, delicate and expensive, attended to by hoards of friends and relatives. But he was neither jealous nor overawed by their displays. He had seen homemade motherboards and distillation towers, wind turbines and plastic models of chromosomes. It was nothing to him, and he had laid his plans with exacting precision. He was going to steal the show. He was not just going to win—he was going to RULE.

It was an exciting time to be a scientist. There was so much happening on so many fronts. The public was enthralled with Star Trek and the "final frontiers" of technology. His stepfather, who chewed tobacco, spat a long, greasy brown arc onto the pavement and said, "A waste of money, if you ask me. If you want to piss money away, get into politics. Politics is where it's at, boy. Anybody who argues like you, ought to make a killing at it. Let everybody else do the work, then you take the credit."

But the boy wasn't listening. He was recounting the details in his mind. He ran down the list. It was like playing chess blindfolded. You just had to remember the details—and it was all about control. That's the scientific method: the controlled environment. And the boy's work wasn't just good—it was groundbreaking. So good, in fact, that he shivered with excitement to think of the commercial potential. He would make a lot of money. He would prove his stepfather wrong.

For two years, the boy labored on experiments patterned after the work of Barbara McClintock, a rising star in the obscure field of cytogenetics—the structure and function of cells, especially chromosomes. It was heady work for most teens, but for this boy, it wasn't all that far-fetched.

McClintock spent years studying the mutation and genetic modification of corn. She had been particularly successful identifying snippets of DNA called transposons, which could be induced to break free and relocate on the chromosome, thus producing mutation. Of particular importance had been her observation that various types of stress could induce the phenomenon, so that, in a sense, species would mutate in response to their environment. The genetic triggers to the mutation were specific individual genes, which she labeled transposons.

The boy's work was relatively simple. Contamination and infection were natural sources of stress. His observation, however, his argument, was that species response to stress (microbial invasion) was not entirely random, but rather, was *intuitive* to or even *guided by* the genetics of the invading organism. Thus, corn exposed to fungus could selectively mutate (and breed) to be resistant to that fungus—a process that suggested an innate intelligence to genetics that went far beyond Darwinian random mutation. To prove his point, he had constructed a sterile, self-contained display into which he had inserted seed and fungus, a display that featured not only the carefully controlled environment but a microscope connected to an overhead projector and display monitor on which could be seen the corn, the chromosomes, and the fungus. The commercial potential was simple: if a field was infected, it was not necessary to breed entirely new seed crops, which would be resistant to the fungus. All that was required was to expose any seed to the relevant *transposon* and the seed would mutate on its own. The process would save manufacturers tens of millions of dollars and years of time. It would save farmers billions, not to mention (in cases of severe infestations), their farms.

The boy and his stepfather turned together and walked into the building and across the cavernous hall to the table and the display and the overhead projector—and there they stopped. The corn kernels—the showcase of the boy's display—glowed a dull, infected pink. The boy stared at the display. It was ruined. All of it. *Fusarium moniliforme*. He knew all thirteen common corn fungi by sight. But how? A suspicion dawned. He checked the display until he found the point of attack. Someone—somewhere—somehow—had punctured the seals with a syringe and injected a contaminant. The work was sabotaged. It did not matter that the infection was not the one the seeds had been immunized against. The viewers and the judges would see only the moldy seed of a failed experiment.

For a long time, the boy stared at the roof of the Kingdome. Eventually, his stepfather laid a hand across the boy's shoulder and said, "Politics, boy. That's where the money is. Let's go home."

They left the ruined display and the equipment behind. Someone would throw it out. The boy would not win the coveted scholarship. He would not go to Berkeley or Stanford or Harvard or MIT. He would not be moved when he learned that the winner was a boy from California with a chintzy display about an influenza virus.

They drove all night to reach Kalispell. In the morning, the boy tore up his college applications and wrote new ones. In his personal statement he wrote: *It has always been my ambition to be a leader of men.* He would view his acceptance to Georgetown with ambivalence. He found only small comfort when, six months later, he attended a science fair where he was able to shake hands with his hero, Barbara McClintock. And on March 26th of the year 2000, when the Kingdome was demolished, the boy, now a full-grown man, paid a lot of money to watch from the observation deck at the Space Needle. He did not join the crowd in cheering. When the blast was over, the dome lay in ruins; he took the elevator down and went to his hotel room alone.

THE OUTSIDER

London, England. August 16, 2009. 6:33 PM. Chris Redfield (the protagonist of the first *Resident Evil* video game) takes a shotgun and blows off the head of a deranged farmer advancing on him with a pitchfork. Chris feels nothing. He is on a mission to rescue the Alpha team. They have been kidnapped by the followers of Los Illuminados, the "enlightened" ones who control the world by means of a mind-controlling parasitic infection. Inside the mansion halls, a mob advances on Chris, and he fires again and again and again. The zombies fall in droves. Chris is on a roll, but time is running out. If Chris cannot rescue them, they will all die, as they are infected with the disease.

The teenage girl is looking over Chris's shoulder. Figuratively speaking. She is also stabbing at the controls that make Chris aim, shoot, and dodge. The girl is obsessed with this.

A computer junkie? She hunches her shoulders and draws closer to the screen.

Behind her, the door opens and a man's voice calls out something muffled and indistinct. He has dropped his briefcase in the hall and thrown his sport coat over the back of a chair, same as always. The girl knows, without looking, that her father will walk into the den and mix a Tom Collins, then call upstairs for his wife, her mother. But before he does, he glances into the living room and says, "Still at that nonsense, are ya? Won't ya give it a rest?"

It's called Resident Evil, she thinks. *Resident. Evil.*

The father stomps off to the bar. A minute later, he calls up the stairs and the mother shouts something down from the sanctity of her bedroom.

Her bedroom—he has his own, now, an arrangement that suits neither of them. The mother wants the father out of their house and the father wants the mother to keep her damn mouth shut and count her blessings. Their list of complaints is as endless as the computer-generated, zombie-like villagers methodically stalking Chris. The father may be called before the court on a tax evasion charge. And the banking regulators are rumbling again over on Downing Street. The mother may have hit someone speeding. There was dent in the grille on the Bentley and bloodstains. They have garaged the car and called for a sleazy Estonian car detailer they know. It is going to cost them a small fortune. Everything costs them a small fortune. The cars, the boats, the home, the time-shares, the clothes, the lawyers, the impending divorce.

The girl is distracted. Chris is almost crushed by a boulder. She mouths the words in sync with the father: "So, I see ya been lolling about in your nightie. Too much trouble to wait for dinner?"

8

There is a chink of glass hitting the marble countertop hard. There will be another drink. And another. And another. The exchange will grow nastier until the father goes upstairs and opens his bedroom door and the mother follows, shouting. What happens then is anybody's guess.

The girl is leaning so close to the monitor that her face almost touches the screen. If it were cold, she would fog it with her breath. Her fingers fly over the controls as if of their own accord. Chris has broken down the door. She has never been to this place. Chris stalks down the hallway toward the chamber where they are chained. He fires the shotgun nonstop. The girl has never felt more alive. She is one with the machine. She is one with the machine. She is one with the machine. Chris has the Alpha team. The whole house can burn for all the girl cares. Chris has the Alpha team. She has won with the machine.

THE DETACHED

Mumbai, India. November 3, 2012. 11:00 p.m. The doctor is gently sewing up a boy's cheek when he asks the nurse to go out of the examination room and see what all the commotion is outside. The doctor cannot be distracted from his patient—the boy fell through a window and his face is cut. But the needlework is almost done. He speaks soothingly to the boy as he sews, in spite of the distraction. The nurse steps away, leaving behind the gauze with which she has been staunching the flow of blood. She crosses the room in two quick strides.

A woman has arrived at the clinic, bypassing the line in the corridor and pushing past the old guard whose presence is intended to keep some semblance of order. The woman is nineteen, maybe, or twenty. She is leading a little line of small ones, a boy of four or five, a girl, and another, a shy one and of indeterminate sex hiding behind the older boy. Besides leading the children, she is supporting a man. The man is drenched in sweat, his chest heaving. He is only semi-conscious.

9

The nurse relieves the woman of the man. The man is dark skinned, a middle-class worker of some sort, dressed in gray western slacks with an open white cotton shirt. He is, perhaps, twenty-six or twenty-seven—no more. He should be the picture of health at his age, but his eyes are glassy, his face almost black with fever. His breath comes in short, pulse-like gasps that neither draw in air nor expel fluid. The nurse takes the man and half-drags him to the examination room and lays him on the bed.

The boy, frightened, sits up. The doctor, in one smooth stroke, follows the boy with his needle and completes the final stitch. He is good. Very good. He cuts the thread, pats the boy on the head, and turns to see the patient. He does not have to ask. The look on the nurse's face says more than the nurse's stammered, "Another one."

"This makes five this week," the doctor says. His tone is matter-of-fact. He sighs. "Fetch me some ice and we'll see what we can do." A new strain of Influenza. No hospital in the world can save this man. In another place, the doctor would roll the man over onto his side and try to drain the heavy green fluid from the man's lungs, but it is too viscous—too sticky to flow. The man is suffocating. It would not even help to insert a tube into the lungs. They've tried that, too, but the thick fluid won't be drawn out. The doctor looks at the wife. He knows that if he does not save her husband, she will become a widow doomed to a life of hell on earth, along with her children. His eyes brim with tears. He has been at the clinic since nine in the morning. With any luck, he will make it to bed by two or three. While the nurse is gone, he reaches inside his shirt and produces a tiny vial carried on a black thread. The vial is almost empty. It is light in his palm. He pries loose the stopper and cradles the man's head in his arms, and shielded from sight, tips some small bits onto the man's bloated tongue followed with a little water. "Try to swallow," he whispers. Then he recites a Buddhist mantra to ensure the mushroom bits administered will heal.

The man, delirious, rasps a sound that may or may not be a reply.

"Just try," the doctor says. He strokes the man's wet hair. "Just try."

THE CONFLICTED

Tollygunj Golf Club, Calcutta, India. January, 1992. Soli and Hutoxi are across the lawn sitting at a table under a tipping green awning sipping tea with Alec and Susan. Their laughter carries to the three children who peek at them through a small gap in the hedge surrounding the tennis club. There are twenty tables clustered on the south end of the courts, and a handful of servants in cream-colored suits with wide red sashes and red turbans and ridiculous, shiny green pointy-toed shoes, to wait on them. The children's scheme has been meticulously planned and rehearsed twice over the preceding weekends. When the order for lunch has been placed, they will have exactly nineteen minutes. Four for the drinks, five more for the salads, and then, ten minutes later (on the button), lunch will be served. The children will not be sought after or missed until their sandwiches arrive. By then, they will have returned—older, wiser, and having settled a dispute that has tormented them all summer. No one will know. There is even a small wager: Amay's prized collection of rare marbles versus the antique French cameo necklace with the profile of Marie Antoinette (that Susan bought from a reliable antique dealer in Prague and gave to Lucky for her most recent birthday). The third child is not invested in the argument. He is Amay's distant cousin, Varun, who is from Mumbai and has been left with Amay's family for a few weeks while his father takes his mother to London to seek treatment for an obscure medical complaint. Varun is younger than Lucky and Amay, a nervous child, a crybaby, and a despised tagalong. He has been alternately threatened and bribed until his silence and complicity are assured. Varun has no interest in the outcome of the bet other than proving his courage to his cousin and his cousin's friend. They have promised to quit tormenting him if he serves his task successfully. His job is to watch the door and make certain that no one ventures down the hall while Lucky and Amay inspect something strange and western—otherworldly, really—called a "sauna." Here, it is rumored, Lucky's hippopotamus-like spinster-aunt is supposed to lounge naked in a large oven, purportedly to help her shed weight. Lucky swears it is true. Amay swears Alec and Susan are pulling Lucky's leg.

The head waiter bends over the table, listening intently to the order even though all four have eaten the same lunch every Sunday for the past six months. With a glare and a warning finger, Lucky reminds Varun to stay put *no matter what.* She and Amay dart for the door. They have been gone only a few minutes. It seems like no time at all. When they return, they know right away that something is wrong. A crowd of adults stands by the gap in the hedge. Beyond them, two waiters run, their backs to Lucky and Amay. One of them carries a small bundle in his arms. On his right side, two thin legs flop like a gull's broken wing. On his left side, cradled like a football, is Varun's head. From the hedge comes a loud thwack and a shout, more of anger and relief than triumph. A moment later, a groundskeeper swings the body of a cobra over his head and cracks it again, like a whip. The snake is dead, but so, too, will be the boy. Over and over again, Soli and Hutoxi ask, "What were you thinking, leaving your little friend like that?" Lucky and Amay could only stare at the pools their tears made on the floor. There was no good answer and no excuse. It was an episode Lucky and Amay would never speak of again. Only once as an adult would Lucky discuss it— with Shanti, her friend and guru.

"Well," Shanti said, after Lucky told her the story, "the snake must have been there for a reason. Maybe they had an appointment."

"An appointment?" Lucky asked.

"Varun and the snake. Stop judging everything, Lucky. Things happen for a reason, and the universe doesn't owe us explanations. Varun was being a boy and the snake was being a snake. It's what we do. We follow our inherent nature. It wasn't personal to either of them, or to you. Sometimes, things like that happen. The real question is, why have you carried around the blame for all these years?"

"What do you mean?" Lucky asked.

"I mean, were you an adult? Did you start this situation just so that Varun would die? Did you know the snake was there?"

"No," Lucky said.

"Okay then. Let it go. It happened. It wasn't like the universe went out and did something TO you. Or TO Varun, either, for that matter. Things happen. Sometimes, we are just in the wrong place at the wrong time. If you have no deliberate fault, then take no deliberate blame. What were you doing again?"

"We were trying to find out whether Aunt Benaifer really sat naked in the sauna."

"And did she?"

Lucky thought about this. "I don't remember," she said. "I don't remember a thing about it. Only that Varun was bit by the cobra and died. That, and for twenty years I thought it was my fault."

CHAPTER 1

Lucky was singing to herself as she entered the wrought iron gate with the inscriptions, "New York State Department of Corrections." It was early morning and she smiled as she mentally went through the schedule of the yoga poses she would give to her class of inmates to reduce their high levels of testosterone. She would make those toughies, who would try to give her a hard time, unwittingly flop on the floor. And there were two of them, both newcomers, Andy and Donald, who constantly mocked her in the last two classes by imitating her and doing the poses standing on their tiptoes and copying her in high, falsetto tones. Suppressed peals of laughter followed. Today, they would be there for class and she had her part well planned. Newcomers were always a challenge in the first few classes but she knew how to flatten their egos with just a few "easy" yoga poses. It was her way of keeping them and her class under control.

For some reason, her ID badge wouldn't work in the card reader, and there were new guards working in the security booth—some sort of institutional rotation thing—who made a big deal about the foul up, despite having Lucky's photo and description in their computer.

"But I've been working here for three years," Lucky said. "And you can see my picture right there!"

"Maybe you have and maybe you haven't," the duty officer said. "Maybe that's you and maybe it isn't. Anyway, we've got these new

Homeland Security directives, and nobody's taking any chances, and I'm not opening the gate without authorization from upstairs. If everybody was who they said they were, we wouldn't need prisons, now would we, sweetie? That's why we have rules."

Lucky's ears tinged red. "Homeland Security? What? Are they worried about people breaking *into* prison now? Is there anything inside so valuable that it has to be protected from foreign intrigue? Or is the food that good? Or maybe there are people so desperate to take a free yoga class that they'd break into prison to do it."

"I'm just following protocol, ma'am," the guard said.

Lucky frowned and crossed her arms, but didn't argue further. It was no use, and besides, it was more important to be on time for her class. After all, she was supposed to be teaching the inmates responsibility, and she couldn't do that if she appeared irresponsible herself. But it didn't matter. The guards had to call their supervisor, write an incident report while they waited for him to call back. The supervisor had to call Warden Capps. By the time everyone was done calling everyone else and the warden had given the go-ahead, Lucky was late.

The two troublemakers she'd anticipated weren't there, and Lucky was told they had detention that week. *Not surprising*, she thought. Still, in their place there were three more newcomers who, judging by their casual postures and leering grins, would ensure that Lucky's tough class plan wouldn't go to waste.

Lucky went to the front of the classroom, spread out her mat, retrieved a belt and stepped out of her shoes. When she turned around to face the class, she noticed the new students were smirking. The way their hands quickly dropped to their sides made it clear why. They were playing the same game, imitating her moves.

"I saw that," Lucky said. *Let them know you know but be calm and fair.*

The trio scowled, slinking off to the back of the room. They stood there with their arms folded across their chests, looking macho and stupid and sullen and defiant. They weren't properly dressed, didn't have their yoga belts, and hadn't even taken off their shoes. Arguing with them would make the class even later. On the other hand, there were many ways to argue.

Lucky smiled. She brought the trio to the front of the class and set them in a triangle pose—feet set wide apart, one hand on the floor by an ankle, the other pointing straight up in the air. Although it looked easy, invariably, novices didn't align their hips properly, and when they finally did, they fell flat on their faces.

"It looks easy," Lucky said to the three, now looking more sheepish than tough. "But strength is not always found in big muscles. Your body has hundreds of small muscle groups, and these are the glue that holds the whole body together. The big muscles sometimes even work against each other. In the end, yoga is not just about strength, but about balance. All the big muscles in the world won't do you any good if you can't stand up. The chain is no stronger than its weakest link, and the body is no stronger than its weakest muscle."

After that, the novices quieted down and made a more serious effort. Still, the class was late, and Lucky had to rush to make up for lost time. *Speed yoga*, she termed it, even though yoga was supposed to be slow, meditative, and unhurried. As she pulled into Ustrasana, the camel pose, she felt a tweak and a burn in her groin. After that, she gave up on the idea of doing the whole workout, settling for quality over quantity in the remaining time.

When they were done and the room had emptied out, she toweled off and tested the sore spot to see if the muscle was torn, or just strained. She decided it was strained, thanking her lucky stars the injury hadn't been worse. "Focus," she said to herself. She took a deep breath. All in all, it hadn't been too bad—except that, well, these days "not too bad" was her mantra. The last six months had been a long series of minor hassles that, when taken together, added up to a stinking pile of aggravation. First, the state had tried to cut the classes altogether; Lucky had had to volunteer to forgo her pay before they relented. When they tried again to cut her class, Lucky had taken on an administrative position in exchange for continued funding of her prison work. So now she had two jobs. Her friends had wondered about her dedication—what, they asked, could possibly be worth all this trouble? Lucky couldn't always find the words to answer. The truth was that she had seen the difference she could make in people's lives. Every time a student came back to her class, every time someone managed a new pose, every time she heard that they found it easier to focus and learn—there was so much joy and fulfillment in this work, who cared about a few hassles? The only downside was that she spent less time with Sean, but, well, few single moms were lucky enough to be able to stay home all day. Why should Lucky?

After the class, Lucky drove home, showered and changed, and caught the train into the city, where her other job was located. The train crept along at a snail's pace, the passengers rocking lethargically as if in rhythm to some mysterious music only they could hear. Lucky had pulled out her special Internet wired laptop, on which she was watching—dare she admit it?—*cartoons*. Old re-runs of *Tom and Jerry*.

She was supposed to be reviewing a presentation, a proposal to revamp the education program run by the New York State Department of Corrections. The idea was to make classes compulsory, rewarding prisoners with privileges for earning good grades. Lucky wanted to make it clear to them that they had skills and abilities that would serve them far better in the "outside" world than whatever shortcuts had landed them in prison. *It's not just about education or punishment but about reformation*, Lucky had written in the proposal. *It's about changing the prisoners' perception of themselves and their place in society. They'll earn their privileges in prison just like we do in the real world. Once they know they can play the game, there's a better chance that they will reintegrate successfully into society.*

Technically, neither classroom education nor prisoner rehabilitation was Lucky's area of expertise. She was an accountant by training, an entrepreneur at heart, and a yoga instructor by vocation. She had run a successful business in Mumbai, and after her divorce, had returned to New York to try running another one.

For a while, that seemed to work—until she found herself entangled and bruised by a con artist. Eventually, she'd ended up here, at the New York State Department of Corrections. This education proposal had grown out of her work at the prison, and her financial background had helped her sell the idea—so far. After all, incarceration was expensive, and if the state could reduce recidivism by even a few percentage points, the program would pay for itself. And as a sharp accountant, she had the numbers to prove it. Lucky had pushed Warden Capps and Barkley, her other boss, until they'd passed her idea up the ladder and made sure it got a fair hearing. Finally, the word came down from Albany: *Show* us. Hence, the appointment and the presentation.

Meanwhile, every time Lucky powered up her laptop, the damn thing went straight to the Web and something called Hulu. Lucky didn't watch much television and certainly didn't want to watch much today (although she had to admit, the cartoons held a certain allure), but she couldn't figure out how to change the default settings on her home page. Here she was, a chartered accountant, volunteering yoga classes for the Department of Corrections, now preparing a presentation to revamp the educational system for the department, and she couldn't figure out how to turn off the cartoons. She was going to have to go home and ask her neighbor's sixteen-year-old daughter how to fix the computer. Perfect. This was turning out to be one of those days. *It happens*, Lucky thought, *a bump in the road*. Still, at the moment, she found the images of the cat and mouse amusing. *Some days*, she thought, *are just made for cartoons*. If only life was as simple.

The man sitting next to Lucky had been watching her since she entered the train station. Although Lucky had spotted him right away, she'd initially dismissed him as harmless. But when she boarded the train, so did he, and when she took a seat, he stood nearby until he could sit down next to her. He wore a red-and-white checkered shirt, jeans, and a cowboy hat. Cowboy boots, too, but they were pretty near worn-out, scuffed to an asphalt gray color. A pack of Marlboros stuck out of his shirt pocket. She tried to ignore him, but when he saw her glance, he elbowed her and said, "Better hold on to that with both hands. Goddamn thieves have been on the hunt lately. They hop on at a station, snatch your computer, and hop off just as the doors close. Peel it out like that." He snapped his fingers. When Lucky did not respond, the man continued, "Happened yesterday morning. Saw it myself. Young lady just like you. Student, I think. Sittin' there with a laptop and the next thing you know, BIM! BAM! GONE! Just like that. Didn't get a good look at the fella. Just a set of gray sweats out the door and down the platform. Too much crime these days, if you ask me. You can't feel safe nowhere no more. Not even in your own house. You just can't tell who's on the prowl these days."

A tiny gray-haired woman seated opposite them nodded and said, "Somebody ought to do something. I saw it, too; yes, it was a young lady. Got off sobbing, poor thing."

"Ought to make an example of 'em," the man said. "Hang thieves along the tracks as a warning to others. Everywhere you go, locks and cops, locks and cops. I got two deadbolts on a steel door at home, and still, the thieves break in."

"What do you suppose he'll do with the computer?" the woman asked.

"Sell it!" the man said, "Or trade it for dope." He laughed a long, loud, deep, obnoxious belly laugh that ended in a smoker's hacking cough.

Lucky sighed. Her sore muscle still burned, and she was starting to remember her mantra 'be great' again. Sean's babysitter, Maria, had been late that morning, her yoga class had been a fiasco, and when she'd practiced her presentation last night, she'd completely blanked and skipped an entire section. Now it was show time, and the train was slow and hot and crowded, and this cowboy wouldn't leave her alone. What was next? He'd ask her for a date? She looked down at her laptop.

The cartoons were gone, replaced by an advertisement for a popular candy. Animated fruit chews pounded apples and oranges and bananas in a game of basketball. The exhausted natural fruits were no match for the faster, taller, and more athletic super-fruits. Blonde, blue-eyed children ran across a lush green lawn toward a picnic table where a smiling blonde woman offered them a plate of candy while a tall, handsome, clean-cut man looked on benevolently. Lucky looked away. Everybody knew the punch line: "Super Moms Choose Super Chews!"

What junk, Lucky thought. She didn't know if it was her Indian upbringing, but to her Super Chews tasted like sugar and chemicals. Lucky was pretty sure that what grew naturally was always better than an artificial product, and although she was trying to impress this upon Sean, it was only creating friction between them. *Kids don't want what's good for them,* she thought.

Now that she'd stopped focusing on her work, a million thoughts raced through her head: *Would Maria remember to take the clothes out of the washer and put them in the dryer? Did Sean take his nap that afternoon? He gets so cranky at night when he doesn't...should I have worn something more feminine than this damn pant suit? Men are so intimidated by women who look professional. Is my blouse going to be sweat-stained? Maybe I should have worn that silk dress after all.* Through the din, her old friend Shanti's words came back to Lucky as clear as if the old woman was sitting beside her: "Don't forget to breathe. Remember, we're human *beings*, not human *doings*. And not breathing is bad for your health." *I'll be okay!* No, Lucky thought. *As Shanti would say, you have to be **great**.*

"I hear you," Lucky said. "I'm breathing." She took a deep breath and rolled her head counterclockwise, trying to relax the tension in her neck. And then she saw the cowboy staring at her like she was crazy.

She needed a vacation. Amay had been trying to pry her away from work for a month to take a long weekend in Maine. He'd had his heart set on the Fourth of July—even had a room at a pricey county inn in Bar Harbor—but Lucky had turned him down. "Too much riding on this presentation," she'd said.

"What do they do with those things they steal?" the old lady persisted, in a gruff, hoarse voice, jolting Lucky back to the present.

"Sell 'em. Trade 'em. It's a joke these days. Cops everywhere and none of 'em doing a thing. Wouldn't surprise me if they were in on the deal. Hang a few—that'll put an end to it. If they could just catch 'em."

"Catching thieves is easy," Lucky said, and then she closed her eyes and bit her lip. *Why did I have to open my big mouth?*

The man stiffened and glared at her. "Sure, if you know where to look."

Lucky shrugged and then began stabbing at her keyboard. "The problem isn't catching them. Thieves get caught all the time. But what do you do when you've got them? If you can't reform them, then in a few months, or years, they're back out on the street stealing again."

The man's expression turned sour. "Reform doesn't work, 'cause crime pays. Ask me, if they killed repeat offenders, we'd be better off. Save taxpayers' money."

Lucky's phone rang. Amay. She ignored it. *In five minutes, he'll text me an invitation to dinner.* She turned back to the cowboy. "Isn't that a little harsh?"

"What's harsh is all of us working night and day while them thieves get three hot meals a day and a cot *if* they get caught. Cops get these small fry while the big bosses get off scot-free. I tell ya, if you've got to steal, dream big and steal big. It's the safe bet. Take my kid brother," he said, "used to be a car salesman. Had a place in Miami. Lost his leg in a wreck. Hit a semi head-on driving drunk on New Year's Eve. No insurance. Couldn't work. Lost his job. Wife left him. Comes to me to lend him a hand. What's a brother to do? I tell him to take his disability and let the government pay *him* for a change, but the wife gets after me about it. "He's your flesh and blood," she says. "You can't just toss him out like trash." "Oh yes I can," I say, but she keeps after me—you know how women are—so after a while I say, "Okay." I got a few bucks in the bank. He says he wants to go into contracting with me so I help him out with some gear, give him the easy jobs, even buy him a truck. And you know what he does? Goes out and bids the jobs dirt cheap—gets a bunch of money from people for deposits, only he never does the work. He splits for parts unknown with the dough. I hadda do all the work—and for nothing. Bunch of lousy, f----d-up bids I couldn't have made a dime on even if they'd been done right to begin with—and minus the deposit money my brother stole. I lost everything: tools, truck, license. All of it. My own goddamn brother."

The old woman said, "People aren't what they used to be. This is my stop." She got up, clutching her handbag tightly.

The cowboy shuffled his feet and watched her.

Lucky looked closely at the cowboy; the tense mouth, a spattering of small white scars on the left side of his face. The way his eyes darted around the train, the way he watched when anyone got on or off, something about him was familiar. And then it hit Lucky. *This guy's an ex-con.*

"You used to be a welder," Lucky said.

"I've struck an arc or two," he replied. "How'd you know?"

"The burns."

He looked at her, puzzled.

"The scars. On your face."

He touched his cheek.

"You worked in a shop somewhere. Then you hurt your left eye and had to give it up. You're not blind, but your eye is shot. Now you do a little mechanic work on the side, or a little construction, when you can get it. I can tell by the grease under your nails and rubbed into your palms. I'm guessing you work under the table. You're not the kind of citizen who pays taxes. You're smart, all right, but lazy. You'll take the easy money. Fencing stolen goods sounds about right. And I hope you're not casing my laptop."

Veins bulged in the cowboy's neck. He jumped to his feet as the train lurched, and he stumbled and grabbed the overhead strap.

"I am only guessing," Lucky said. "And it's none of my business so long as you leave me alone."

The old woman backed away toward the door.

The cowboy narrowed his eyes.

"I'm not a cop," Lucky said. "But I am in Corrections. I teach in prison, so I can spot a con a mile away. But some of my best friends are inmates."

The man kept staring at her. "Really?"

Lucky nodded while studying his face. He looked so out of place in New York. In her experience, people looked out of place for three reasons. Either they *were* out of place, they wanted to attract attention to themselves, or they wanted to divert attention away from something else. Nothing else seemed unusual about the commute, though.

The cowboy said, "So you're good at spotting jailbirds?"

"Yes," Lucky said. "I am."

"And what do you do when you see them?"

"Nothing," Lucky said. "Or, maybe that depends. It depends on if some action is called for. Sometimes, I say something to try to help them—point them in the right direction. If they're up to no good, I might say something to let them know I'm on to them. Once in a while—a very long while—I might let the cops know. But only if I think there's something bad about to go down. Mostly, I try to help people. I mean, criminals are people, too. Sick or challenged, but still people. It's not for us to judge."

"Help, eh."

"That's what I said."

The man scratched his chin. "So you got connections?"

Lucky nodded.

"Prove it."

"Prove it? Why? I don't owe you anything."

"What I meant was, maybe you could help me."

Lucky bit her lip. *Here it comes*, she thought. "And what can I do to help you?"

"Can you find my brother?"

"Your brother? The one who ripped you off?" Lucky leaned back on the bench and looked at the man. "Sure. Why not?"

The man grunted. "Right here," he asked. "Just like that?" The train was grinding to a stop. The old woman did not get off but crept back close to Lucky.

"Maybe. If you have a little information about him."

"Information like…"

"A name. An ID. A job. A former address. I can't find people without something to go on."

The man looked around the car, then nodded. "Finch," he said. "Mike. Used to work for Finch Car and Truck. Had a house down in Miami. That enough?"

Lucky sighed, then clicked on an icon on the desktop of her laptop, and paused while the program loaded. "Age?" she asked.

"Fifty-two."

"Birthday?"

"February 18th."

"That makes you Jim, right?"

A shadow crossed the cowboy's face. He nodded.

Lucky punched at the screen, then turned the computer for Jim to see the photo.

"That's amazing," the cowboy said. "How'd you find him?"

Lucky shrugged. "A little intuition, a little help from the Web. You'd be surprised at how much information is out there these days if you know where to look."

"So, where is he?"

Lucky looked at the laptop and read quietly. "You'll not see him again," she said.

The cowboy's face brightened.

"But whoever Mike Finch is, he's not your brother. And I know you're not Jim."

The cowboy grinned. "You didn't think I'd give you *my* real name, did ya?"

"No," Lucky said, "I didn't." She looked at the cowboy. "But how's this for finding people? It will take a couple of minutes."

Lucky turned her screen away from the prying eyes of the cowboy and after a few minutes, exclaimed, "Ah ha, your name is Gordon

24

Bolton and you're from Ashbury Park, but guess what? You've been living in Jamaica for a while now—at least four months. You got a parking ticket there in April. And there's a warrant out for you. Something about a liquor store and a little thing at a camera shop. Looks like somebody got hurt in that one, but like I said, don't worry. I'm not interested in you."

Without taking his eyes off Lucky, Bolton stood up and edged backward toward the door. The train slowed and he jumped off at the next platform.

They were in Manhattan proper now. Lucky looked at the old woman. "Wasn't that your stop back there?"

"Oh," she replied, "I'm in no hurry. The train goes both ways. I got time to kill, you know. This is much more interesting than mall walking. Did you really find his brother?"

"Mike Finch wasn't his brother," Lucky said. "But I did find a Mike Finch."

"But how did you know he would never see him again?"

"Mike Finch died two years ago in a car accident. I don't know why Bolton was looking for him. Maybe Finch owed him some money. Who knows? Whatever it was, I'm guessing it wasn't good."

The old woman nodded. Her eyes were glassy. "It's going to be hot today," she said.

Lucky looked down at the text message she had just sent the transit police—the one with the name and picture and the time and the stop where Bolton got off. "Yes," she said. "And it's going to get hotter."

Her phone buzzed. A text message.

Amay. *Dinner?* he asked.

CHAPTER 2

The government building that housed Lucky's other office was a clunky 1970s brick punch card of a building in lower Manhattan. To get there, Lucky had to cross an awkward, five-way intersection, where one wedge contained a bit of a lawn and a large, drooping pin oak surrounded by a low, cast iron fence of indeterminate age. It was a sight better suited to a Gothic cemetery or an Edgar Alan Poe poem than to a bit of green in downtown Manhattan. Eyeing the complicated path she'd have to take, Lucky decided not to attempt it on an empty stomach and detoured to a cafe at the end of the block to purchase mocha and a croissant. The café had a trendy New York way about it—the sign, for one thing, was like an old-fashioned eye chart, so that it read:

A STAR CALLED LUCKY

Inside, the baristas and wait staff wore white lab coats, and a TV set was playing Alfred Hitchcock movies—currently, *Vertigo*. The staff, if they were paying attention, added their screams to the movie at the appropriate moments. Fortunately, they weren't paying attention. When she'd first started working in this area, Lucky had been surprised that Cafe Vision did any business at all. Then she'd discovered that they made a great mocha, with a choice of a dozen different gourmet chocolates from around the world and topped with whipped cream from an organic dairy in Vermont, and decided some things were worth braving Alfred Hitchcock for.

When Lucky emerged, she saw that in the time it had taken her to buy her mocha, a crowd of protestors had occupied the sidewalk and blocked the street in front of the office building. A cacophony of signs proclaimed that they were PETA activists. The signs bore images of animals in cages, animals in various stages of vivisection, and stacks of carcasses—stomach-turning stuff. The protestors seemed to be mostly young student-types in college tee shirts, but with a smattering of housewives, artists, aging hippies, and priests. Some handed out tracts to passers-by, while others gathered around a guitar player and sang. Someone had splashed buckets of what looked like blood all over the steps leading into the office. Lucky wondered why the heck PETA activists would be picketing a state office and why they had to pick *today*, of all days. But there they were.

In this age of bombings and mayhem and Occupy Wall Street, the NYPD was not taking any chances. A cop on horseback was standing by, and a line of squad cars was arriving with reinforcements to block off both ends of the street and to direct traffic around the event. Traffic had already backed up out of sight in both directions, and the drivers seemed to be getting unruly. *Of course, we are in New York. When aren't drivers unruly here?*

As Lucky zig-zagged through the crowd, one protestor in particular caught her eye: a youngish-looking man of indeterminate age with short, flax-colored hair and piercing gray eyes. He was startlingly attractive—handsome face, square jaw, not a spare pound on his lean frame. He could have been a movie star, and Lucky couldn't help but notice that he sat quite still in Lotus Pose, cross-legged on the concrete, hands resting palms-down on his knees, entirely unmoved by the noise and heat and confusion around him. Despite his European features, he wore the red saffron robe of a Buddhist monk. Lucky was sure as she passed that the man's eyes followed her. For a moment, she involuntarily stopped as she passed him.

Then she turned, looked at him in the eye, and asked, "What's the fuss all about?"

He shrugged his shoulders. She felt awkward and stupid—anybody could see what was going on. They were protesting cruelty to animals. Still, she could not escape the feeling that when they held eye contact a deeper communication had passed between them.

As she turned to go, he said, "You can help or walk away."

Lucky nearly stumbled but quickly recovered and kept going. Once she reached her office, Lucky decided to take care of one last detail from her train ride. Gordon Bolton had been quite the shady character, so Lucky wanted to track him further—and she had the tools to do so. The program was called Bloodhound, and it had been developed by the state with help from Homeland Security to keep track of parolees, sex offenders, and men and women on bail awaiting trial. Lucky had been recruited to participate as part of a control group from the Department of Corrections when the software was being tested. She had done well so she had been drafted to continue to work with the implementation team as a tester. With its 1,558-point topological contour facial recognition, Bloodhound was as accurate in identification as a fingerprint. And it was eerie in the way it connected search preferences, personal correspondence, phone and email records, credit card use, and social networking to track people's habits. The statistics it compiled told Bloodhound where to search, and its success rate was astonishing. It was as close to intuitive as a machine could be. Lucky played only a small, advisory part in Bloodhound's testing, but she'd still shared in the accolades, and she'd held on to her beta version on her laptop. Nobody had told her to erase it and besides, who knew when it might come in handy?

A STAR CALLED LUCKY

Using a photo she had surreptitiously snapped with her laptop, she began tracing the cowboy. The blue light fluttered as Bloodhound raced through online databases of surveillance photos and public records, Facebook pages, and Google search histories. Almost immediately, a series of surveillance shots appeared—at the airport in Jamaica, getting off the train in Manhattan. But what she couldn't find was a picture of Bolton in handcuffs. Bloodhound showed her a security feed from the train station, showing that Bolton had simply waited at one side of the platform while the cops rushed down the stairs. After they passed, he jumped the turnstile and fled upstairs behind them. *Idiots*, she thought. *He was right there!* She pulled Bolton's record. A three-time loser. Narcotics. Armed robbery. He wasn't any purse-snatcher or petty thief, like she had first imagined. He was a real menace, and he had been on the run for *five* years. How on earth did he escape detection? Why couldn't the cops nail this guy? And when they did, how on earth had he gotten bail on his own recognizance? *I should have looked closer at his file on the train*, Lucky thought. Then it dawned on her that, had she known the whole truth, Bolton might well have harmed her. She shivered. Now what?

Her finger hovered over the Bloodhound icon. She could track him further. She could call the cops again. But then again, it might raise some ugly questions she wasn't quite ready to answer—like: How did she know he was a con? And how did she find him? If she found Bolton, she'd have to find a way to make it look like an accident. Besides—she looked at her watch—ten minutes to the presentation.

On a whim, Lucky typed in an address and the street outside appeared on the screen. She tried to pick out the monk who had made eye contact with her—he should have been easy to spot in his robe. But he was nowhere to be seen, and Lucky realized why when she saw that cops were loading the protesters into police vans. Horrified, she pictured a cop pointing with his nightstick and saying, "Hey, Brickowski, get the shit hole in the red robe. Let's give him a thumping on the ride downtown." Well, if he had been arrested, there would be a name to go with it. Maybe there was more than one way to help.

Five minutes until the presentation. Lucky checked her e-mail, and saw that she had thirty-seven new messages. She sighed. The first was from Lucky's boss, Chad Barkley. The e-mail contained a link to a news article about the newest strain of drug-resistant influenza in India. Evidently, it had mutated, becoming both highly virulent and resistant to treatment. Barkley wanted Lucky to be ready to offer an impromptu supporting opinion that Bloodhound could be used to track down potential carriers of disease. None of the actual programmers were available on such short notice, and since she had been involved in the testing of Bloodhound, she could demonstrate its capabilities adequately. Well, that seemed easy enough. It was all about connections. Lucky sighed and closed her eyes. In her mind, she could already see the red, root-like tracks Bloodhound would draw as it collected data and connected the intersecting lives of patients and those who might have been exposed to the disease. With any luck, the flowing red lines would intersect and merge until they formed a single thread—a line that would lead to patient zero. The authorities could round up the victims and isolate them, and that would be that. Bloodhound was perfectly suited to that kind of information crunching. Compared with criminals, patients would be easy.

It was time. She gathered her things and took the elevator to the conference room.

As it turned out, she needn't have worried at all. The meeting was delayed because the office was expecting a visitor: Clevis Coleman, director of the US Global Wellness Council (GWC), a board of medical experts and public health officials who formulated and directed global health policy for the US Department of Health & Human Services (H&HS) and the FDA. Coleman, who had unexpectedly asked to attend, was almost an hour late. Barkley was mystified at the request and what a person of Coleman's stature would possibly want at the meeting. But despite his perplexity, Lucky's presentation on education was tabled for a later date.

Coleman arrived in a fury and launched a tirade against the activists who had created the traffic jam that delayed him. He was tall, lean, and energetic, his back was straight, his expression was humorless. His hair was thick, very straight, and pure white. He wore it combed up and back from his forehead. His appearance was impeccable: a light gray business suit, almost military in its cut with wide lapels and smartly starched-and-rolled cuffs, with a plain white shirt and dark blue tie. At first glance, Lucky took his cufflinks for brass, but after a moment, her jewelry training kicked in and she realized that they were gold, or at least, gold-plated. Coleman wore narrow, rimless glasses—little more than slits to peer through. No laser surgery for him, Lucky thought. She wondered whether Coleman was afraid of doctors. If true, it would be ironic, given his current position, but not unlikely. The fear of doctors was a common behavior exhibited by men obsessed with control. And Coleman was most certainly obsessed with control.

Upon being introduced, he said, "I hate being late. I'd apologize, but the problem is these damn activists. Here we are trying to cure diseases and help Americans live longer and better than people anywhere in the world, and they insist on interfering because they think trying vaccines on mice before we give them to children is immoral. If you ask me, what is immoral is blocking public roads and interfering with good governance."

Lucky shrugged. *Get over yourself. What else were you going to do today?*

"After I leave here," Coleman said, "I'm going to Washington to report to the president about this little situation developing in India. A strange strain of Influenza, which kills in forty-eight hours. But a handful survived healed by a local doctor. I presume you have heard about this? The BBC broke the story last week, and CNN picked it up yesterday. We're putting a team in place to deal with contingencies. Your work was mentioned. It sounds interesting. It sounds like something we could use." He turned to Barkley. "Tell me about this Bloodhound thing, which can trace the interaction of people so the sick can be quarantined."

Barkley began to explain about the origins of the project and its importance to the Department of Corrections, but Coleman waved him off. "I don't have time for a history lesson," he said. "What I'm talking about is a demonstration." He looked right at Lucky. "I hear you're pretty good with this thing. Care to show me?"

Lucky wasn't paying any attention to Coleman at all, and it wasn't until Emil, her secretary, elbowed her in the ribs that she realized Coleman was speaking to her.

"Me?" she asked.

"Yes, you. You were on the implementation team, weren't you?"

Lucky nodded. "Sort of. Though I was more of a tester."

"But you've used it?"

"Yes, sir."

"And it works?"

"It works very well."

"Well, I suppose that means that any idiot can use it." There was a round of laughter and Lucky frowned.

"Show me," Coleman said.

Lucky looked around at Barkley, who nodded in affirmation. Mentally sighing, she pulled out her laptop and started it up.

Coleman looked at his watch. "I don't have all day here."

Lucky kept her expression calm. "This will only take a few minutes, and you can tell me more about what you'd like to see. Whom would you like me to trace?"

"I don't know. Make up some names. What difference does it make?"

"If I make up names, then I might as well make up the data, too."

Now Coleman flushed red. "Oh, I don't know," he said. "Can't you just pick two random people?"

"I can't research random people," Lucky said. "I have to have something specific to go on. You won't be researching random people in real-time, either. You'll have names, addresses, ages, driver's licenses, credit cards, something. You have to start somewhere. Even a picture will do."

"Okay," Coleman said. "Then pick someone you know."

"But who?" Lucky asked.

"I don't know!" Coleman snapped. "Pick anyone. Pick yourself. Just give me a demonstration."

"Could I have your driver's license?" Lucky asked. Coleman scowled, but dug in his wallet and handed the license to Lucky.

Lucky entered the license number into Bloodhound but found that Coleman's data was blocked as CLASSIFIED. She relayed this to Coleman.

"Of course it's classified," Coleman replied. "I'm the head of the Food and Drug Administration."

Lucky frowned. For some reason, she felt Coleman *wanted* her to fail. She bent over the keyboard again. "Give me five," she said. Coleman started to look annoyed again, but Barkley came to the rescue, and soon, Coleman had launched into his description of what would happen in a killer influenza epidemic and how the NSA had refused to help him track it.

"Their stuff is so super-secret they won't take any chances with the source code getting out or that someone could backwards engineer any changes that we made to protect the military end of things."

Meanwhile, Lucky started with the photo of Coleman she'd just taken. He would have just come from the airport. What time? What gate? What flight? From where? Coleman's face wasn't classified. Bloodhound picked up the image, and she watched the lines unfold from there. A few minutes later, she took out a piece of paper and wrote down a list of names.

Clevis Coleman. Director, GWC

1. Roger. (Your neighbor.)
2. Daphne. (Your neighbor's wife.)
3. Emma (Daphne's best friend.)
4. Sonya (Emma's daughter.)
5. Jill. (The daughter's kindergarten teacher.)

I should count these three as one, since Daphne has met Jill. But the strongest connection is…

6. Peter (Jill's brother.)
7. Clay (Peter's son.)
8. Nancy (Clay's teacher).

I should also count those two as one, as again, Peter has met Nancy…

9. June (teaches in Lucky's neighborhood).
10. Collette (My neighbor).
11. Me. Lucky Boyce. *And if I looked long enough, I've probably met June, too.*

Lucky handed Coleman the paper. He read the names then stared at Lucky for a moment.

"I could bring it down to the proverbial six degrees of separation," Lucky said as she waited for his reaction.

"Enough!" he said as he tucked the paper into his pocket and went on with his message about how the new influenza strain could wreak havoc on its own. Lucky caught puzzled glances from Barkley and Emil, but no one wanted to interrupt the man. At the end of the meeting, Coleman said, "But the real danger is the possibility that this agent could be used as a biological weapon by terrorists."

Lucky grimaced. *Can't we have a meeting about <u>anything</u> that doesn't drag terrorism into the mix?*

After the meeting, Lucky met with Barkley in her office. "You realize," Barkley said, "that you erred in your presentation."

"I have no idea what you're talking about."

"I peeked over your shoulder while you were working."

"You're right. Roger's name could have been left out." Lucky said, "But if I'd worked it a little longer, I'm sure I could've cut it down to six."

Barkley shook his head. "You know exactly what I mean. There were only ten names on that screen to begin with."

Lucky sat back in her chair and looked at Barkley. She sighed. "But it would have been bad form to point out that Coleman *also* visits his neighbor's wife."

"And how did you know this?"

"Email. Facebook. Airline reservations. A weekend in Guadalajara. The program is good."

Barkley nodded. "And I have noticed you using this on your *personal* laptop too, when we were researching Barry for the assistant supervisor position."

Lucky winced.

"No harm," he said. He winked, and then added, "Isn't Coleman's file—as a senior government official—supposed to be confidential?"

"It is," Lucky said. "But his neighbor's isn't. And neither are their pictures. They were smiling when they came through customs together."

"Be careful, Lucky. Coleman is not someone you want to rile. He carries a lot of weight in Washington."

"I didn't keep any of the pictures, if that's what you mean."

Barkley smiled. "Of course not," he said. "But then again, you might want to. Who knows? They might come in handy some day."

CHAPTER 3

It was 6:00 p.m. when Lucky walked out of the office. Behind Café Vision was a narrow side street where a number of book, bric-a-brac, and antique dealers traded. Lucky turned the corner and went to see if her friend Grant, who tended a shop halfway down the block, was in. Grant was a wiry, middle-aged Irishman with an exaggerated Irish accent and a fading thatch of reddish hair—he certainly had the mark of an Irish rover. Some days, he was open and some days he wasn't. One could never be sure with Grant, and he himself didn't seem to worry about the shop, or money, or anything, so far as Lucky could tell. Lucky had long ago given up arguing with Grant about how to properly run a bookstore. "Wh'a do a' look like?" Grant asked, "Barnes 'n 'oble? The way books sell, you're lucky I'm here a'tall."

The last time she'd seen Grant, they'd argued about Walt Whitman, and he had promised Lucky an antique volume of *Leaves of Grass* in passable condition. Of course, Lucky could download practically any book that had ever been printed to her computer in seconds, but there was something about the feel and smell of real leather binding and the texture of old paper that appealed to her. Physical books were also much more easily shared with others, and if there was one thing Lucky never missed out on, it was reading to Sean. Every night, she read to him. And even if he didn't understand *Henry IV* Parts I and II, he appreciated the time Lucky spent reading to him and the little explanations she made. He even named his teddy bear Falstaff.

She looked through the window of the bookstore. Grant was bent over a parcel, his back to the counter. When she went in, he looked up and smiled as soon as he saw her. He set the parcel he had been unwrapping onto the floor, reached into the books stacked on the counter, and produced a green, cloth–bound volume of *Leaves of Grass*. Lucky reached for the book, but Grant held it away. He opened the book and flipped a few pages, cleared his throat and read:

> Here is the test of wisdom;
>
> Wisdom is not finally tested in schools;
>
> Wisdom cannot be pass'd from one having it, to another not having it;
>
> Wisdom is of the Soul, is not susceptible of proof, is its own proof
>
> Applies to all stages and objects and qualities, and is content,
>
> Is the certainty of the reality and immortality of things, and the excellence of things;
>
> Something there is in the float of the sight of things that provokes it out of the Soul.

"Beautiful, eh?" he said, closing the book and passing it to Lucky.

"Wonderful," Lucky said. "Where was that?"

Grant smiled and shook his head. "Have to find it yourself, now. Wouldn't want ta spoil yer studies."

"In the float of the sight of things," Lucky said. "What do you suppose he meant by that?"

Grant smiled and closed his eyes, and with a look of sublime pleasure on his face, said,

> Here is realization;
>
> Here is a man tallied—he realizes here what he has in him;

The past, the future, majesty, love—if they are vacant of you,
you are vacant of them.

"Do you know," he asked, opening his eyes, "what you have in you?"

"If you're talking about a physical soul, I know it exists."

"Can you prove it?"

Lucky had been distracted looking at the book. "I'm sorry, prove what?"

"That the soul exists."

"Of course I believe it exists."

"That's not what I asked. I asked, 'Can you *prove* it?'"

Lucky looked around the store. "I guess I can't *prove* it, but that doesn't make it untrue."

"My pointh exaactly!" Grant exclaimed in his heavy Irish accent. "But try telling that to tha average man on the street! People have this childlike insistence on proof. If they can't see ith they won't believe ith."

Lucky felt drawn to play the skeptic. It wasn't that she disliked arguing with Grant—on the contrary, she found his wit entertaining. But he had a way of leading her into arguments from positions she neither believed in nor felt she could win. She took a deep breath and said, "But isn't it natural to demand some kind of proof?"

"Prooof!" Grant said. He made a face like he had bitten into a sour apple. "Thinggs may fall, but can ya prove gravity?"

"But things fall," Lucky said. "You can see it."

"You can see them fall, but you can't see *why* they fall. You can't see gravity—only tha effect it has on matter. And what is matter? Get rightt down to it; physicists reduced all matter to bits of stringg with gravity but no mass. Bits of nothing held together by strong and weak forces. Vibrations in the ether, they are."

"It is only a way of describing how matter behaves," Lucky said.

"Exaactly," Grant replied. "The more ya examine it, the less substantial it tis. Yet there it tis, matter, which consists of nathing, and gravity, which we can't see and which pulls bits of nothin together. And we call that reaality, in all its glory. But me point is that we can describe haw matter behaves, and haw gravity behaves, and haw the soul behaves, but we can neither see nor proove any of them. But people don' question the existence of matter, or of gravity. But when it comes ta the soul—'Off with ya,' they say."

"And that means?"

"It means that Whitman, tha poet-physicist, intuited that all things arise from tha soul and float, light as air, so that we may delight in themm. Matter did not give rise to life that gave rise to tha soul. Soul gave rise to life, which gave rise to matter. 'In the beginning,' the Good Book says, 'was The Word.'"

Lucky nodded. Grant was much like Shanti, in an affable, drunken, Irish kind of way. He was one of those curious people who seemed to know a little about everything, despite his lack of formal education. Maybe that was what came of working in a bookstore. Their arguments ran in circles, with Grant asking questions and trapping Lucky into defending answers she knew weren't true. It was humiliating, like losing at chess to a child. Even if the child was a prodigy, it was of little consolation.

"Okay!" Lucky said. "I'm off."

"Could I interest ya in a copy of Sun Tzu's *The Art of War?* It's a classic—and unique copy once owned by Omar Bradley, himself. It's got his ex libris inside the cover. More practical than Whitman, perhaps, but no less valuable."

"Not today," Lucky said, making a mental note to Google Omar Bradley. She headed out, the book tucked under her arm.

As she turned the pages of the Whitman on the train she imagined making her PowerPoint presentation on her proposal to revamp the education program at prisons and someone in the committee asking, "But Miss Boyce, what credentials do you have to make such an outrageous proposal?" and herself—slowly turning red—saying, "But it just *feels* right? Isn't there something to be said for common sense?" Maybe she could just quote Whitman: "Wisdom is not finally tested in schools." *That* would go over real well. No, she would just have to stick to her guns. The plan would save the state money in the long run. It sounded like voodoo until you actually sat down and looked at the numbers—and *that* was exactly what Lucky was qualified to do.

The next morning, Barkley stopped by her office. Lucky figured he was there to talk about her presentation, but he went to the window and tapped the glass. The protestors had started gathering. The cops were there, too, waiting to load them into police vans. "There's no bail for them this time," Barkley said. "They're going to be charged as domestic terrorists—can you believe that. They'll all do time. Do not pass go, do not collect two hundred."

"How do you know?" Lucky asked, standing and looking out of the window. It wasn't a challenge so much as an honest question.

"Coleman told me. He's excitable that way. And he hates religion. He hates pseudo-religious types. And he *especially* hates PETA activists. They've been badgering him for months now. Seem to have made a pet project out of annoying him. Never mention anything that remotely resembles animal rights to him. Or religion. Or anything else left of the NRA, for that matter."

"So that's it? Coleman gets mad and due process goes out the window?"

"Oh, they'll get due process," Barkley said. He laughed. "They'll give 'em a fair trial and *then* hang 'em."

"Tell me about Coleman…"

"Well, he's basically a good man, or so I've heard. Eccentricities aside. He's done some good things—twisted some insurance company arms, come down on some pharmaceutical firms, even hamstrung some of the malpractice lawyers. He's the consummate politician. He claims his goal is workable, affordable healthcare for everyone. Science and medicine—that's his mantra."

"A noble ambition," Lucky said.

"Yes, noble." Barkley sighed. "A *lofty* ambition. Not the same thing as noble, necessarily. Don't let him fool you. Coleman sits in the inner sanctum, the inner core of the Directive Board of the

GWC that drives Health and the FDA. He has the president's ear. Right up there with the Joint Chiefs and the CIA and Homeland Security and the Feds and what-have-you. He could have had any job he wanted, he's one helluva politician. A good administrator. A real terror to his staff. If he has one fault it's that he's ruthless. Ruthless, but good. Always in control. He *chose* the GWC and not because his background is science, either."

"Then why?"

"It's where the *real* power lies, Lucky. These guys rule the Department of Health and Human Services (H&HS) and the FDA, I may add." Barkley said with raised eyebrows.

"And it sanitizes him. It suits his ambitions. He's not military and he's not an academic. He's a pure politician. He wants to be visible, but in the right places. His role at the GWC fixes that. He's not a doctor, but people seem to forget that. They think he is, and who better to trust than your *doctor?* After all, he has your *health* foremost in mind." Barkley placed his right hand over his left breast, "And your best interests at heart. He's a climber, Lucky, and unconventional. He's dedicated to his profession, but he wants more."

"What more could he want?"

"Rumor has it he wants to run the World Health Organization."

Lucky stood up and stretched. The muscle in her calf was aching again—a small burning pinpoint pain. *The smallest muscles*, she thought, *sometimes cause the most annoyance*. Big muscles had plenty of oomph to deal with pushing and pulling, but the small ones, despite being just as useful, are more delicate. That is one of the things about yoga—it makes one work on one's balance. And what is balance but fine control, the small muscles guiding the big ones? Take the triangle pose, for instance: feet wide apart, one foot aligned north/south, the other on the east/west axis. Bending to the side, stretch those big lats and deltoids and trapezius muscles, as well as the smaller muscles of the neck. Even the calf and hamstrings, and to some extent, the abs and psoas muscles. But the pose simultaneously stretches the thighbone into the hip socket—

deepening the bone into the socket in a kind of stretch-in-reverse. And maintaining balance while doing all this involves a myriad of small muscles from the neck right down to the toes. Invariably, when Lucky taught this to new inmates—as she had that morning—they fell. It took new practitioners a month or more of doing the triangle pose with their backs to the wall for support before they had the small muscles tuned so they could support the weight of the whole body. And the more muscular the inmate, the longer it took him or her to develop this fine control. Funny how it was the little muscles that worked like hinges to turn the whole door.

Ambition, Lucky thought, *is like the big muscle. But what's the balance point?* Maybe that was where conscience came in.

Lucky bent down and touched her palms to the floor and held the pose for nearly a minute. Then she straightened up and slipped into an extended triangle pose, her legs wide, her left foot pointed out, the right forward. She held her arms wide and leaned as far to her left as she could, finally resting her left hand on her left ankle, her right arm pointed straight up toward the ceiling.

"You knew I taught yoga?" Lucky asked.

"Of course."

"I taught a class of inmates this morning."

"I've often wondered if there was any benefit to your work. Yet, somehow, your students seem to leave early and return less often."

Lucky laughed. "Yoga is not just about the body. It is also about the mind. Maybe *primarily* about the mind."

Barkley frowned, puzzled. "Like a counselor?"

"A little bit, maybe. You have to work with the *whole* person." Lucky changed sides and looked Barkley over. He was middle-aged and overweight. He would have gone bald long ago but for hair replacement therapy. At sixty, he still sported a thick, black, natural-looking head of hair, and a flat, black mustache hung over his upper lip. On his right hand, he wore a large silver ring, inlaid with lapis lazuli that Lucky remembered was only found in Afghanistan. His left hand was bare, however, as he was divorced. He was a good enough boss, in a quiet, unobtrusive kind of way. He preferred to manage from a distance and let his people do their jobs. As long as things got done, he didn't fuss about the details of how. It made him seem, in some ways, dull-witted, but Lucky wondered if it wasn't a deliberate ruse. What difference did it all make, anyway? Aside from work, though, he was a total mystery. Lucky didn't know if Barkley fished or collected stamps or Hitler memorabilia or cooked or owned a pet rock. Nothing. His personal life was unknown to her.

He patted his belly. "Afraid I could never bend like that," he said.

"No one can when they start," Lucky said. "You never know what you can do until you try." The words came back to her: "Here is realization; Here is a man tallied—he realizes here what he has in him…"

"Hmm," Barkley said. "Some sage of the East?"

"Walt Whitman," Lucky said. And then it hit her that she understood what Whitman meant about the past and future, majesty and love, and being vacant of them and their being vacant of you. He was talking about *attachments*. He meant that if people were too attached to the past or the future, they restricted their options and limited themselves to what they knew or what they did not fear. *But*, Lucky thought, *majesty and love aren't attachments, only attributes of being, qualities that know no fear, the possessions of a man or woman who knows no fear. Or, at least, who is not ruled by fear. These are the kind of attributes that are worth being attached to.* "The point is," she said, "that you never know what you can do until you try."

"And why would I want to do that?" Barkley said. "I've gotten along quite nicely for sixty years without it."

Lucky sat in lotus pose on the little rug in front of her desk. Then she lay all the way down onto her back in full fish pose. She took a deep breath and exhaled slowly. "Your right leg is an inch shorter than your left," she said, "So your hip and lower back hurt all the time. Sometimes the pain spreads to your shoulders because of the tension in your back. You'll pay fifty or a hundred dollars for a massage—I can always tell when because the next day you feel better. You're chipper, more alert, and you move around more. There's a little bounce in your step. You'll spend money on massage, chiropractors, orthotics for your shoes, an ergonomic chair, and a back brace, yet you won't invest a few minutes every day in taking care of your body."

"What I need," Barkley said, patting his stomach again, "is an exer-cycle and a weight machine. I used to play lacrosse in college, did you know that?"

"No," Lucky said. "I would not have guessed that."

"I was a defenseman, and a rather good one, if I say so myself. Second string all-American my senior year. Strength and endurance—*that*'s the key to fitness. If I tried that stretch now, I'd probably break something I might need later." He laughed.

"Anyway," Lucky said, "the point I started to make is that through yoga, I teach my students how to straighten out their lives. Sending people to prison with no hope, no plan for their rehabilitation, no knowledge of what they need or how to help them, just because you have the power and they piss you off, practically guarantees they will reoffend. It's all connected."

"So by teaching them to sit like pretzels you help them straighten out?"

Lucky couldn't tell if Barkley was joking or serious. She bent down and placed her palms flat on the floor. Carefully she aligned her knees to her elbows and then rolled forward so that she balanced on her hands and her head, her knees resting on her elbows. Then, she slowly straightened into a headstand, and then a handstand.

"Good God!" Barkley exclaimed.

"This is nothing," Lucky said, and slowly she shifted her weight to her right hand and, holding her left off to the side, executed a perfect one-handed pushup.

"Wow!" Barkley exclaimed. "No wonder those inmates come to class!"

Lucky stood up, feet apart, bent forward, arms stretched, palms upward facing the walls, and placed her head between and beyond her knees. She smiled and explained, "This is my pose—*a lucky pose*." As she took a breath to continue, her phone rang.

It was Emil, her secretary. "Lucky," he said. His voice was quavering.

"Nobody else better answer my phone."

"Clevis Coleman is on his way to your office."

"What? *My office*? Coleman to see *me?*"

"Yes and nobody else is supposed to be in it."

"Touché. Did he say why?"

"He didn't call for an appointment. The front desk called me. They tried to reach you but you wouldn't pick up."

"Thanks." Lucky hung up.

Barkley nodded. "I'd best be going." But he stood by the window looking at the protestors until Coleman burst through the door. Lucky was smoothing her blue pantsuit and hair with one hand and offering Coleman a handshake with the other.

He ignored her. He looked from Lucky to Barkley and back again, then snapped to Barkley, "Don't you have something important you were about to do?"

Barkley swallowed and nodded. "I was just about to—"

"Then I suggest you do it."

Barkley nodded and left.

"Sit down," Coleman said. He looked at his watch. "I have ten minutes."

Lucky sat. "Shall I call for—"

"No time for that. I read your file. You're a smart girl. I've had my eye on you for a while now. Really pissed me off with that stunt yesterday, so I won't beat around the bush. If you don't know Daphne and I are lovers, you soon will, so keep your mouth shut, understand?"

"I'm pleased to meet you, too," Lucky said.

"Pleased has nothing to do with it, does it?" Coleman said. "I'm talking about job performance. So we can dispense with formalities. The one thing I can't afford right now is a public divorce. These things have to be handled delicately—especially in my position. I'm sure you can understand, having had a very public divorce yourself."

Lucky squirmed in her chair.

"You're not the only one who can research." He lit a cigarette and exhaled a thick cloud of blue smoke in Lucky's direction. "Do you mind?" he asked. "Another of my vices. In a week, you'll know all of them. And you'll probably hate me. So what? I'm not here to be liked. And at least I'm not hypocritical. With me, what you see is what you get." He gestured to Lucky with his cigarette and grinned. "When I was a boy growing up in Kalispell, my stepfather told me to climb a tree and walk out on a limb. He stood underneath, held out his arms, and said, 'I'm going to teach you a lesson about *trust*, boy. Now jump and I'll catch you.' I jumped and he stepped aside. I landed flat on my back. While I lay on the ground gasping for air, he said, 'The lesson is, *trust no one*.' I don't make a move before I cover all my options." He crushed the cigarette out on the strap of his wristwatch and threw the butt into Lucky's trash.

"Most people think relationships are founded on integrity, idealism, and all that emotional kitty litter. What a crock! Sun Tzu says, 'Those who are puritanical can be disgraced.' So I don't waste any time appealing to religious sentiment. That was Reagan's angle. I've got my own. Healthcare. It'll be the miracle of the 2000s. Communism is dead. Gangs are on the run. Terrorism will fade as well. So what else are people afraid of? Death! The final frontier. The ultimate enemy. People are scared shitless of it. And death and taxes are the only things constant in this world. We're going to make health care the Marshall Plan of our generation. Universal healthcare. Vaccinations. Cures. Genetic engineering. People want to live forever and I'm going to give it to them. And at a price they can afford. Or least," he said, checking his watch, "at a price they are convinced they cannot afford *not* to pay.

"As for my vices, everybody's got vices, and the more they deny them, the more vulnerable they are. Successful relationships are founded on three things. One, an-iron clad understanding of power dynamics, i.e., I have it and you don't. That's not hard for a bright girl like you to fathom, now is it? Two, clear communication, of which the explanation of the preceding item is a prime example. Still with me? Of course you are. That's because I communicate clearly and effectively. And item three, fear. Not trust, not love, not devotion or respect or any of that emotional kitty litter, but a simple understanding that I-won't-tell-on-you and you-won't-tell-on-me, and if you screw up, I'm going to nail you to the wall and watch you bleed. 'What restrains competitors is harm.' That's why the Allies won World War II. Am I right? Am I?"

Lucky had barely digested the "hate me" part of Coleman's speech. She nodded.

"So you and I, we have our secrets, I'm involved with Daphne and you're a divorcee who's adopted a son with a background better unknown than known. His father, Steve is a convict who escaped while out on bail. Wonder how that happened, Lucky?" Coleman straightened up and glared at Lucky.

Lucky defiantly scowled back, saying, "Nothing to do with me, check the records and before you insinuate me please show me the proof."

Coleman replied in a calmer voice, "I am merely stating facts here. All I want is that you keep your mouth shut and we'll get along fine."

Lucky's blood ran cold.

Coleman then smiled a tight smile and continued. "Now that we have it all settled, we can move on to the real reason why I'm here." He looked at his watch. "Eight minutes. May I?" he asked, nodding in the direction of Lucky's computer. Lucky got up, letting Coleman insert a small gold-plated flash drive into the laptop. "I actually came to ask for your help," he said. "I had my doubts, but your little demonstration convinced me that you might be onto something."

A grainy black-and-white photo appeared on the screen. In it, a group of men stood in front of what appeared to be a stone building with a backdrop of high mountains. A line of fluttering prayer flags hung in one corner. There was nothing remarkable about the men; the photo could have been taken almost anywhere: the Andes, the Himalayas. Their square, flat, dark, slightly Asian faces bore humorless expressions. One of the faces was circled in red and, as Coleman clicked away at the keyboard, that face enlarged until it filled the screen, blurring as the program approximated his facial features and filled in the missing pixels. Eventually, there was the unremarkable face of a middle-aged man staring impassively into the camera. He was thin, thinner than the others perhaps, and possibly a few years younger, as well, though his hair was graying and his face was lined with deep creases—the kind of lines Lucky associated with care and worry. The man did not appear menacing. A fatherly face, Lucky thought. A man who understood pain. He wore glasses in a cheap black plastic frame. His eyes, Lucky noted, were bright and alert. They seemed to look right through her, even as they appeared on the screen. It was the face of a man who had no secrets but knew yours. A man who was at peace with the world and his place in it. A man of conviction. A man without fear. He was waiting patiently for you to begin. You would tell him everything, and he would listen. Then he would give you the answer. The photo disappeared and was replaced by a sketch showing a similar, but perhaps slightly older, man.

Coleman said, "This man is Lobsang Telok. He was born in Dharamsala in 1959; his mother fled from Lhasa to India with the Dalai Lama's entourage earlier that year. This is the only photo we have of him. He's kind of in hiding. It is said that he is shy of cameras, in fact, resistant to all technology." He pulled the memory stick from Lucky's laptop and put it back in his inner jacket pocket, giving his chest a final pat, and continuing:

"His father was the personal physician to the Dalai Lama, but he was murdered right as the Dalai Lama fled to India. The boy and his mother escaped."

"All right."

"I'd like to find this man. I'd like to meet him. I need your help."

"I'm sorry," Lucky said, "I'm an accountant and a volunteer yoga teacher and work for the Department of Corrections. I just don't…"

Coleman stood up and placed his hands palm down on the desk. He leaned across at Lucky and said, "I need someone smart to help me out with a small project. It won't take long, and I'll pay you very, *very* well. And I want someone from outside of my organization, someone familiar with Mumbai. I've already asked your boss if I can borrow you for a few weeks. Didn't he tell you? I know this isn't your line of work, but you've got some kind of gift when it comes to this software thing. I'd like you to help my people find this man, Lobsang."

"But why me? Why not someone on the software team?"

"Because you're from Mumbai, you have lived there and that is where Lobsang visits. He runs a temporary clinic there."

Lucky laughed. "So are half the engineers writing code. They could have fielded a cricket team!"

"Yes, but only two of them actually *lived* in India recently. The rest were born in the USA or moved here young with their parents. Believe me, I've checked. You weren't on my radar at first, but I did my research. You would have connections with your business background there, I mean, you know the lay of the land, the culture, the people, and can perhaps charm them into talking." Looking deep into Lucky's eyes, he continued, "And that demonstration I asked for was no accident—it was a test. Shall I say you exceeded my expectations? Besides that, there's something else—the guys here are all engineers. They're good as far as their thinking goes, but they *think* like engineers. You don't. Where I'm asking you to go, and what I'm asking you to do, they wouldn't have a clue. You think out of the box, and I need people who see things differently. I have boatloads of engineers at my disposal. Buildings full of them. You're intuitive in ways they're not. And you already showed me that you could use the software intelligently. I can't ask my local staff, this is 100% confidential."

"I don't know," Lucky said. "I've got a home, my son to think of."

"I'm not asking you to go away for months, just a few days or weeks." He sighed. "If it works out, then perhaps something more—later, down the line. Who knows? Maybe I can find a place for you in Washington. Leave this little side-show burg."

Lucky looked at Coleman. His expression was both grave and sincere.

"What's so important about this guy, anyway?" Lucky asked. "Why is the GWC interested in a poor Tibetan refugee?"

Coleman walked around the desk and sat on the edge, right in front of Lucky. "This influenza we talked about today—it's not a theory. Have you ever had the flu? Or heard about the new strain of Influenza?" Coleman paused and looked Lucky over. "Of course you've had the flu. Everybody has. But not like this. The first flu epidemic was in 1918. Spanish Influenza, they called it. Killed more people than the First World War. Twenty million died. And you know what was strange about it? It wasn't the old and the young and the sick and the lame and so forth who died—it was mostly healthy men and women between the ages of eighteen and thirty-five.

"Why them? Why the healthy and not the old and the sick and the weak? That was what was so frightening—so unexpected about it. We've studied the epidemic for years, and the gene sequences of the virus, and now we think we know why that was.

"Picture a tickle in your throat. Just a tickle, mind you, a little feather of goose down in your esophagus. Five, maybe ten minutes later you cough, just a little 'hut-hut' to clear the airway. But it doesn't go away and so you get a drink of water and think that will help. And it does, for maybe fifteen minutes or so. Then you get hot. You get hot so fast you might even feel dizzy. You want to go lie down but you're young and strong, maybe you're at work, so you tough it out. But in an hour or two, you go lie down anyway. You cancel your plans for the day. You're not hungry, you just want to sleep. You don't know it, but your metabolism has been hijacked. Not just hijacked—enslaved. You see, your body has been taken over by this virus and now that virus is launching a coordinated attack. Anywhere there's mucus, your cells are churning out new viruses, and those cells burst and die. The body's response is to swell. Your chest tightens, you feel like someone has cinched a belt around you. Worse. With every exhale, you find that you cannot fully inhale. You struggle to breathe. And at the same time, you begin to cough in earnest. You throw up lung-oysters, fat gobs of sticky green mucus. You are trying to inhale and trying to cough at the same time. Your heart races. You've become oxygen deficient and you don't even know it. You're no longer thinking clearly. Now, if you're old or sickly, or if you're young and mommy is still watching over you, right away you ask for help, or someone asks for help for you. Your chances might not be good, but if they rush you to the hospital and a nurse inserts a tube in your throat to keep the bronchial passages open, you might live. They'll start an IV to keep you hydrated, bathe you in ice to control the fever.

"But suppose you are young and healthy. Two things work against you. First, you don't seek help right away. Second, your body's defenses, the very ones that are supposed to purge your lungs of contagion, have become the instruments of your destruction. The healthier you are, the more your body tries to kill you. In a few hours you are gasping for breath. Your chest tires. You cannot draw air and you cannot clear the mucus. You drown, Miss Boyce. Or you suffocate. By the time you realize that you are in over your head— it's too late. You might get out of bed, but you haven't the strength, you haven't the oxygen, to walk. You drop to your knees if you feel it coming, and then to your face on the floor. Or maybe you just topple like a tree in whichever direction the wind blows you. They'll find you like that in morning. Onset to mortality in as little as six hours.

"Recovery, if one is so fortunate, may take months. And the hell of it is, Miss Boyce, that you have been quietly incubating the virus for weeks. Who knows how many people you have infected? By the time you are well enough to tell someone where you have been, what you have done, and who you might have come in contact with—in all probability they're already dead."

"And this Lobsang…" Lucky said. "Let me guess. He has the cure?"

"More than the cure," Coleman replied. He got up and walked around the desk, stood facing the screen where Lobsang's picture was displayed. "Lobsang's father was the personal physician to the Dalai Lama. I'm not one for medical fads, Miss Boyce, but do you realize how many discoveries happened by accident?"

"Like Fleming and penicillin?"

"Yes, yes. And Archimedes. And Rontgen, and Plunkett, and Mistral, and Brandenberger, and Chesebrough. History is paved with accidental discoveries." He looked at his watch.

"And Lobsang?"

"What do you know about Ayurveda, Miss Boyce?"

"It's the oldest practice of medicine in the world."

"How old?"

Lucky shrugged. "The writings go back 5,000 years."

"Yes," Coleman said. He turned and faced Lucky. "And we know, now, that much of what they learned 5,000 years ago was right."

"Okay."

"So, tell me, have you heard of the ice mushroom?"

Lucky arched her eyebrows. "No."

Coleman nodded. "Neither had I. As as far as I know, neither had anybody else—until some time in the early 1960s."

"Is this some kind of *psychedelic* thing?"

"Far from it. What happened was, there was an outbreak of dengue fever in a refugee camp. The people, you see, had no natural exposure or resistance to dengue. They should have died. But a few of them didn't."

"Let me guess," Lucky said. "This happened in a Tibetan refugee camp?"

Coleman nodded. "It did. There were some stories, a few people came back with wild tales about this stuff, but in the West, it was dismissed as bullshit. Except that it *wasn't* bullshit. Apparently, somewhere high in the Himalayas, there really does exist a mushroom or fungus or something that, well, extends life. Unnaturally."

"The fountain of youth?"

"Not exactly," Coleman said. "But apparently there is something that boosts the immune system in ways that we don't yet understand. If administered, in most cases, say 80%, it prevents disease. But mainly if taken before one is infected. And that is why I want to find this man."

"Because you think he has this thing?"

"Or knows someone who does. Or where to get it. That's classified."

"I don't know," Lucky said. "It sounds pretty far-fetched to me. I mean, I lived in Mumbai for years and I never heard of this 'ice mushroom'"

"Nor would you have, if it was a closely-guarded family secret."

"Well, sure," said Lucky. "But that doesn't mean it exists." Coleman scowled. "Look, can you imagine what a thing like this would be worth if it could be grown, studied or synthesized, or in some way reproduced? Imagine we can take the properties and make it into a vaccine. Imagine being injected with this vaccine every year, year after year and then staying fighting fit for the rest of your life. No illness, no disease. Just perfect health." He narrowed his eyes. "Think of the pain and suffering that would be alleviated. Imagine a world without cancer or disease. Imagine a cure for AIDS or hepatitis C, ebola, or Spanish influenza, or any of the myriad ills that plague mankind. What does the old song say, 'What a wonderful, world this would be.'"

Lucky pictured Sean in the emergency room. Worse, she pictured herself in the ER, choking to death on her own mucus while Sean watched. "And you believe this stuff exists? And that it could do all that?"

"I know it exists," Coleman said. "And I think it can do a great deal. Who knows what? Our guess is it would contain complex sugar molecules called polysaccharides, which studies show stimulate virus-fighting cells in the immune system. But who knows what secrets it might unlock, just studying it?"

"And you want to do that?"

"It's my job," Coleman said. "And I do it well and sincerely."

"But you're not a doctor or scientist, you're a *politician*."

Coleman smiled. "Somebody's been talking about me, have they? Yes, I'm a politician. And as such, it's my job to get things done. It doesn't mean I do them myself. But I do get them done. Can you imagine, Miss Boyce, what the 'Discovery of the Century' might do for mankind? Can you imagine what it might do for my career? Or yours?"

"But this…mushroom…if it exists, it would be…"

"Worth its weight in gold?"

"Or something like that?"

"No, Miss Boyce, it would be worth much, much more than gold. What was it Jesus said?" Coleman smiled a wry smile. "'What would man give in exchange for his life?'"

Lucky shivered. "But you say you're sure this stuff exists? It's not just another bullshit story about miracle drugs from the Amazon?"

Coleman stood up. "There may be drugs in the Amazon, too, but what's different about this is that we *know* it exists. I've met a man who's taken it."

"Who?"

Coleman fidgeted. He looked Lucky over carefully. "His name is Sun Lin."

"So why don't you ask him?" Lucky asked.

"We did," Coleman replied. "But his knowledge is limited. The epidemic was raging. Sun Lin was the head of the camp and was given a few mushrooms to distribute, although he can't remember the doctor who gave them to him. It was done at night. It was all very chaotic. The mushrooms were made into bits and distributed, and the people not infected were all saved. It helped some of the sick, although he claims there were only three survivors. His daughter was one. That's why I give it only an 80% chance. But again, that is the best clue we have. It's not mythology. We know this thing exists— only we don't know how to find it."

Lucky thought about this. "How is he so sure it worked?"

"Three things," Coleman said. "Sun Lin said his daughter knew what happened because she was dead and looking down from above. We have her testimony."

"Great," Lucky said. "Maybe she can predict the next Kentucky Derby winner while she's at it."

"They had no other medication available."

"That's a bit more reliable," Lucky said. "And the third thing?"

"And the third thing is that we tested Lin's immune system. He has near-perfect immunity against everything from the common cold to the AIDS virus. His daughter was also tested, but she had lower immunity levels."

Lucky frowned. "You tested them?"

"Yes."

"What's so interesting about that?" Lucky said. "With immunity."

"Because," Coleman interrupted, "In 1950, Sun Lin was the Commander of the People's Liberation Army at Qamdo."

"Wait a minute," Lucky began counting on her fingers.

"That's right," Coleman said. "Add it up. In 1950, Commander Sun Lin was already 42 years old."

"Do you mean to tell me that Sun Lin is *still alive*?"

"Yes," Coleman said. "He's 105 years old, in near-perfect health. He has *never ever* been ill since. Then he tried unsuccessfully for years to find the doctor and the mushroom and that's why he finally came to us through a friend as a last resort. Someday, he'll die. He knows that. An accident or perhaps his body will just give out. He didn't want to die without the world knowing, so he came to us personally with a plea to find this medicine."

Coleman paused as if deep in thought and then said, "In fact, he also gave us a warning that we are not the only ones looking for it."

"You mean the Chinese?"

"Again, that's classified," Coleman said. "And I'm trusting you not to repeat this to anyone. But there's another reason why we want to find this Lobsang. We have reason to believe that the Chinese were looking for the drug when they killed Lobsang's father. And that also might explain his desire to remain hidden all these years. We think he's in Mumbai, but when things heat up he moves in and out. Hard fellow to catch. His clinic is mobile. It has no fixed address. His followers guard him with their lives. They're devoted to him. Now you know why.

"My people will call you. We'll double your salary. Meanwhile, I need you to come to Washington for a few days and get up to speed with my staff. We'll set you up with a nice little office there. You'll have plane tickets in the morning.

"Remember," Coleman said, "you heard it here first. Anyway, I can use a few closed-minded, tight-lipped, smart people on my staff. Hitch your wagon to me and you'll go far."

"Mr. Coleman—" Lucky said.

Coleman straightened up. "Call me Clevis. After you leave, you can call me Mr. Coleman again." He turned to go. At the door, he looked back. "Not a word of what you're working on, understand? What I have just told you is of the highest level of national security. If you leak a word of this—you'll end up in some place that'll make Guantanamo look like a Carnival Cruise."

And then he was gone.

CHAPTER 4

Lucky stared for a long time at the door. She shook her head. Perfect immunity? A long life? A race with the Chinese? Bad luck to even think about it. But Coleman was right about a few things. She was good with Bloodhound. At least somebody had finally noticed her talents. Her mind raced as she thought about the possibilities. If what Coleman said was true, this was a worthy project. Even if it wasn't true, she could hitch her wagon to a rising star. A lot of good could come of this—even if the Lobsang story turned out to be complete bullshit, which she was sure it would be. She would have to make arrangements for Sean, though. Perhaps Amay would look after him.

There was a knock at the door. Barkley. "Has the devil vanished with a flash and a bang?"

"He's gone."

"So what's the new assignment?"

"I can't talk about it, but I'm not sure I want it, either."

Barkley sat down in one of the chairs opposite Lucky's desk. "What's to think about," he said, "Hate to lose a fine worker like you, of course—won't find another. Someone will take your desk, but nobody can take your place." He laughed.

Lucky looked around the office. Coleman's offer was looking more appealing by the minute. Here in New York, what did Lucky have to look forward to? A bulging, bureaucratic middle age of meaningless assignments in a decrepit state government office? Then again, there was something creepy about Coleman. Lucky felt like she had been hustled into taking the post. "What happens," Lucky asked, "if I don't want the assignment?"

"What's *want* got to do with it, Lucky Boyce? Who wants *any* of these assignments?" He gestured with his hand toward the door. "Do you want what's on my desk right now? You can *have* it." He turned and stared out the window. It was already drifting into late afternoon. He suddenly looked back at Lucky. "You can't be serious? You're not thinking about turning Coleman down? The only thing I can think of worse than working for him would be crossing him."

"What would happen if I did?"

"Why on earth would you?"

"I've got Sean to think about, and my house. Coleman wants me to go to Washington for a few days. Tomorrow. I don't know. It's a lot to think about."

"Sean? Get a babysitter! Your *house*? If they move you around—and to my knowledge nobody has suggested that they will—then you can find a house wherever he sends you."

Lucky paled.

Barkley paused and looked her over. "Oh, all right. That house of yours. So it's nice. I'm sure you'd be happier and better off in an apartment like...ahhhh," Barkley said, breaking into a grin. "Nobody's said anything about *money* yet, have they? Got the old accounts book to think about, don't we? I'm sure if Coleman wants you *that* badly there'll be a raise and a promotion. Might even buy you a house. At least they'll pay some hefty relocation money. Wouldn't expect them to toggle you around for nothing, now would we? I'm sure his boys have already cracked the details."

"That's not what I said." Lucky stood up and walked to the window and looked down at the street. It was clear now, just the usual traffic. But there were a handful of policemen loitering around on the front steps, just in case. Coleman and his detail appeared from the entry. They had no sooner reached the street than a caravan of black SUVs, preceded and followed by NYPD cruisers, roared around the corner. It took only seconds for the entourage to pile into vehicles and race off. But Lucky noticed another black SUV facing the opposite direction, parked on the other side of the street. It wasn't going anywhere. "Money's not an issue for me. Hell, I work for you for nothing. But what if I don't want the job? What if I refuse? What happens then? I've got this education project, and I've put six months into it. I believe in what I'm doing, and I'd like to see it through."

Barkley stood up and placed his hand on Lucky's shoulder in a fatherly gesture. "Of *course* you do, my girl," he said. "We *all* believe in what we're doing here. And a splendid job of it you do, too, if I must say so myself. No wonder Coleman swoops down and snatches you out of the nest." He turned and crossed the office to the door and looked up and down the hall. Then he stood with his hands clasped behind his back, looking at the floor. "You're a strange duck, Boyce. You're not like the rest of us, what with your chartered accountancy and multiple degrees…"

"Just a double major in accounting and psychology," Lucky said.

"Okay, pysch, then. But you'll get bored with this work. And you'll get tired of bureaucracy—dealing with Albany and all that. This education thing is near fruition. One thing you'll find is that if you get too attached to your projects they'll only cause you grief. Know why everyone complains that politicians are cold, stodgy, and insensitive?"

"Why?"

"Because they *are* cold, stodgy, and insensitive. Have to be. Only way to survive in this business. If your program gets funded, the first thing that happens is that a hundred men and women not half your equal all want their say in things. Where it goes, how big it grows, how much goes into it, how long—you may create the thing, but in the end it won't be yours. It won't even resemble it much. They'll name it after somebody famous and dead, you know, another Lincoln Project or Washington Something or other. As if a name makes it any better. Somebody else will take the credit. You'll only get mentioned if something goes wrong and they need a scapegoat."

Lucky shrugged. "It doesn't matter," she said. "I said I'd take it. I guess I was just getting the usual cold feet, that's all. It all happened too fast."

Barkley smiled. "What was that crap you were spouting earlier? We don't realize what we can do until we know what we have in us? Or something like that?"

"Something like that."

"Well, you better start realizing, young lady. You're running with the big boys now. So unless you want to spend the rest of your life teaching yoga to inmates, when Coleman says 'Jump!' you'd best ask, 'How high?' Though I wouldn't mention any of that yoga stuff to him either."

"Yeah, I gathered that already."

"Good luck," Barkley said. He checked his watch. "I suppose you'll want to leave straight away and get cracking on this. Go on. We'll do fine here." And with that, he disappeared out of the door.

Lucky got up and surveyed her office. She looked around at the little Indian trinkets dotting the wall: plaster of Paris elephants set with colored glass stones, a tapestry from Rajasthan stitched from fragments of old wedding dresses, a painting of Ganesh, a collection of old sepia-tone photographs of maharajas from the 1800s. Only a few years ago she would have written to her mother excitedly about her prospects, but now, well, she had an uneasy feeling about all of this.

"It is simple to promise the moon," Shanti used to say, "but another thing altogether to deliver. Beware of men who make promises that sound too good to be true." But now, Lucky's mother was dead, Shanti was dead, and Alec and Susan would not understand her reluctance. She wondered, "What would Shanti say about longevity?"

Be careful what you ask for? Who wants to live forever? No, more likely she would say, What makes you think that we don't? What is death but a part of life?

Lucky started to go but then went back to her desk and opened a browser on her computer. She Googled *ice mushroom*. A games forum came up. Great, she thought. It read: *Obtain Ice Mushrooms in Battle Quest: Big Horn Yeti*. Wonderful. The yeti. Lucky sighed but kept staring at the monitor. On a whim, she connected to the NYPD website and started a search. Misdemeanor arrests. Male. Under 40. Blond hair. Arrested before noon yesterday. Manhattan.

The search returned multiple pages, at twenty photos to a page. Who would have thought there were so many blond troublemakers in Manhattan yesterday? Luckily, he was on page two, staring into the camera with that same, calm, unperturbed look. What a mug shot. He might just as easily have been ordering a latte as being booked into jail. His name: Usko Tahti. *What kind of name is that?* Lucky wondered. She Googled it, and found that it was Finnish, meaning "faith star." She smiled, hearing his voice again: "You can help or just walk away."

He was thirty-five, and a newly enrolled doctoral candidate at Columbia working on a PhD in Comparative Religions. He was also a writer with a half-dozen articles in journals and another dozen or so poems. She read two of them, "Starlight over Bones" and "Red Dust Kandahar." In the first, a young soldier was writing home to his sweetheart and child while standing guard over a mass grave. In the second, a sniper watched a boy planting an IED (improved explosive device) in the road at night but couldn't bring himself to pull the trigger. *What the hell?* Lucky wondered.

She dug deeper. Thanks to Finland's universal male conscription, Usko Tahti had been in the army for years, rising to the rank of Lieutenant Colonel and obtaining two college degrees along the way: mechanical engineering and psychology. He had served with distinction in Bosnia and Afghanistan. But something had happened. The articles weren't very forthcoming about what. He had disobeyed orders. Mutiny? Insubordination? *What orders?* Lucky wondered.

She kept reading. Usko had nearly been court-martialed. Even his acquittal was tainted with political implications; according to the articles, Usko had *wanted* to go to prison. He had threatened to testify—against himself. Had been ordered by the courts to keep silent. Here was a front page article in *Helsingin Sanomat* and another in *Kuukausiliite*. The latter had a picture of Usko in uniform in front of a tribunal, with exactly the same expression as his mug shot. Lucky checked the date; that was in 2004. Well, here he was, six years later, sporting a saffron robe and protesting institutional violence against animals. *What happened to you, Usko Tahti?* Lucky wondered.

She shook her head. Why should she care? Why should she get worked up over whether a bunch of PETA activists went to jail? He was nothing to her. But communication had passed between them and she'd looked deep into his piercing grey eyes while he looked into hers. For a man who had—allegedly—stared down the scope of a sniper rifle, he didn't look like a killer. He didn't even look that old; he might have been thirty. What could he have known or done that was so dangerous as to deserve a court-martial? Ignorant, foolish, impulsive, naïve, idealistic, misguided, there were any number of things Lucky would have believed about him. But a criminal?

She thought it through. Was it worth the risk? Her finger hovered over the SHUT DOWN icon, but finally, she clenched her teeth and emailed her attorney, John Black.

John,

Would you do me a favor?

There were some protestors arrested this morning in Manhattan just outside my office. PETA activists, I think. I heard they are going to be tried as terrorists and held without bail. Sounds crazy, I know, but there are some politicians involved and maybe some ruffled egos. Will you see that they get bail—at least one of them—if you can't get them all out? The whole thing is ridiculous, really. His name is Usko Tahti. He's a student at Columbia. Please send me the bill. And don't mention my name. Thanks,

Lucky.

She hit send. *There*, she thought. *You've done it now.*

CHAPTER 5

A platform; a line; the press of swearing, sweaty bodies; a careless child and a drink spilled; a gummy red stain that probably won't wash out; a fat, angry woman in a multicolored blouse hustling a cute little runny-nosed boy out of sight for a beating. "It's okay!" Lucky called after her. "It's just a… an old pant suit. I was going to throw it away anyway." No reply. "Or give it to Goodwill." Her voice trailed off as the woman and boy disappeared. *Goodwill.*

A train going east, the air-conditioning working (thank God!), a rocking click-clack and murmur of glazed-eyed banal conversations. Some pro sports draft or another—a lottery of lucky new millionaires. Lucky tuned it out. Was there anything less important than knowing who in Los Angeles was going to make fifty thousand dollars a minute playing a stupid game? Weren't there enough hungry people in the world? The train slowed and Lucky stood, almost the last passenger off. To the west, she saw the pale glow of the sky over the horizon; to the east, a hazy dusk. Suburbia. Connecticut. Further east, a half-moon would be rising over the Atlantic. Dawn in New Delhi, dusk in Manhattan. Lucky smiled.

Her phone rang. Maria was cooking chili rellenos for dinner; could Lucky stop by the grocer for some milk and oatmeal and fruits and fresh cilantro? She could and would. *Oatmeal and cilantro?* Lucky wondered. *I hope the oatmeal isn't going in the tortillas.*

In the checkout line, the woman just ahead of Lucky dug through her purse for loose change. She was a few dollars short for her groceries. A teary-eyed little girl clung to the woman. A gum-chewing clerk eyed them indifferently while a long-nosed manager with a brown mustache and a poorly fitted wig hovered in the background. On the counter before the woman was flour and salt and oil, a lump of hamburger, a few tomatoes, a dozen eggs, a box of donuts dusted with powdered sugar. "I'll pay," Lucky said, proffering her card. The manager eyed her suspiciously, the woman gratefully. The clerk didn't seem to see her at all.

"I'll put these back," the woman said, removing the donuts.

"Those, too," Lucky said, nodding to the clerk.

The little girl clutched them to her chest.

"It's her birthday," the mother said—whether by way of apology or explanation, Lucky wasn't sure.

"Happy birthday," Lucky said, bending down. "How many?"

The girl held up three fingers.

"You're four now," the mother said. She lingered beside the manager while the clerk rang up Lucky's things. The woman was attractive, in a curvy, motherly kind of way. "I changed my handbag and left my wallet behind," she said.

"Happens to us all," Lucky replied.

"Thank you," the woman said again, "if you give me your address I'll repay you."

"Happy birthday," Lucky said. "Pass it on." When the woman was gone Lucky thought about the child. There was something only a woman could understand about carrying a baby for nine months. It was inside of you, a part of you. She had Sean, but was it the same? Why did she yearn for this experience that most women complained about and suffered through? How many women had Lucky heard say, "If we didn't forget the pain, we'd never do it again."

Thinking of children made Lucky think of Amay, and she frowned, realizing she'd never replied to Amay's text asking about dinner. Well, she was too tired to go out now.

A Star Called Lucky

Poor Amay. He was steady, predictable, trustworthy—a real Boy Scout. Lucky and Amay's parents had been good friends, and they'd grown up together. They'd lost touch for a while, and finally reconnected in New York. But since his divorce from Leila, he'd been following Lucky around like a little lost puppy, turning up at her house, at her office, inviting her to his gallery for every sort of opening and lecture. Now he was pestering her to come to Europe with him. He wanted to open another gallery there—one dedicated entirely to children's art and supporting some kind of charity for war orphans. "Why don't you marry me and help me run it?" he'd asked. *Right. Just what I don't want to be. A pet wife. Again.* Why couldn't Amay get it through his head? Was it that hard to understand she would never again put herself in a position where she was not in control of her own life?

"I'd rather be kidnapped by terrorists," she'd said. He'd sulked for a week or two, and then the invites began again. *On the other hand*, Lucky thought, *if it weren't for me coming back to New York, they might have still been married. And Leila was such a sweet girl.* Lucky knew how it felt to lose a husband to another woman. It was not how she wanted things to turn out for Leila and Amay, but sometimes, life was like that. Mistakes were made.

She picked up her groceries. It was less than a mile from the grocer to the road that cut through a little swatch of woods and down a hill that led to her house. Lucky always enjoyed the walk, unless it was pouring cold rain. And sometimes, she liked it even then. *Walking*, she thought, *is good for the soul.*

Along the way, Lucky stopped at Collette's. Collette was the punky sixteen-year-old daughter of one of Lucky's neighbors. She was a skinny girl with hair dyed jet black and a gold ring in her nose. She was, Lucky thought, the kind of teenager who made you glad you weren't her mother. Not that she was involved in anything seriously bad—Lucky hoped—but she was exasperating. Which was why Collette's mother had never minded Lucky's being sort-of friends with Collette.

Analise Kennedy-Skyles—Collette's mom—was an ambitious hot-shot PR consultant, always jetting around the country from this city to that, from one corporate office to another. Collette's father, Wayne Skyles, was a London-based corporate raider and a borderline alcoholic. The parents had met on the job, but their whirlwind romance had plummeted from glossies on the society pages to nasty write-ups in the gossip columns as they battled through a bitter divorce. All kinds of rumors had swirled around them. From what Lucky gathered, Analise was now somewhat on the rebound. Meanwhile, Collette was a teenager in New York with her mother and prided herself on being a computer junkie. She'd practically raised herself—along with a circle of computer friends with names like SLoPoə☼99, acidf8ce, and εϋχ. Not only had Collette never met any of these people in person, she had never even *seen* them, since they all conversed through 3D graphic renditions called *avatars*. Their world was an electronic playground of pseudo-cloak-and-dagger intrigue. They were always tinkering with their computers and Internet connections. Collette had showed Lucky her avatar, once, a donkey made into a parody of a unicorn. It had deer horns, bat wings, and a scorpion's tail. It looks dorky, but watch out for the sting," Collette said.

"Aren't you worried about online predators?" Lucky asked.

Collette yawned. "They're the ones who should be worried about me. Do you know how many pervs I've reported to the FBI?" Lucky didn't know and didn't ask.

Lucky set down the groceries and knocked on the door, and after a moment, her phone rang. She took it out and Collette sang, "Hi, Lucky. What can I do you for today?"

How had Collette known who was at the door? Lucky looked up and down the porch. In one of the hanging plants she saw a glint of glass and red LED. *A camera.* Lucky looked for a wire, but there was none. Wireless? The number on her phone said UNKNOWN. "I was wondering if you could take a look at my computer for a moment?" she said.

"K," Collette replied. A moment later, Collette opened the door and led Lucky into the kitchen. She poured two glasses of cherry Kool Aid, forgetting as usual that Lucky never drank it.

"How come you're not showing up on my caller ID?" Lucky asked.

"It's a new application I downloaded on the bird. It turned our microwave into a pirate cell tower."

"On the bird?" Lucky asked.

"Cheep, cheep. Cheep, cheep," Collette replied.

"So you hacked it?"

Collette shrugged. "Somebody might as well do it. I mean, it's not like they're going to sell this for iPhones or anything. What's up with your 'puter?"

Lucky handed it to Collette, who sniffed it, then turned it over and squinted as she read the specs. "So what'd you do to it?"

"Nothing, I just can't get it to open right. It sometimes keeps defaulting to Hulu."

Collette sniffed it again then eyed it curiously.

Funny, Lucky thought, her feet barely reach the floor when she sits in that high chair, but here she is, about to fix my computer.

"Kind of a virus-y thing, huh?"

"No, it just keeps coming up to Hulu."

"But you keep resetting it and it keeps doing something you don't want?"

"Yeah, I guess."

"Uh huh." She took a long swig of Kool Aid and looked at the clock on the wall over in the breakfast nook. "Sounds like you got a virus."

"I don't know how, the computer's brand new."

Collette yawned. "Who knows? You got antivirus?"

"Of course."

"Well, that's good. But it still might have picked something up before you installed it."

Lucky sighed.

"I got this friend in Bulgaria, Yazma, but he doesn't get up until midnight—his time. That'd be about…" she looked at the clock on the wall, "now. We're seven hours different, I think. He has something that scans hard drives for buried code. But it takes time. I'll ping him and see if he's around. When did you say you need this?"

"Well I," Lucky began. She hadn't intended to leave it, just to get the settings fixed. "Are you sure you can't just…" Then she stopped. Coleman would have a computer for her in Washington—so it wasn't a big deal. "I'll be out of town for a few days," she said, "so there's no hurry. And by the way, do you think you might have some free time to look after Sean? I mean, Maria may need some help around the house."

"I got tons of time," Collette said. "All the time in the world."

Lucky got up to go but turned at the door and looked at Collette. "Are you okay, sweetie?"

Collette followed Lucky to the door. "Never been better. I hacked into the school computer yesterday and posted my grades for the year. I'm not going back."

Lucky blanched, and Collette smirked a bit at the expression.

"Don't worry, I didn't give myself the kind of grades that anybody'll notice. B's and C's, mainly. And nobody there'll miss me, anyway."

Lucky reached out and stroked Collette's hair. "You're such a sweet girl," she said. "Promise me you'll at least read and do your math every day?"

"Math's easy," Collette said. "Do graphic novels count?"

"Graphic? Oh, you mean, with pictures. No. Real novels. Why don't you try something like *Anna Karenina*?"

Collette rolled her eyes. "What's that about?"

"It's a story about a family in Russia a long time ago. A love triangle, sort of. Mostly about two sisters, Kitty and Anna. Levin loves Kitty, but Vronsky, an army officer, wins her. Then Vronsky dumps her and runs off with Anna Karenina. Anna is married but her husband won't give her a divorce. Kitty eventually realizes that she made a mistake and agrees to marry Levin. Their life turns out happy. But Anna, doubting her lover and trapped in a loveless marriage, throws herself under a train."

"But what does it all mean?" Collette asked.

"What do you mean, 'What does it mean?'"

"What's the point?"

"It's about love," Lucky said. "What is true love? And how does one find it? I guess you could say it's about not judging by appearances."

"Love," Collette said, "is the biggest crock of shit ever pulled over a girl's eyes."

So that's the problem, Lucky thought, as she walked home. *Collette's boyfriend dumped her.* She made a mental note to call Analise and to drop a hint to the school counselor.

Perhaps it was Alec's and Susan's, her godparents, palatial colonial home with the carefully manicured grounds (grounds that Lucky sometimes referred to as the 389th National Park) that inspired Lucky to purchase a tiny house clinging to the edge of a ravine on a piece of wild land that nobody else wanted and nothing could be done with—literally at the end of the road. But she liked the quiet and privacy. The inside of the house was civilized enough, reminding Lucky of the quaint cottage behind Alec's and Susan's and all the happy weekends she had spent there conversing with Susan and watching Alec teach Sean to read Dr. Seuss, build Lego castles, and fold origami cranes.

This house had borne little resemblance to the cottage when Lucky purchased it. Then, it had been an old 1940s concrete-block house with a tilting foundation and a leaking roof. Over time, and with much love, she had transformed it into something special, once spending a whole week sleeping in a tent in the backyard while the old roof was torn off and replaced right down to the joists and rafters. And she had the walls insulated and energy-efficient windows installed. She laid the natural flagstone tiles herself, everywhere but in the kitchen, where she used hand-painted ceramic tiles. To keep the floors warm, she laid Kashmiri rugs, three mostly red and one mostly blue, housewarming presents from Alec and Susan. The rugs, Lucky knew, were collectors' items. They probably cost as much as the house.

But there was another reason Lucky wanted the property. There were eleven acres that wound along the inside of the steep-sloped ravine. The ground here was too soft for heavy construction. The creek—designated a wild bird preserve—could not be dammed or piped or diverted. The ravine trapped cold air in winter, which was bad, but it was also shady and cool in the summer, which was *very* good. It had at least a trickle of water most of the year; only in late August, in the driest of summers, did the spring fade to a wet, moldy smudge on the rocks from which it sprang. Along the banks of the creek were a number of old silver maples and cottonwoods, and among them grew a profusion of ostrich ferns and stinging nettles and grasses and weeds and wildflowers. Cattails grew in the deeper pools in the creek, and in the spring, the thin, new leaves filtered the sunlight into a bright, fresh green. In the summer, the thickened leaves canopied the ravine into a dusky and sedate shade of dark gray where Dragonflies whizzed by in the evening, and tree swallows and butterflies flitted in the mornings. Lucky had once seen a deer in the ravine, a doe, alone. And on another occasion, a red-eared slider turtle had bobbed up in the pond. There were occasional herons, too, and at least one raccoon had taken up residence somewhere in the area. Sean had spotted it and taken to leaving treats for it on the back patio.

"In other words," Lucky had said, as she showed off the remodeled house to Alec and Susan before the housewarming party, "it's perfect."

"Except if you have an emergency," Susan replied.

"You are soooooooooo dramatic," Lucky had retorted.

Now Lucky peered through the open window across the living room and into the kitchen, where Maria worked over something floury on the counter. As she watched, Maria pushed back a lock of hair that had fallen into her eyes. She wore her favorite apron—sky blue and white—the colors of the Guatemalan flag. She had made chili rellenos (although not Guatemalan, they were still Sean's favorite—he called them "ray-nos") with rice and beans and strips of steak with onions and green chili on the side. Lucky wanted to slip in through the door unnoticed and sneak up on Sean from behind, playfully spooking him in the kitchen, but before she was halfway across the living room, Maria called out, "Hi, Luck-eeeee," and the plan was ruined.

Maria was short and broad and mahogany-skinned, her face long, wide at the eyes, narrow at the chin, with pronounced cheekbones and a wide, triangular, hawkish nose. In some ways, she looked almost Indian—South Indian, anyway, or Tamil. Her hair was thick and black and very long and shiny. It was Maria's eyes that made Lucky hire her—they were so dark, yet full of life. *Like water sparkling in a cave*, Lucky thought at the time. Although Maria had lived a hard life, there was not a hint of anger or bitterness in her eyes. They were, Lucky thought, like deep pools of love. Maria was not the kind of woman one sees once and forgets.

The bad part was that while a few of Maria's relations were documented aliens, the rest were refugees. Where did they all come from? Mexico? Guatemala? El Salvador? Really, other than Maria's word, Lucky had nothing to go on. It was no use tracking them. There were no databases in Mexico, not like here in the good old U S of A.

And when the night was finished and Maria had gone home, Lucky realized she hadn't told her about the trip to Washington. *Tomorrow*, she thought, and sighed. Or maybe she'd just send Sean to stay with Amay. She decided to call Amay and arrange it.

"Hey, sweetie," he said, sounding sleepy.

"I got your text," Lucky said, "but I was busy. It was a strange day. I was mega-busy."

"I figured you were."

"Look, I have to go to Washington for a few days and I was wondering if you could look after Sean. I'm sure he'd love to see Murzban and Ava."

"Washington? Why? What's down there?"

"I'm going to work on a little project at the Food and Drug Administration. Just for a few days, a week or two at the most. But who knows? It might turn into something permanent."

"Wow," Amay said. There was a long silence.

Lucky listened. There was a sound like rustling in the sheets. "Are you in bed?" she asked.

"Yeah, I was tired. I went to bed early. Washington, eh? I was not expecting that."

"Me neither. It came out of the blue."

"I suppose that means it might not turn into something?"

Lucky frowned. "I guess so. But it sounds interesting. Wouldn't you want to be doing something good?"

"I'm just being selfish," Amay said. "I don't want you to go. But of course I'll look after Sean. You want to drop him off or should I pick him up?"

"Can you pick him up? Maria will be here in the morning, but I'll give her a week off while I'm gone."

"You leave *tomorrow*?"

"Yes, tomorrow. I told you this came out of the blue."

"I guess so," Amay said. "What will you be doing?"

Lucky bit her tongue. "I really can't say right now," she said. "But I'll tell you about it after I get back."

CHAPTER 6

That night, Lucky dreamed she was at the controls of a bulldozer. How could this happen? She'd never even seen inside the cab of a bulldozer, much less operated one. She woke at dawn drenched in sweat. She'd been grinding her teeth and her jaw hurt. She struggled to remember. There was a protest—PETA activists with signs—but they were all tall blonde men in maroon robes, a river of them washing down the road toward her. The vehicle was out of control and she tried to warn them, to push them back, but she did not know how to handle the joysticks that guided the machine, or the accelerator, or the brakes, and she toggled this way and that and stamped on the pedals, but the machine was crushing the protesters underneath the treads with a sound like dry leaves underfoot in the fall. "I'm sorry!" she shouted over and over again. "I can't stop! Nobody showed me how!"

She climbed out of bed and dressed quietly, stripped off the sheets and threw them in the washing machine. In the kitchen, she lit a stick of incense and sat for a few minutes in lotus pose then made coffee for herself and oatmeal and toast with butter for Sean and mixed a pitcher of orange juice. Sean came into the kitchen rubbing his eyes and dragging Falstaff, his slowly disintegrating stuffed bear, behind him. He wore his Superman pajamas and crawled up into Lucky's lap and hugged her, sucking his thumb. He had stopped sucking his thumb for a while a few months ago, and this was the second time in a week that Lucky had noticed him doing it again.

"Did you sleep okay?" Lucky asked.

Sean shook his head. "Falstaff had bad dreams," he said.

"Oh. That seems to be making the rounds this week. And what did Falstaff dream?"

"'Bout lolygaters."

That was Sean's word for *alligators*. Ever since he'd watched a show on the Discovery Channel about alligators, and how they lurked in ponds to eat whatever came down to drink, Sean had developed a phobia for water. The tub, the toilet, and Alec's and Susan's duck pond. Everything these days came down to 'lollygaters. Lucky spoon-fed Sean his oatmeal and sewed up a little tear in Falstaff's neck. Maria came—on time, thank goodness.

Lucky packed, threw the laundry into the dryer, and said goodbye to Sean, feeling a sudden pang of regret as she kissed him and promised to be home soon. She quickly informed Maria of the situation, telling her Amay would be there soon, then hurried out of the door. But Lucky paused at the rose garden on the way to the subway station. How many times, she wondered, did people say goodbye to their loved ones, walk out the door, and never see them again? She shook it off. Bad omen, thinking things like that.

She caught a train to downtown then hurried along down quiet streets, stopping only at Café Vision for a mocha and a cinnamon roll. On impulse, she went around the corner to see Grant. He was sitting at his place at the counter reading. "That Sun Tzu," Lucky said, "do you still have it?"

He did. Lucky bought it before she could change her mind then headed for work.

She was surprised to find Barkley in her office, sitting at the chair behind Lucky's desk. "I didn't expect to find you here so early."

"I had an idea you'd flit in and out." He tossed Lucky a Fed-Ex envelope and Lucky did not have to open it to know that it contained a plane ticket.

"Well," Lucky said, sitting down in the chair opposite Barkley, "We'll see how it goes." She rested her chin in her hands.

"Where's my bright-eyed girl?" Barkley asked.

"I left her at home."

"Still not sure about the job?"

"Somebody once told me if something sounds too good to be true…"

"It's an opportunity some people would kill for," Barkley said.

"Well," she said, looking up, "I'll try my best."

"Of course you will, dear girl. Really got swept up in the drama yesterday, didn't we? Hate to lose someone like you. I mean that. You realize that, technically speaking, you're being promoted to a higher level than *me*. Hard to accept, but not hard to believe. Obviously talented. Not like I'm currying favor or anything, but I do hope you remember me when you crack the top."

"I'm not leaving for good, for God sake!" Lucky said. "I don't think…"

"What I mean to say," Barkley said, "is that you'll be missed, when you eventually move on to Coleman's team." He pushed a small parcel across the desk to Lucky.

"What's this?"

"A remembrance."

"I wasn't expecting anything. Besides, I'll be back here in New York in a few days."

"Of course not, no one never expects anything. But you never know, do you? What fun would there be in that? It's the sheer unexpectedness of things that makes them good, isn't it? Go on, open it."

Lucky opened the package to find an ornate, gold-plated frame bearing an old, hand-colored photograph of a Rajput king. The image was impressive: A tall, white mustachioed man in a short blue jacket with baggy pink pants, a pink turban, and a sweeping white cape. His left hand was extended in a gesture, which could be interpreted as either a welcome, or a gesture of finality. His right hand clutched the silver haft of a short, wide, curved sword, the scabbard of which was thrust into his belt. "This is really old," Lucky said, lightly touching the glass overlaying the photo. "Where on earth did you find this?"

"I found it at an antique shop on my way home yesterday. Knew you had a thing for Indian stuff, so I wrangled it for you."

"Thank you," Lucky said. She rose and extended her hand.

Barkley stood up and shook it. At the door he paused. "Mind yourself, Lucky Boyce," he said. "Be careful in Washington. That crowd would boil and eat their children for a promotion."

Lucky nodded. For some reason, one of Shanti's old sayings came to mind. She used to say, "When the hand is empty, there is nothing to grasp." Lucky thought about this and said, "I mean, what have I got that anyone would want?"

Barkley arched his eyebrows. "That kind of thing sounds good on paper, Boyce. But I wouldn't trust them. Not for a while, at least. Magicians always show you an empty hand, but then they pull a coin out of your ear. It might not be so much what you have as who you are, or where you are. Be at the wrong place at the wrong time and you might get run over by a truck. It's not personal, it's just timing. There are some people who think they only look good when they tear somebody else down for comparison, you know?"

When Barkley was gone, Lucky opened the Fed-Ex envelope. A first-class ticket on the 1:00 PM flight. There was a letter, too, with the address of her new office. It confirmed her wages and benefit package (which was eye-popping) and that Lucky had hotel reservations at the Marriott Residence Hotel. *He moves fast*, she thought. And while she was re-reading the letter, her phone rang. It was Collette. "Call me back from a pay phone," she said.

So dramatic. "I thought you were supposed to be—" The line disconnected.

Pay phones? Do they even have those anymore? She checked her watch. Almost 10:00. *Plenty of time*, she thought, as she left her office for JFK.

She stopped by Emil's desk, said her goodbyes, then walked out of the building, noticing a crowd on the sidewalk. *The PETA protesters are back again.* As she walked down a step further, a flash of maroon caught her eye. In the distance, she saw four monks—three short, one tall. She looked again. Three dark, one very pale. *It can't* be, she thought. But then again, how many tall, pale, handsome Buddhist monks were in New York City? She hesitated, then walked closer—yes, it was definitely Usko. She stopped in front of him and met his gaze.

"Hello," Usko said. "Have we met?"

"Not exactly," Lucky said. "I mean, we haven't been properly introduced. But we have met. Sort of."

"Ahh," he said, nodding. "And how do people meet—sort of?"

"You were here yesterday—at the demonstration. I walked by and asked what the fuss was about and when I turned to go you said I could help."

He pointed at her and smiled. "The lady in the blue suit."

"Very observant. Yes, that would be me. I mean, I was wearing a blue suit. I had a premonition. I mean a presentation. But I had a premonition about the presentation, too. I don't usually wear suits. I mean, but you know how business is. Or," she looked at him, staring impassively at her. Then realizing she was making no sense said, "Oh! maybe you don't. But you were easy to remember. Yesterday you were the only one here in a monk's—what do you call those, anyway? Habits?"

"Robes," Usko answered.

"Yes. A robe. And a nice color, too, I might add. It suits you."

"We don't get to choose the color, though. That's traditional. But thank you."

"You're welcome."

"And the suit?"

Lucky blinked. "The suit?"

"The suit you had a premonition to wear. Should you have worn it?"

"I think so, yes, but the presentation was canceled anyway. That was my premonition, that the presentation was going to be canceled."

"I see. And you often have these premonitions?"

"Sometimes. But they're usually spot on when I do."

"That's a good sign," he said. The other monks, all three of whom were short, thin, old, and Tibetan, looked quizzically at Usko.

"Do you know where I could find a good cup of coffee around here?" Usko asked.

Lucky pointed at Café Vision. "Right there," she said.

"Would you like to join me?"

Lucky checked her watch. She had a little time. "Okay," she said,

Usko turned to his fellow monks. "Will you excuse us?" The monks nodded and shuffled off.

They walked to Café Vision, where Usko ordered mocha for himself while Lucky got a latte. They found a table by the window.

Lucky cleared her throat and shuffled her feet.

Usko took a sip and smiled. "Do you work for the government?" he asked.

"No," Lucky said. "I mean yes, but probably not the way you think I do. Why do you ask?"

"You mean, besides that you were suited and were headed into a government office?"

Lucky smiled. "I was working for the State Department of Corrections. The New York State Department of Corrections, I mean. Not *the* State Department." She winced.

"I see."

"But I was just hired at the Health Services. Sort of. I'm on my way to JFK to go to Washington. And you?"

Usko smiled. "Regrettably, I was *not* "sort of" hired by the Health Services. I will also be on my way to Minneapolis. Washington is nicer, but Minneapolis is cooler."

"Yes, it is. Much cooler. Washington has more art and more music and more museums. But Minnesota is cooler. Weather-wise, anyway."

Usko looked at Lucky. "So you're going to work for Clevis Coleman?"

"How did you know?"

"He runs the Health Services. And he was here. And there are important FDA meetings going on inside. He's the reason we're protesting. It wasn't hard to guess he would be the reason you were attending."

Silence. Usko sipped his mocha but his eyes were penetrating. Lucky shifted in her seat, crossed, and then uncrossed her legs. "So what are you really doing?" Lucky asked feeling rather odd.

"Well, besides protesting, I'm raising funds for a special school for children maimed by landmines. I have a presentation at a Lion's Club convention tomorrow."

"Really?"

"Yes."

"And how's that going?"

"Not very well. Since most of the children live far away, and people in America don't have much experience with landmines, nobody around here cares much about them. But the Lions care about children in general, at least in theory, although they mostly support charities for the blind. I might get a token donation. If I'm lucky, I'll touch some rich veteran's conscience and he'll write me a check worth cashing."

Lucky thought about Usko's poem—the one about the boy planting the improvised explosive device. She wondered how much he really knew about explosives. *A lot, I bet*, she thought. Hadn't he been in the Balkans? And Afghanistan?

"Since I'm not having much luck soliciting donations, I was thinking about suing the companies that manufacture the mines. Do you know mines only cost a few dollars to make but almost a thousand dollars each to remove?"

"I did not know that."

"And mines laid in conflict zones are often not mapped—they're laid in a hurry and often by foot soldiers who don't write things down—so they're difficult to find. In fact, we frequently don't know where the minefields are until people step on them. Most often, that means children, because they're the ones running around in the forest. And mines are designed to maim, not to kill. So long after the war is over, we have children losing their feet and hands and eyes to landmines."

"But why maim?"

"Why? Because a dead soldier is a dead soldier. He can be left and buried later. But a wounded soldier—preferably bleeding and screaming in agony—his brothers won't leave him. They'll carry him to a doctor. That takes at least two more men out of action. And the sight of all that generally stops the rest. Hard to find a man who'll knowingly walk through a minefield."

"I see."

"These corporations make millions manufacturing mines, then do nothing when it comes time to remove them."

"So, who makes mines?"

"You'd be surprised. GM used to make them. Mercedes used to make them, until we outed them and a protest ensued. Lots of companies make them. Nowadays, they are mostly made by rogue traders. Arms dealers and Mafioso with little factories on the side."

Lucky nodded. "If you need help with this," she said, "With a lawsuit, I mean, I know a good lawyer…"

"John Black?"

Lucky caught her breath.

"So you're the mysterious stranger who posted my bail."

For some reason, Lucky expected Usko to be angry with her—to call her a meddler or some kind of do-gooder—but instead he bowed slightly and said, "Thank you." He leaned closer and looked straight into Lucky's eyes.

She blushed.

"Why?"

"Why what?"

"Why post my bail?"

"Well, you're a student and all, and I didn't think you had a ton of money to pay for a lawyer—not that Columbia wouldn't go out and find you a good one—but John owes me a favor, so I called him. I mean, you don't look like a criminal. You're just out there for your cause, you know? You don't even look dangerous and you don't belong in jail. I mean, are you? Do you?" Lucky bit her lip. There was something about Usko that she found both incredibly disarming and unbelievably alarming. She couldn't stop talking and she couldn't make sense. "I'm not very good at this kind of thing," she said. "Talking to guys I mean. The opposite sex. I guess that's why I'm pushing thirty and single."

"Me neither," Usko said. "The opposite sex." He leaned back in his seat and crossed his legs. "Maybe that's why I became a monk. So what do you know about Clevis Coleman?"

"Not much, really. I only met him yesterday. He hired me to be on his team. Just yesterday. You said you know him—"

"Sort of," Usko said. "Sort of, sort of, sort of. Sort of *in passing*." He scratched his chin absentmindedly. "I try to cross his path as often as I can."

"Why?" Lucky asked.

"Coleman is ambitious. I don't mind ambition if it's tempered with ethics, but Coleman runs the world's largest institutional torture of animals. Since *the animals* can't ask him to stop, I'm asking for them. And I'm going to keep asking until he does. I've made him a symbol, a target. Kind of like we did with Mercedes. If he doesn't want bad publicity, he's going to have to mend his ways. And bad publicity is the one thing he doesn't want."

"But the government doesn't torture animals."

"You can't be that stupid, Miss…."

"Boyce. Lucky Boyce. But you can call me Lucky."

"The experiments the FDA now approves–under Coleman's personal direction, mind you—are not very different than those that the Nazis performed on Jews and Gypsies and other unfortunates. Give them x amount of this drug and see if they die. If they do, cut them open and see why. If they don't, cut them open and see if they might have died, if you hadn't cut them open."

"But the work is scientific research—I mean, it saves lives. Doesn't it?"

"Does it? If that were true, wouldn't we be healthier today than we were fifty years ago?"

"But aren't we? I mean, life expectancy has gone up, hasn't it?"

"Prolonging life and improving the quality of life are two different things. Many of the things that used to kill people we have learned how to treat. But many other things that used to be statistical blips are now major killers—things like cancer and heart disease; diseases that thirty years ago were virtually unknown in many parts of the world but are now as common abroad as they are here—thanks to diet and medicine."

"You mean the things tested at the FDA?"

"Precisely. Tell me…Lucky. Do you know anything about sociology?"

"Sure. It's the study of systems and societies. Much like psychology but at the group level."

"Nicely put," Usko continued. "Societies, like people, operate on many basic assumptions. For instance, that the purpose of schools is to educate."

"But isn't it?"

"Could be. We'd like to think so. But if that was the purpose, no student would leave school without an exemplary education. No student would earn, say, a 70%, a C. Only when a student mastered a course would they move on. Some might finish sooner, some might finish later, but they'd all graduate with full subject mastery. Sociologists looking at schools without any idea what the stated purpose was would conclude that schools exist, not to educate but to stratify students—to break them down into groups. *Some* students get educated, but *all* students get classified. Classified and stratified."

"But isn't that just a measure of achievement?"

"Not necessarily. Often, the brightest students are the ones who fail. Take Einstein, for instance. Failed math. He was a genius at math—knew more than his professors. He's a perfect example. He could have skipped ahead ten years. The same principle is true with the FDA. If scientific testing was to find out that things were *safe*, we wouldn't eat or consume or use half the things we do. Rather, testing is to find out how *unsafe* things are, to quantify the risk, classify the risk, and proscribe acceptable levels of risk. That way, when people get cancer and die, the manufactures can shrug their shoulders and say that they were acting within the law. Sort of like making landmines and then not cleaning them up."

"In other words," Lucky said, "the whole thing is a sham to keep the blame for deaths away from the producers, and to shift the blame onto the consumers?"

"Pretty much that, but I think *scam* is a better word."

Lucky looked Usko over. "I don't know," she said. "Is it wrong to make an animal suffer if it helps a human being?"

Usko moved closer to Lucky and lowered his voice. "Have you ever heard an animal scream in pain? I have. A deer. I was eleven. I was hunting with my dad."

Lucky remembered a dog she saw run over by a taxi when she was a little girl. It lay in the street yelping for several minutes until another car finished it off. "I guess so," she said.

"That scream was the loudest sound I ever heard until…well, maybe not in volume, but it was a sound I never forgot."

"Until what?"

"Come again?"

"Until what. You said it was the loudest sound you ever heard *until*."

Usko looked away. "Never mind. The thing is, is that a sound you would enjoy listening to? Would you, say, buy a CD of cats screaming in death agony and listen to it over dinner?"

"Of course not."

"So what would you think if I told you that sometimes they surgically remove vocal cords so the experimenters can't hear the animals scream?"

Lucky looked down at her feet. This wasn't why she had followed Usko, and things certainly weren't going the way she had imagined. "Look," she said. "I don't believe in torturing animals. Is there a middle ground between testing and torturing?"

"Not really," Usko said. "Even if there were, corporations and the governments that serve them are not so much concerned with doing what's right as doing what they feel is legally necessary—and doing it as cheaply as possible. Ethics are expendable—just like the animals they kill. It is about respecting life," Usko said. "We have no right to cause any being to suffer. If I won't respect the life of an animal, then I won't respect the life of a man or woman, either. It is about *respect for life*, Lucky."

"You sound a lot like an old friend of mine," Lucky said. "But just for the record, I'm not involved with any of that testing stuff."

"And what do you do?"

"I was hired to research people, I mean a person."

"Who? Me? Is that what he sent you to do? To get close to me? To spy on me? 'Bail him out of jail and see if you can strike up a conversation.'"

"Sent? Spy? Nobody sent me. I'm on my way to the airport."

"And I never said anything about being a student at Columbia, either, so I suppose you just saw my maroon robe and deduced that?"

Lucky blushed. "You're not hard to find," she said. "All I had to do was Google you."

"And how did you know my name?"

Lucky stammered. "Look, the truth is, I wanted to help you. Believe me, I don't always help strangers."

Usko stood up, frowning. "Tell Coleman I said 'Hello' and I'll see him again soon."

Lucky caught his hand. It was warm. "I *wasn't* sent. Seeing you here was just a coincidence. I looked your name up in the arrest records—that's public domain. It wasn't hard to find. And I meant what I said about bailing you out. You don't look dangerous and you don't seem like a criminal."

"Well," Usko said, "You're wrong on both counts. Go back to Google and read some more." He walked away for a moment then turned and looked back at Lucky. "And the dress would have suited you better. Green, yes. Blue is not your color."

When he was gone Lucky thought, *Do I know how to pick 'em, or what? How can I be such a lion in the office and such a lamb on my own?* She hailed a taxi and headed for the airport, realizing as she arrived that she could have almost missed the plane. She was the last person to board.

As she settled into her seat and buckled her belt for takeoff, her phone rang. She struggled to retrieve it while surrounding passengers glared. "Hello?" she said.

Collette. "How come you didn't call me?"

"Collette, sweetie, I've been *really* busy. I just barely caught my plane and I can't talk right now—we're just about to take off."

"Well call me," Collette said. "From a pay phone. And be careful with your phone. You've been hacked."

"I'll call you when I get to Washington, okay?"

There was a sound like someone smacking chewing gum. "I gotta go."

Lucky turned off her phone.

As soon as they landed in Washington, Lucky turned her phone on and it rang before she could even check for messages. At the other end was a deep, melodious, slow Southern baritone voice, "Miss Boyce?"

"Speaking."

"Evan Cotton. Clevis sent me to meet you. When you pick up your bags, I'll be by the exit."

"And how will I recognize you, Mr. Cotton?"

"I'm six feet seven inches tall, black, and I'm wearing a red, green, gold, and black knit cap. Do I need a sign?"

Lucky laughed. "I think I can manage that."

Evan drove—another of those annoying black SUVs.

"Why do VIPs always drive SUVs?" Lucky asked.

"Beats me," Evan said. "Me—I'd have me a Beemer or a Benz. I s'pose they're worried about crashes. And you can get an SUV armor plated."

"So, is this armor plated?" Lucky asked. She looked around self-consciously, suddenly feeling important.

"No—we're expendable. But you can bet the boss man's is, top to bottom. I bet that sucker weighs four tons, all the stainless steel it carries."

Lucky sighed.

"But don't repeat that. Me—I can get away with it. I am, as you will soon figure out, Coleman's token black man. I'm in all his photo ops. But often, I feel like I'm just a glorified gopher."

"Gopher?"

"You know—go fer this, go fer that. Like pickin' you up. I s'prised he didn't tell me to wear a blue suit and little chauffeur hat. Go fer a ride, Miss Daisy?" Evan laughed.

"Come on, it can't be all that bad."

"Oh, it is. Oh, yeahhhhhhhhhh," Cotton said, exaggerating the yeah.

"I've heard that before. Who was it? Soupy Sales?"

"Timmy Rodgers. But it works for me, too."

"I don't remember him," Lucky said.

"Probably best that way," Evan said. "He was a sad Uncle Tom, but he had a good punch line."

They dropped Lucky's bag off at the Marriott—it was on the way to and very near the office. Evan checked his watch. "We've got a half-hour until the next staff meeting. Anything you need?"

"I could do with a coffee."

Over a latte, Evan explained that his background was in immunology—he was a medical doctor (Brandeis, 1997, Magna Cum Laude) whose specialty was tropical diseases and their prevention. He had been with Coleman for almost three years, but he wasn't happy about it. "I came here to do science, but instead, I'm wasting my time," he explained. "You'll find Coleman unbelievably demanding. He'll ask the inconceivable, settle for the impossible, and when you've done it, he'll berate you for taking so long. But trust me, that's all a façade. Underneath that hard exterior beats a heart of stone-cold granite. The man has toxic waste for blood. It would freeze, if it wasn't for all the radioactivity he carries around."

Lucky laughed, but inside she began to wonder, *What have I got myself into?*

The meeting was in a spacious conference room on the 20th floor. A dozen staff gathered around a C-shaped table, pens and cups clattering and phones beeping as they were switched off. Lucky came in last. Evan did not introduce her, and no one asked who she was or even seemed to notice her at all. Lucky wondered if visitors were common, or if Coleman's own people came and went so often; there was no sense trying to get to know them.

Coleman walked in at five on the button. He took his place at the head of the table. "I'll get to the point," he said. On the video screen appeared the same sketch Coleman had showed Lucky the day before. "We haven't had any change or new developments regarding this Telok….Lobsang fellow," Coleman said. "There are, however, reports of eleven new influenza cases in Mumbai. Given the state of the pertinent ministries, that means there could be anywhere from ten to a hundred new cases, and God-only-knows how many fatalities." He looked at Lucky. "Miss Boyce has been brought on board to lend her expertise. She knows Mumbai and she's good at what she does. Unlike most of you," Coleman said, "who couldn't find their elbow given a mirror and an anatomy chart."

A dozen faces turned to Lucky. She blushed.

"So what do you think," Coleman continued. "Is it possible to find this guy?"

Lucky shrugged. "I don't see why not."

"Do you hear that?" Coleman said, looking around the room with a wide grin on his face. "She doesn't see why not."

Lucky looked at the sketch. "This isn't a lot to go on," she said.

"What do you need?"

"What have you got?"

"I've told you about everything. He's a doctor. He's shy about people and technology. He's hiding out somewhere, we presume in Mumbai, where he runs a mobile clinic."

"You trust this?"

"Yes. Later on we got other images. Some old photos. They're on file, but this is the most recent. We paid a high price for this one," Coleman said.

"If information has to be purchased, can you be sure it's genuine?"

Coleman hesitated. "The price I mean," he said, "is that the man who took it paid with his life. He was killed shortly after he sent this to us."

Lucky sucked on her lip. "I assume you suspect the Chinese?"

Coleman nodded, his expression grave.

"Still," Lucky said. "Why couldn't Lobsang or his people contrive to give you a picture to throw you off? How do you know this is Lobsang Telok, at all? I mean, the picture could have been of anybody. In fact, for all you know, and from what you tell me, the Chinese might have given you the picture to throw you off—and then killed the courier to make you think the likeness was authentic."

"Sun Tzu says, 'Dead spies are those who are fooled by their own leaders into passing on false information.' My spies tell me the truth."

"Yes" Lucky said, "and dead men tell no tales. I ask you again: Why should I believe that this picture is accurate? *Especially* since you say the man who gave it to you is dead."

"Sun Tzu also says, 'One cannot use spies without sagacity.' There are many approaches to finding out what you want to know. I believe our man told us the truth. He came to us. We didn't have to ferret anything out of him."

Lucky shrugged. "That's even worse. He came to you. Be that as it may, you have no idea who the man in this sketch was. Or is. Even if there's a resemblance to other photos, it still doesn't mean you were close to the guy."

"I know exactly who's in the pictures," Coleman said. "It's just that the man who helped us with it is dead now, so there's no way to talk to him anymore."

"He was Tibetan?"

"Indian, living in Mumbai."

"Where? When did this all happen? Tell me everything."

"He showed up at the door of a monastery in Hubli. That's in south India. This was in 2005."

Lucky frowned. "What was he doing in south India?"

"The usual, I suppose," Coleman replied. "Working or looking for work. Or smuggling, or something. He took ill and, being Buddhist, showed up at the monastery asking for help."

"Sounds just like the story you told me about Sun Lin."

"Sort of. And that in itself lends credibility to the story."

"Why? Because it's familiar? If someone wanted to throw you off, the best thing they could do is mislead you with something familiar."

Coleman looked around the room and frowned. The group was watching the debate quietly. "The man's name," Coleman said, "is Somasundaram. Was Somasundaram. That's all we know. He went to the south of India, got sick, went to the monastery and was mysteriously healed. When he recovered, he asked what happened. He kept asking questions, but everyone was evasive. Finally, a houseboy told him the story. After that, he began looking for Lobsang. He had no luck at all. That's when he got him when he just walked right into the embassy in Mumbai and said he had a secret. We spoke to him. What concerns us," he said, "is that shortly after that, Somasundaram was found dead in his bed."

Lucky sighed. "You said you paid for the information."

"That's right."

"What was it you just said about dead spies?"

Coleman frowned.

"But this man, Somasundaram, he contacted you?"

"He wanted to know what we knew."

"And then you paid him for a picture?"

"Yes."

"I think a more likely scenario," Lucky said, "is that this Somasundaram fellow somehow found out you were looking for Lobsang and concocted a story about meeting him. He picked a story he thought would interest you—or else conned you into telling him what you expected to hear—and then took the money and ran. Mr. Coleman—"

"Clevis."

"Clevis. If you are looking for a doctor in Mumbai, I think there are better ways of finding him than going on wild goose chases."

"But just for one minute," Coleman said, "pretend that the sketch is real. What might that tell you about Lobsang?" He leaned forward in his chair. "This *Bloodhound* thing, can it be made to run in India?"

"Not quickly," Lucky said. It would take a year, maybe more. Your best bet, in India, is to do things the Indian way. I could go to Hubli or Mumbai."

Coleman shrugged, and after a moment, Lucky continued.

"From this picture, I suspect that Lobsang is older than he looks. Frankly, I think the drawing tells us more about the artist than it does of the subject. In other words, it's worthless.

"I would deduce that Lobsang must depend on others for transportation, and that necessitates that he seldom operates outside of a very limited territory. I suspect that you are dealing with a man who presides over a very small territory and avoids confrontations."

"So what action plan does Wonder Girl suggest?"

Lucky shrugged. "I would approach this from the angle of mobility. He has to move sometimes, somewhere, so how? If he avoids technology, you have already divided up the territory, Mumbai—if that's where he is—into a kind of grid. You can look where the technology isn't."

"And if we had a crystal ball, we would know where he was next," Coleman said.

"That's not as far-fetched as it may seem," Lucky said. "Have you heard of the Monty Hall problem?"

Coleman shook his head.

"The name was taken from the TV show, *Let's Make a Deal.* Here's how it works. Bear with me. You are shown three doors. Behind one door is a big cash prize. Behind two doors are goats. You choose a door. Monty Hall asks, 'Are you sure?' 'Yes,' you say, yes, I'm sure. Then he shows you that behind one of the doors that you did *not* choose, there is a goat. He asks, 'Are you still sure?' What do you do? Mathematicians all agreed, the odds started at one in three, right? What difference could it make? But a damn old gossip columnist named Marilyn Vos Savant figured out that, actually, you are more likely to win the prize if you switch. This seems counterintuitive, but the odds have changed since Monty showed you the door with the goat. You made a selection when the odds were one in three. He has given you another choice—one where the odds are two in three. So you are better off switching. Your odds of winning have doubled. They've tested and retested this with little mock-ups, and it works like a charm. Try it some time."

Coleman looked flabbergasted. "What the hell has Monty Hall got to do with finding Lobsang?"

"Simple," Lucky said. "When people tell you where he is *not*, they are inadvertently increasing the odds that they are telling you where he *is*."

"Enough," Coleman said. "You make me dizzy."

One of Coleman's men then stood up and talked about a contingency plan for a targeted epidemic—one that might force Lobsang into the open to seek medical treatment himself or to reveal his secret for the good of the masses. What was needed was a germ that was mild, which would be harrowing but not fatal for a man of Lobsang's presumed age. Something perhaps affecting the kidneys, lungs, or heart. Viral, not microbial. Even better would be a kind of poisoning that would require blood chelating. Lead, cadmium, or some other heavy metal would work……

Lucky breathed out and was thankful that Coleman shot him down midstream with, "Nonsense! Preposterous! The Health and Human Services doesn't do such things."

For the remainder of the meeting, Lucky remained quiet. This kind of stuff was not only over her head but she thought it was an odd conversation for a group of staff members working for GWC to even raise the point.

Coleman ended the meeting by saying, "You guys get together and update me, everyday same time, right here. I want concrete pointers and suggestions," He turned to Lucky and added, "Not imaginary ones."

When the meeting was over, Evan showed Lucky to her temporary workstation, an office, he explained, kept for visiting researchers.

The office was spacious, with a broad bank of windows facing west and overlooking the Potomac. The room was flooded with bright evening light. There was a standard office desk and a set of green upholstered chairs clustered around a coffee table. In one corner stood a mini-fridge, a sink, and a small convenience stand furnished with coffee and tea and an electric kettle, a small coffee machine, sugar, sweetener, paper towels and a tin of tea crackers. Two tall, gold dust dracaenas in green ceramic pots were placed on either side of the windows. The computer on Lucky's desk had a 21-inch monitor and was faster than fast. It was already on and, according to Evan, would stay that way 24/7. There was no password, no boot up, nothing was required on her part. Apparently, the system was a closed network that was secured to the highest levels. She should note that any correspondence going outside of the building would be automatically logged and monitored, as was anything inbound.

After Evan was gone, Lucky tried out the desk by sitting down and checking her e-mail. She called Amay. He was at work, but the babysitter put Sean on the phone. "Hi, sweetie," Lucky said. "Tell me about your day."

When she was done talking to Sean, Lucky looked around the office. It was nice. Very nice. She went to the door, but—*Collette. Damn*, she thought. She went back to the phone, but Collette's warning buzzed in her ear. A pay phone. *Right. Do they even have pay phones anymore?* But if Evan said all outgoing Internet was monitored, no doubt, cell connections were as well. Lucky decided to call from the hotel. But when she arrived and settled in, she laid down for "just a minute" and promptly fell asleep.

CHAPTER 7

6 a.m. The phone rang. *Where am I?* Lucky woke, still dressed from the day before. She had been deep into a dream about India. She was at the Hanging Gardens in Mumbai, with Shanti, but it wasn't the Hanging Gardens. There was the hill and the path and the bench where they met, but the path had led around the park and then into a building in which there was a swamp. Lucky was terrified of the dark, shadowed water—or, more precisely, of what might lurk below its surface. Shanti was not afraid of the water at all. She sprang from lotus to lotus, landing on the bright pink flowers without causing so much as a ripple. Lucky wanted to call out to her, but no words came. She wanted to run after her, but her feet felt weighed down, as if she were dragging iron bars through the mud. Shanti was almost across the pond. She turned, pirouetting on one toe like a ballerina, and beckoned Lucky on. "Travel light! You're carrying too much of a burden."

What burden? Lucky wondered. The phone rang again. *Where am I?* She found the receiver. "Hello."

Collette. "You didn't call me," she said.

"What time is it?"

"Six a.m."

"Why on earth are you calling me at this hour?"

"It's important, with a capital M."

"Are you all right? Where's your mother? Does she know you're calling me?"

"I'm fine. Mom's in bed with her boyfriend—but I'm not supposed to know. I'll have to act like I've gone to school today so she can sneak him out. And she doesn't know I'm calling. Call me back from a pay phone right away, okay? I gotta talk to you before they get up."

"Okay, Sweetie." Lucky said. She sighed. "I have to get up and get dressed first."

6:05 a.m. Lucky staggered into the bathroom and turned on the water in the tub to warm it up. She was greeted by a heavy spray of cold water. Some joker had pointed the showerhead over the side. She shut her eyes. She was dripping wet and freezing cold. *At least I'm awake now.* She showered, patted on a little makeup—not too much for the first day in a new office, dried her hair, then stood in front of her suitcase and looked at her clothes. *What the heck was I thinking when I packed?*

In her mind, she heard Shanti, "You weren't thinking, and that's the problem. Mindful in the little things. What were you doing?"

Lucky had been thinking about Sean and Maria and Amay and Collette. Anything but the task at hand, which should have been, *What do I wear on the first day of work in a new office in Washington freakin' DC?* Laid out in the suitcase were all of what Lucky called her *lawyer clothes*: severe pants suits in military grays and greens and browns. She sighed. *Someday, I'm going to have a job where I can wear whatever I want to work.* Almost immediately she heard Shanti's voice, "Be careful what you ask for—you might get it."

Downstairs, the coffee shop was open. Fifteen bucks for a sticky cheese omelet, some dry hash browns, and a cold cup of coffee that managed to be both bitter and weak at the same time. "Do you have a pay phone?" Lucky asked the waitress.

"In the bar," she replied.

The bar was shut, a padlocked iron gate separating it from the hotel lobby. She asked the receptionist, "What time does the bar open?"

The receptionist looked at Lucky. "It's six thirty, ma'am. Did you try the minibar in your room, or does it need to be restocked?"

Minibar? Lucky scowled. "I don't need a *drink*. I'm looking for a *pay phone*. The waitress said there's a pay phone in the bar."

"Oh, sure. A pay phone. I should have known. Well, the bar doesn't open until eleven, but there are courtesy phones down the hall by the elevators, or you can make free local calls from your room. Long distance is a bit pricey, though. You'd be better off using your cell. You do have a cell, don't you?"

"Forget it," Lucky said. "I'll find one outside." But there were none between the hotel and the office. She walked on and, realizing she had found the office, sighed as she stepped toward the gate. She would try again later.

For most of the morning, Lucky pored over Coleman's Lobsang file, having asked for time to update herself that morning before she met with the team for discussions. Coleman had made this file available for the team, along with some other findings stamped "strictly classified, locked, password needed." There was a lot of background in the file, none of which, so far as Lucky could see, was sensitive. Much of it consisted of newspaper clippings.

The Tibetan diaspora. Primary school in McLeod Ganj. Secondary school on a scholarship to British International School in New Delhi. University College of London. Medical school at Oxford. *Oxford*? Lucky leaned back in her chair. This did not compute. A man who purportedly eschewed all technology sporting a medical degree from one of the finest — and most technically advanced — universities in the world? A man reputed to be dealing in — dare she say — *magic* mushrooms?

There were, as Coleman said, some old photos. Outdated. Lobsang in the back row of a group photo with a gaggle of grinning scholarship recipients. A blurry, white-lab-coated Lobsang squinting into a microscope. One photo was of another student — Lobsang was just caught in the back, slightly out of focus. Here he was in jeans and a Grateful Dead tee-shirt, his hair grown long and swept back over his shoulders, standing with a blond girl outside of what could only be Royal Albert Hall, in the rain. And here was an earnest-looking Lobsang in glasses, standing alone, framed in a doorway of what might have been a library or a dorm. He was short, his head large and square, his hands swinging awkwardly by his side. Lucky stared into the photo displayed on her computer screen. There was something familiar about Lobsang's expression. The narrowing of the eyebrows, the tight mouth, the light in his eyes, the way he cocked his head slightly to one side. He looked like he was about to say something important, something that was weighing on his mind. Something he had thought about for a long time. He looked like he was about to say, "Goodbye."

And evidently, he did, for there were no more photos. Not one in thirty-one years. Not even a drawing until a man named Somasundaram caught dengue fever in Hubli — *allegedly*.

Lucky leafed through Coleman's research, looking at what he had done, and wondering what he might have missed. Medical colleges in India and Tibet. What had he done there? There were satellite images of India dotted with possible sightings or the locations of possible acquaintances. Shipping records for medical supplies. Excerpts from telephone conversations and e-mails of suspected associates, although not one of them mentioned Lobsang by name. Where did all of this stuff come from? And how did the U.S. government have that much clout? There were even sections about suspected Chinese activity. None of it was especially useful. *If they listened to my phone conversations, and if they read my e-mails, what might they infer about me*? Lucky wondered. *If you're looking to find the Virgin on a tortilla, then sooner or later you'll find the Virgin on a tortilla.*

But the difficult thing — and the point Lucky kept coming back to — was the idea of how a man with an aversion to technology would act. That thought intrigued her. It had to narrow down his options.

Lucky folded her hands and rested her chin on her knuckles. She thought about the Monty Hall problem. If you knew where someone *wasn't*, you increased the odds of knowing where they were. Really, the odds were best if you looked where he had never been and where nobody thought he was. Lucky sat bolt upright. She looked at the map. What was the *least* likely place for him to be? In Mumbai? At first, she had dismissed the idea, but maybe it had merit after all. Coleman had said Lobsang was based mainly in Mumbai. It was easy to hide in Mumbai, and everyone seemed to know somebody there. It would be easy to hide in a densely populated area — and Mumbai certainly was that. Somehow, though, she felt he was not in Mumbai. Too much technology. She slumped, defeated, and thinking of Shanti saying, "When the world goes upside down, you need to stand on your head." Instead, Lucky went to lunch.

When she returned, she found Coleman sitting on her desk, considering the volume of Whitman.

"Hello…Clevis."

"Afternoon, Boyce." Coleman replied. He did not look up. "Knew you were eccentric. Didn't think you were subversive."

"You're kidding me?"

"I hear the carpenter singing. The mason singing, the boatman singing, the woodcutter singing. Singing with open mouths their strong, melodious songs. Tell me, Boyce, have you ever heard anyone sing *without* their mouth open?"

She looked up, puzzled.

"Didn't think so. Some editor should have struck that line."

"I like poetry," Lucky replied. "Mark it down as one of my vices. And if I wasn't subversive you wouldn't have hired me."

"Done and done. And you have no idea how right you are about that. Whitman was gay, did you know that? He and his robust young friends partying through the night. You know why people read books, Boyce?"

"To learn?"

"There you go being idealistic again. And naïve. Have to wean you off that. Whitman knew. Try this one." She turned back a few pages. "*I myself often think I know little or nothing of my real life.* There. Ignorance. That's why people read, Boyce. They are ignorant of their real life. Do you think books can make people sing, Boyce?"

"I suppose you're going to tell me no."

"Precisely. You were going to argue that books could teach you music, but that's not the same thing. You know what makes people sing? Happiness? Contentment? That's a lot of crap. What was it Maya Angelou wrote? *Why does the caged bird sing?* Birds sing to attract mates. And people? People sing because they are blissfully ignorant."

"Perhaps people sing for different reasons?"

Coleman frowned, then looked back at the book. He idly flipped pages. "We make people sing, Boyce. You and I. The leaders of this sorry pack. We can make them happy and we can make them sad. We can make them work like bees in a hive or riot in the streets in protest. And the beauty of it all is that we yank the chains and they think it's their idea. Have you heard this one?

> To find a new unthought of nonchalance with the best of Nature!
>
> To have the gag remov'd from one's mouth! To escape utterly from others' anchors and holds!

"What do you make of that — A new un-thought? What the hell is that?"

"He said 'unthought-of.' He was talking about the nonchalance —"

"Or this…."

> To have the feeling to-day or any day I am sufficient as I am.
>
> O something unprov'd! something in a trance!

"Something in a trance? He's got to be mad! Boyce! Hear this one…."

> To drive free! to love free! to dash reckless and dangerous!
>
> To court destruction with taunts, with invitations!

"To drive free! To love! To dash reckless! To court destruction! He was a sadist, of sorts."

> To feed the remainder of life with one hour of fullness and freedom!
>
> With one brief hour of madness and joy.

"To feed the remainder of life with one brief hour of fullness and freedom! With one hour of madness and joy! Was the man prescient, or what, Boyce?"

"I find it rather amusing."

"Amusing? In what way?"

"In the same way that all fanatics are amusing. Nature has no power —"

"Who said anything about nature, Boyce? He's talking about *television*. Of course *nature* can't satisfy our demands. That's why men invented technology. If nature were all that great, we'd still be running around in skins and eating whatever could be dug, picked, snared, clubbed, or shot with a bow and arrow. Man and machine were made for each other. To cast off this husk of a body. Why, in one hour of television you can have the experience of a lifetime. Think of it, Boyce, the loser on the street — Whitman's fishermen and housewives and stonecutters and whatnot — for an hour they can be anybody! They can sleep with impossibly beautiful people, visit exotic places, fly, dream, live! Thoreau said, 'Most men lead lives of quiet desperation.' We, Boyce, the *upper* crust, we relieve them of their misery. We've done more for mankind in the past fifty years than was done in all the preceding millennia. How can real-life compare with what we offer? Ordinary life is — or was — as Shakespeare would say, 'a fishmonger's wife.' We offer sex with a supermodel."

Lucky looked out the window.

As if he read her mind, Coleman got up and walked around the desk. "People are happy because of us." He licked his lips. "We give them food and shelter and entertainment. What else is there? For a few hours, they can be anybody. Indiana Jones! Luke Skywalker! Batman! Superman! Think of it! A magic carpet ride to anywhere, for free, right in the comfort of their homes! You wouldn't want to mess with that, would you, Boyce?" There was a trace of menace in his voice. Coleman snapped the book shut.

"No sir," she said.

"Yes, I know all about you. And your prison work, your yoga, your rather endearing ability to know a little bit about everything. And nothing at all about what really matters."

"What matters?"

"Yes." Coleman stood up and went to the window. "What matters? How long has television been around, Boyce?"

"Farnsworth, 1927."

"BBC began broadcasting in 1937. NBC in 1939. If we allow, say, twenty years for the diffusion of the technology to reach a saturation level at which it could have a real impact, then in the West we have had, say, five or six generations that have grown up on it."

"That sounds about right."

"What do you know about McClintock's Constant?"

"He was a molecular biologist."

"She. *She* postulated that knowledge becomes genetically encoded in seventeen generations. Fruit flies taught for seventeen generations will spontaneously acquire that behavior without training in the eighteenth. Knowledge itself can act as a kind of *transposon*."

"A what?"

"A transposon — a gene that jumps around in DNA. Brings me back to the time when I was a boy graduating from high school."

"And your point is?"

"You have a colorful past, Miss Boyce. A climber. A shark in business. A society marriage. A few scrapes with the law. Perhaps I've misjudged you."

Lucky looked out the window, then back at Coleman. "How so?"

"Have you any interest in politics, Boyce?"

"I suppose everybody has thought about running for office."

100

"I'm not talking about running for office," Coleman snapped. "Any jackass can run for office. I'm talking about *politics*. Real politics, Boyce, played the old-fashioned way."

"And which way is that?"

"Would you lie to the press if I asked you to?" Lucky started to speak but Coleman held up his hand. "If I said it was important. If I said it was an issue of national security?"

"No sir."

"Would you plant an illegal wiretap?"

Lucky shook her head.

"Would you hack into someone's computer?"

"No sir."

"Would you plant evidence on a man to advance your cause and hurt his? If you knew your cause to be just?"

"Wouldn't that go against —"

"Fair play? That's what I mean, Boyce. When it comes to causes, there is no fair play. Would you sleep with a man to gain his confidence?"

Lucky's eyes bulged. She stammered, "Of…of…of course not."

"Would you kill a man without judicial review if he was a clear and present threat to your nation?"

Lucky hesitated.

"That's what I wanted to know," Coleman said. "If you would act decisively for a cause and *without hesitation*."

Lucky's eyes were suddenly dry and irritated. She blinked, but no moisture came. She said, "In Vietnam, in 1968, a U.S. Army Major, Phil Cannella, supposedly told a reporter that we had to destroy the village of Ben Tre in order to save it. Isn't that what you are asking? That I should destroy the values I hold dear in order to save them for others? What sense does that make?"

Coleman smiled. "According to McClintock, we have twelve generations to go before people stop thinking for themselves entirely. Won't that be marvelous? Think about it. There will be a ruling class, an *intelligentsia* to think for them. They will rule benevolently, but firmly. Everyone will be better off. *Especially*, those at the top of the food chain. In politics, Boyce, there are two kinds of people. Those who play the game and those who read the rules. Those with their noses in the rule book are generally taken for fools and left in the dust, or worse. Are you certain you don't want to play the game?"

"Is this some sort of a joke?" Lucky asked.

Coleman smiled. "Of course it's a joke. Just a little test of integrity I give all my people. Don't worry, you've passed." He stood up to leave, crossed the office, but paused at the door. "People have been praying for world peace for generations," he said. "Only — until now, we never understood how to make that happen. Once people are properly domesticated, then and only then will we have world peace. I'd like to think that my great-great-great-something-or-others might grow up in that kind of world. How about you?"

"I can't even visualize that," Lucky said.

Coleman shook his head. "Work on that. You have to be well prepared for the meeting this afternoon."

When he was gone, Lucky fixed a cup of chai and went to the window. The day was hot and humid, the air hazy. Across the Potomac was Arlington, and to the south, Alexandria. This was all Civil War country. Strange, Lucky thought, to think of Americans fighting each other, much as Indians did during the days following the Partition. More than half a million men died in that war. Mostly, Lucky noted, of disease.

She returned to her desk and opened the volume of Sun Tzu. Choosing a page at random, she read: *Good warriors cause others to come to them. They do not go to others.* Now, there was a possibility that nobody had seriously considered. Maybe there was a way — besides a disease or a poison or necessary piece of machinery — maybe there was a way to make Lobsang come forward, come up for air, come to them with a request. *Wouldn't that be a corker?* he thought. But what would he want?

The way to reach Lobsang was to find out what he wanted. But what does a man who has renounced the world want? That, Lucky realized, was the one thing Coleman had never said: What does this

Lobsang want? He had something of great value, and he had to know that. Why, then, wouldn't he share it with the world? Wasn't that what any normal person would do?

Lucky opened a file on psychological forensics—case studies as varied as Jack the Ripper, D.B. Cooper, Shakespeare, Che Guevara, Joan of Arc, and Saddam Hussein. There were many enigmatic people whose motives were easier seen posthumously than while they were alive. All the deduction required was certain basic facts from which conflicting possibilities could be sorted out. These were:

1. Circumstances of birth
2. Family life
3. Physical health
4. Education
5. Employment
6. Life experiences

The date of birth told you someone's age, and the maternal and paternal details of the circumstances of birth provided information on the environment the child would have been likely subjected to — as well as the issues they would have had to confront during their formative years. Age progression was unavoidable, and although class could change, there were certain *facts* of class, which tended to leave signatures — habits of speech, diet, clothing, even habits of thought. Not to mention the number of siblings and the order of birth.

Physical health also said a great deal about a person's potential for action. For example, some historians' claim that Joan of Arc had to be a man was based on the assumption that no woman could ride, wield a sword, or command soldiers, as Joan had. On the other hand, there was nothing concrete to rule out that Joan was a woman — provided that she was in excellent health. Thus, overall health was an important key to understanding behavior.

Education. Almost all those who contended that Shakespeare could not have written Shakespeare did so on the grounds that his education was not considered sufficient to support such an ambitious body of work. On its surface, this was a good argument. But when one considered other factors, and the number of factual and historical errors in Shakespeare's work, the reverse became evident. It was not his education that enabled his work but his upbringing and life's experiences. In reality, his lack of advanced education *hindered* his work, as the upper class almost always appeals to an innate superiority when attempting to discredit upstart rivals from the lower classes.

Employment. That was easy to trace for any individual.

The last of the six factors was life experience. Would it be possible to understand Mother Teresa or Che Guevara or Mahatma Gandhi without understanding the events that triggered their devotion to their causes? Sleuths cited military experience as a factor in D.B. Cooper's selection of parachutes. But the real question — the one no one could answer — was: what prompted a man to risk his life for a suitcase full of $100 bills? Was he trying, as some argued, to fund a revolutionary organization? By the same token, Gandhi, who was born into a wealthy family, renounced wealth as a *hindrance* to his idealistic goals. Thus, opposite behaviors might be triggered by similar events. What was necessary was to understand how the person interpreted those events in relation to his or her own life experiences.

It was not what was known about people that created these mysteries, but rather, what was not known about them. And the means of inferring what was not clear was what fascinated Lucky.

"Who," she said out loud, "am I looking for?"

Lucky reviewed what was known about Lobsang.

Birth: Tibet. Age, estimated 52 years.

Family: Fled Lhasa. Raised as a refugee. Alienation? Disaffection? Outrage?

Physical health: Presumed excellent. Past injury to leg or hip?

Education: Non-traditional. Religious. Medical college in England.

Employment: Charity. Hobbies ???

Life experiences. Little known?

He's a Buddhist monk who has renounced the world as an illusion. Where would he be? Would he be in Mumbai? Did that make any sense?

Lucky went to her computer and brought up her address book. She had a list of friends and suppliers from her days in Mumbai and from Lockwood Enterprises in New York. She shot off e-mails to all her contacts in Mumbai describing Lobsang and enclosing two snapshots of him, one as a student in London and the other the sketch they had. Coleman might not be very pleased, this being "strictly confidential," but what the heck, she reckoned. It was better than sitting and dreaming about him and where he could be.

At the afternoon staff meeting, Coleman was insistent in hearing what progress had been made toward finding Lobsang. He glared at Lucky.

"It is less efficient," Lucky said in defense, "for us to look for him than to create conditions in which he will look for us."

Her observation provoked a round of sniggers from the staffers gathered around the table. Even Coleman was taken aback. "What the hell am I paying you for?" he asked. "You're not an accountant anymore. Resources are not the problem. We have all the resources in the free world at our disposal."

"It takes years to find the major leaders of drug or terrorist outfits, even when we know a great deal about them. And when we succeeded, in most cases, it was through an act of betrayal by one of their lieutenants. Take Saddam Hussein, for example. One of his former lieutenants led to his capture. Not spies, not spy satellites, not hi-res photos and X-rays and infra-reds. And we knew a lot about Saddam Hussein. We know next-to-nothing about Lobsang's recent past."

Coleman frowned. "He's a man, goddammit, and he puts his pants on one leg at a time."

"Actually," Lucky said, "he might not even wear pants."

Another round of laugher.

"What do you mean?"

"For all you know, he might dress in flowing white robes. Or a lungee. We really don't know what he wears."

"That's beside the point."

"No," Lucky said, "That's *precisely* the point. You're looking for a man and you don't know the first thing about him. What he wears. What he eats. What he might do for recreation."

"I don't care if he wears fishnet stockings and high heels, the point is that we are going to catch him, and damn soon, and your job is to work out how."

"What have you done so far?" Lucky asked.

"We've read everything he's written and we've analyzed the paper and the ink and the words. We've even taken DNA from skin samples we found on the page."

"Is it his DNA?"

Coleman shrugged. "Who knows? But we think he is using scribes—no two samples have been alike."

"All that, and you haven't got close enough to snap a photo."

"If we were close enough to snap a photo," Coleman said, "we'd have the key to immortality."

Lucky nodded. "Have you ever gone fishing?" she asked.

Coleman said, "Of course I have."

"What kind of fish?"

"Everything from green cutthroat trout to swordfish, why?"

"When you want to catch a fish, do you jump in the water and swim around with a knife? Do you spy on them from the sky? Or, do you use bait? Sun Tzu says, 'What causes opponents to come of their own accord is the prospect of gain.'"

106

"Enough!" Coleman said. "I'm paying you for data: charts, graphs, maps, names, and places. And to quote Sun Tzu again, 'Those skilled in defense hide in the deepest depths of the earth. Those skilled in attack maneuver in the highest heights of the skies.' Lobsang is hiding while we soar."

"He also said," Lucky said, "that a wise governor does not keep his men in the field."

Coleman looked incredulous. "Remember what I said, Boyce. If the troops do not obey, it is the fault of the officers. You'll do what I tell you or your stint here will be shorter than either of us imagined. I have the feeling you are going to be working some long hours."

As she trudged back to her office, Lucky thought, *This is a strange assignment.*

CHAPTER 8

After failing to make any more headway on the mysterious doctor, Lucky decided to take a break by calling Amay, only to hear a familiar greeting on the other end of the line.

"Heeyyyyyyyyyyy, Luckee!"

Lucky almost dropped the phone in surprise. At first she thought she had dialed her home number by mistake. Even though it wasn't the first time Maria had done double duty as a babysitter, her voice came as a surprise. "Oh," Lucky said. "Hey. What's up?"

Maria was cooking spaghetti for the kids. Lucky pictured her pinching the phone between her ear and shoulder while she stirred the marinara sauce. "Why didn't you just order out?" she asked.

"I like cooking. Besides, it's more fun for the kids. Here. Sean wants to talk to you."

He missed his mommy. "Come home," he said.

"Soon," she replied. "How's Falstaff?"

"He stumped his toe."

Lucky thought about this. How does a stuffed bear with no feet stub his toe? Must have been one of the kids. "Is he all better?"

"A little."

There was a crash of breaking glass and a sharp shout in the background.

108

"What was that?" Lucky asked, but Sean didn't answer. A moment later Maria took the phone. "It's under control," she said, "but I have to run. Is there something you need?"

"No," Lucky said. "I just called to say hello. Where's Amay?"

"He had something to do and he had to go out for a while. Didn't say how long. I think he's got something on the side, maybe a woman? Ha!"

Lucky frowned. "Right," she said.

"You can call back later."

Lucky hung up. Now what? She stared at the picture of Lobsang for a few minutes, then closed her programs, turned off the monitor, and trudged back to the hotel. As she crossed the lobby to the elevators, a voice called out, "Hey, Lucky!"

It was Collette. *Collette*. She was dressed in all pink; on her shirt was a picture of a phone that had skulls on the keypad instead of numbers. Below the image, it read: DIAL "M" FOR MISFITS. She was carrying a small suitcase and a My Little Pony backpack.

Lucky did a double take. "What are *you* doing here?"

Collette blew a bubble. "*You* didn't call me."

"I… but… I…"

"I *said* it was important." She sighed and rolled her eyes.

"I keep looking for pay phones, but do you know how difficult they are to find anymore?"

Collette folded her arms and frowned. "There's one right there in the bar," she said.

Lucky looked over at the bar, now open. "But the bar was….oh, never mind." An elevator arrived, and they got in.

Lucky asked, "Honey, does your mother know where you are?"

"No, but it's not like she cares or anything. She left some stuff in the fridge and said she'd be back by midnight." She checked her watch. "Don't worry, I got a round trip ticket. I'll be home before she misses me."

"Collette, what's going on?"

Collette smacked her gum. "I told you it was important that you call me, but nobody listens to what I say. After all, *I'm* only a teenager. Unless I'm carrying a gun to school or getting pregnant or using dope, I'm supposed to be *seen and not heard*."

The elevator door opened and a couple of men in suits got in. Collette made a zipping motion, running her finger across her mouth, and stayed quiet. Lucky decided she'd ask later; right now, she was grateful for the chance to assess the situation and decide what to do next.

When she and Collette got off, Collette said, "Did those men strike you as odd?"

Lucky shook her head, fumbling in her purse for her room keys. "No, why should they?"

"They got on at the fourth floor."

"So?"

"They were going up."

"And?"

"Who gets on an elevator from their room and goes up?"

"Maybe they were on their way to see friends or co-workers? Maybe there's something on the roof — a bar or a pool or something."

"And what floor were they going to?"

"I didn't see."

"You didn't see because they didn't push a button."

Lucky finally found her room key and opened the door, vaguely hoping that if she and Collette could just sit down and have some tea, everything would make sense. But as soon as they entered the room, Collette began looking closely at the screws on the light switch.

"What are you looking at?" Lucky asked.

"Fresh scratches." Collette paused, then turned to Lucky. "Don't say my name or reveal any details about me out loud."

"You're paranoid."

"You're not paranoid enough." Collette looked around the room again. "Meet me outside, and then we can talk." And she went back out into the hall.

Lucky stared after her and then looked around the room herself. *I guess I'm not getting that tea after all.* Well, at least she had a chance to freshen up.

A Star Called Lucky

After changing into jeans and a light green cotton top, Lucky went out to the hall and found Collette sitting on the carpet between two potted ferns, reading a spiral bound manuscript with a photo of a keyboard on the front. It was called JAVA, AGILE, AND SCRUM FOR HACKERS. "Let's take the stairs," she said.

They walked down to the garage and then back up the ramp and out. "Where are we going?" Lucky asked.

"To eat. I'm starved. Airline service is NOT what it used to be. They give you salty peanuts and then they charge you for water. Capitalists."

"How did you get here, anyway?"

She rolled her eyes. "I bought a ticket."

"By yourself? How?"

"Online. I used my mom's credit card. She'll never know. She doesn't check her statements. She just pays them and complains about the money."

"And you flew by yourself?"

"Isn't the Internet age great? Miss Kennedy sent her unaccompanied minor daughter to Washington to meet her father. All I needed was a credit card. United gave me my own private escort and everything. He was cute, too. I thought about getting a wheelchair or a sign-language interpreter, you know, saying I'm deaf. But then I figured that might be laying it on too thick. I gave him the slip at the baggage carousel. There's a Wendy's. Want a cheeseburger?"

Lucky didn't, but they crossed the road, dodging traffic, and Lucky winced as Collette ordered them cheeseburgers and fries. How long had it been since she'd eaten junk food? She couldn't remember. They found a reasonably clean table and sat down.

"Is this about my computer?" Lucky asked.

"Sort of."

"Couldn't it have waited until I got home?"

"What if I told you that you might not get home?"

Lucky set down the burger.

Collette said, "There was nothing really wrong with your computer."

"No virus?"

"Not exactly."

"But the home page —"

"Oh, the home page was nothing. Just a little old crappy malware script. That took me about two minutes to sniff out."

"Okay."

"The real trouble is this." Collette dug in her pocket and produced a flash drive.

"That's not mine," Lucky said.

"Neither is what's in it. But that was what was in your computer."

Lucky leaned across the table and looked at the flash drive. It was nothing—just a black and gold, eight-gig stick. "And what was in my computer?"

"It's kind of hard to explain," Collette said. "Have you ever heard of a mirror server?"

"A what?"

"A mirror server."

Lucky sighed. "What's a mirror server?"

"It's a connection to a dupe site. It makes it look like you're online doing whatever you usually do, but it actually copies everything you do. Somebody is reading or storing everything about you. Everything you'd ever done, written, every picture, all your contacts, everything."

"But what…how…?"

"I don't know. I was kinda interested to hear what you had to say about this."

Lucky shook her head. "But my laptop is practically new. I haven't done much with it at all."

"So you're not surfing porn or anything?"

"What?? Of *course* not."

"I mean, it's not like it's any of my business, and far be it from me to judge…"

"Collette!"

112

"I'm just checking. I suppose no online gambling sites. Those are real holes, too."

"No," Lucky said. "I don't know anything about online gambling."

"Have you opened any weird attachments in your e-mail?"

"No," Lucky said. "I haven't."

"Has anybody put anything into your computer?"

"No, nobody has…" and then she stopped and covered her face with her hand.

Bloodhound. "Well, there was one thing. But there's no way it was infected with some virus."

"A pen drive?"

"Yeah," Lucky said. "A pen drive."

"Some kind of download?"

Lucky sighed. "Yes." She was wondering how she could explain this to Collette, and to her bosses, who surely must know by now about the purloined software. She should have known better.

"Well, there you have it," Colette said.

"You figured this out?"

"Not me. Not entirely. I told you, I got this friend in Bulgaria."

"Collette, please just tell me everything."

Collette stirred the ketchup on her plate with a French fry. "Well, once I got in your computer, I started fooling around. Nothing mean, I mean, I was just gonna do a few things to enhance your performance. Really. I was just gonna fix a few things for you and not say anything about it. Just for fun. But when I checked the system usage, it was way over what it should have been — and that meant something was running. Something I couldn't see or find. And I got kinda pissed about it cause I think I'm pretty good at this stuff. And so I called Yazma and he gave me a few pointers, and then we found that this thing was echoing everything we did. But to find that, well, you don't want to know. We had to kind of trick your computer into thinking it was online and then watching what it did."

"So you tricked my computer?"

"It's not that hard. Anyway, Yazma got really, really excited; said he'd never seen anything like it before."

"Look," Lucky said. "We have to be really careful about this. There's this program on my hard drive…if it gets out, a lot of people could get hurt."

"You're telling me! Yazma said it was like, the Holy Grail of hacking. He can even go after Swiss bank accounts now. He said to say, Thank you. That's pretty unusual for a Bulgarian. He said he owes you a favor."

Lucky buried her face in both hands. "Goodbye, career," she said. "Maybe I was meant to be in prison after all."

Collette slurped her milkshake. "Huh?" she said.

"You're telling me some teenage Bulgarian hacker just got a government program from my hard drive and I'm not supposed to react? OMG," she said.

"Oh, it's much worse than that," Collette said. "You see, whoever did this to you—as soon as they go to the mirror site to check you out, they're going to know that you know about them too. It's called the magic mirror."

Lucky sighed. "So I guess I turn myself in and get it over with?"

Collette looked puzzled. "Get what over with?"

"I have a program from the state government. I mean, I didn't exactly steal it, but I borrowed it without official permission. And now, if I lose it, then I'm going to be the fall guy for the whole thing getting loose. They'll throw the book at me." And then it really hit her, and she began to cry. "They're going to send me to prison."

"What the hell are you babbling about?" Collette asked. "I'm not talking about that bloodsucker thing."

Lucky looked up. "Then what?"

"The program that hacked you. It was still running in your computer. It's on your hard drive. Bloodsucker was nothing. Yazma said that thing had been around for years. *This is something else.* This program can hack into any computer – and it's top secret! It's all so simple. It's designed to be used on a pen drive—you insert it into someone's computer, it copies itself on and does its thing, and then it gets deleted. But whoever it was pulled out the flash drive too soon, before it could delete the program. Must've been a real amateur! But Yazma and I love him for it."

Lucky was stuck. *This is something else*? And then — "Oh!" *Coleman*. He had used the flash drive on her computer when he showed her the sketch of Lobsang in New York.

"What is it?" asked Collette.

"There was something else," Lucky said. "My new boss. He put something in my computer. But then," her face brightened, "he just gave me a new computer. Why would he spy on my old computer if he gave me a new one?"

"Well, if somebody wanted to spy on you, they could give you a new computer all set up for them. But sometimes people want more."

"I see," Lucky said, even though she didn't.

"If somebody wanted to know *all* about you, the best way is to get your old computer. Sounds to me like they killed two birds with one stone—they can look into what you've done and spy on what you will be doing." Collette shrugged.

Lucky frowned. "Look. This isn't a spy movie, and nobody wants to bug my computer." But even as she said this she realized that it was, well, entirely possible. Why wouldn't Coleman want to know everything to maintain a high level of security?

Collette, evidently, registered Lucky's hesitation. "Yes? Correct?" she asked.

"But I don't have any secrets. And he wouldn't have to steal my computer to spy on me—if that was what he really wanted to do."

Collette shrugged. "I don't know. But someone definitely has it out for you, and this boss of yours sounds like a good candidate. If I were you, I'd quit right now and get away from these guys. Whatever they're up to isn't normal. Yazma said he could fix something up to cover you for a while. If you want. He can make it look like you've been mirrored, but he said the best thing was just to let it go and then set up some new accounts and anything you don't want people to know, well, if you buy a new computer and stay out of your old accounts, you can have a second life. And then use your old accounts for anything you're not worried about people knowing.

Anyway, that's why I was worried about you. And that's why I came to warn you. If I were you, I'd clear out of town until this dies down." Collette looked at her watch. "Speaking of clearing out, I gotta get to the airport."

"You came all the way to tell me this? Why didn't you just call me?"

"I *did* call you, remember? Besides, I like flying, and I figured anybody who'd go to that much trouble to hack you is probably tapping your phone. And they have the room bugged, too. It's in the light switch. Amateurs. Duh. And those two guys—five minutes after you got off they came back down the elevator, got off, saw me, and got right back on and left. You missed that. If they find out who I am, I'm dead meat."

Lucky shook her head. "They may be checking me out, Collette. I can't explain it, but I'm working on something classified, so they might just be doing a routine security check. They may need a background check, too. Who I know. Whom I talk to. They're just making sure I'm okay. There's no conspiracy."

"Yeah, and I bet you don't believe in black drone helicopters, either."

"Oh, I believe in black drone helicopters all right, just not the kind you're talking about."

Collette fumbled in her backpack and took out a black string with a translucent yellow pebble strung on it. She handed it to Lucky. Lucky looked at the stone closely. A mosquito trapped in amber. "Cute," she said.

"Will you wear this for me? Just for luck? I'd feel better if you did."

"It hardly goes with my suits."

She looked at Collette looking at her.

"Okay," Lucky said. "Just for you."

"Yeah, but, just in case, you know…"

"Just in case what?"

"Just in case I'm right."

"Sure. You're sixteen and if I believe you—which I *don't*—you dropped out of school and hacked into your records so you won't get caught." Lucky sighed. "I'm probably contributing to the delinquency of a minor."

Collette looked at Lucky, stony-faced. "You know, you're my only real friend. Nobody else gives me the time of day. I mean, who else would hang out with some nerdy girl who keeps serving cherry Kool-Aid even when you never drink it? I just don't want anything to happen to you."

Lucky looked down at the table, trying not to show how touched she felt. Instead, she hung the stone around her neck. "Okay, just in case. For you."

Collette stuck out her hand, and they hooked pinky fingers.

"I got that online. You know amber's been around for, like, sixty million years. Imagine that. One day you're sucking the blood out of a dinosaur, and the next thing you know, you're set in stone and hanging around somebody's neck. Against all odds. You know, reaper drones fly at 60,000 feet and can stay up for days at a time. You can't hear them, or see them, but they can see you and hear you. They can listen in on any cell phone they want. They use them in Afghanistan."

"I know," Lucky said.

"And I know you know. You know how I know you know?" Without waiting for Lucky to say, she said, "Because Yazma told me you knew, and he's read your hard drive. We use them in Afghanistan and wherever. Who's to say we won't use them here, too?" She looked out the window. "If I wanted to keep my eye on what went down in Washington, that's how I'd do it. But what do I know? I'm just sixteen."

"There's a lot you don't know," Lucky said.

"Yeah," Collette replied, "and sometimes we don't know what we don't know because to really know what we don't know would be too scary."

Lucky looked at Collette. *You're sixteen and you've already figured that out?*

Outside, Collette caught a cab to the airport, and Lucky walked back to the hotel. The more she thought about it, the more it seemed like she was going to have to tell Coleman she knew about the hacking and the Bulgarian. After all, if he'd just asked, she would have told him anything. Why the subterfuge? So she'd tell him she knew. Then one of two things would happen: either he'd fire her, or they'd go on. She almost wished he'd fire her; she could go back to her yoga gig and working with Barkley. It suddenly seemed like the saner of her two choices.

A helicopter passed overhead. No, three of them. Hey, it was Washington. They were headed toward the White House. Maybe the president was inside. Lucky waved.

Long after the choppers were gone, she stood on the sidewalk staring up at the sky. *Would they? Would they dare?*

She was crossing the hotel lobby when a voice called out, "Lucky!"

What the hell? Lucky turned. It was Amay. *What is this, National Let's Surprise Lucky Day?* "What are you doing here?" she stammered.

Amay took her in his arms and kissed her. "I'm glad to see you, too," he said. He pressed a bouquet of roses into her arms.

"I'm sorry it's just… it's been a long, weird day. Bizarre."

"Maybe I can make it longer, weirder, and more bizarre?" he said, and winked. "Have you had dinner?"

Lucky thought about the cheeseburger. "Just a snack," she said.

"I've got reservations for two at L'Auberge Provencale." He checked his watch. "We still have time."

"You might have told me you were coming."

"Something came up. There's this artist from Bosnia doing an exhibit at the Hirshhorn."

"I thought you *hated* the Hirshhorn?"

"I do, but this guy's really good. I don't know why they booked him. His name's Berber. We've corresponded. He called me at the last minute." Amay sighed. "I'm not much of a liar, am I? The truth is I came to see you."

Lucky softened, then kissed Amay again. Maybe a night out would do her good. "I need to take a shower and change. I can't go someplace swanky looking like this, can I?"

CHAPTER 9

Lucky woke in the middle of the night to find Amay propped up on one arm and watching her. For some reason, the sight irritated her. "What's the matter?" Lucky asked.

"I love you," Amay replied.

Lucky wondered, *Why do the wrong guys always say this?*

The only light in the room was what filtered through the white liner sheets that hung behind the darker, heavy curtains, which they'd left open. In the half-light Lucky could almost see the boy with whom she had played in Calcutta as a child. She remembered that they had once pledged as children to marry. Lucky had cut a finger, and on impulse, Amay had sliced his own and they had pressed the wounds together. Romantic, perhaps, but not all that sanitary.

But therein lay Lucky's dilemma. Amay was there for every cut and bruise, but over time, she'd come to find his attention stifling. It was almost like he needed her to be wounded in order to love her — or to prove his love for her. But who wanted to go through life being wounded? Or rescued, either, for that matter? Maybe it was an insecurity that sprang from Amay's being a skinny, sickly, nerdy boy. He always made a point of saying, *I'll always love you*, as if he felt *he* would never be loved again. *Just once*, Lucky, thought, *I wish he wouldn't say it. Just once I wish he'd argue with me, or call me a bitch, or tell me that I don't know what I'm talking about. Or make me feel normal!* Would she love him more if he just rolled over and snored like Viki, her ex? How might she react if he ignored her? Would she be inspired to pursue him for a change?

"I'll always love you," Amay said.

"I know," Lucky replied.

The next morning they ate a rushed breakfast of runny omelets and soggy hash browns in the restaurant downstairs, and Lucky was late to work. She rushed to her office and found Coleman sitting behind her desk again. "Looks like you had a late night," he said. "You look like hell."

He must know, she thought. *Maybe Collette was right.* "My boyfriend came down to surprise me. I guess we slept in."

"You can't spend a week apart?"

"It was a surprise. I didn't know he was coming."

"Helluva first impression. I expect my people to be punctual and responsible."

Lucky sighed. "You're right, of course. I'm sorry."

Coleman clicked on the overhead projector and walked around the desk as the picture of Lobsang appeared. "I've been thinking about what you said yesterday. I don't like being put on the spot like that, but I'd be a fool to dismiss your ideas without considering them. You're a bright girl, Lucky." Coleman stood in front of the video screen. "That's why I asked for your help." The colors of the image splashed across his face as he gestured for Lucky to sit. "The question is, are you too smart for your own good?"

Lucky sat on the edge of the desk, a few feet away from Coleman. His face was now almost perfectly superimposed over Lobsang's. Coleman said, "Suppose we were to 'fish' for this man, as you so aptly put it. What would we use for bait?"

"I can research that."

"I bet you can," Coleman said. "And you will. How can we get to him? What does he want? How do we make him come up for air?"

"I really don't know much about his beliefs," Lucky said. "I mean, I know a fair amount about Buddhism, and I know something about the conflict between China and Tibet. But that seems to be more

120

about politics and people than a conflict of religions. But my," she shook her head, "the story changes depending on who is telling it."

"What do you mean?" Coleman asked.

"Well, according to the Tibetans, Tibet was an independent country with a long and honorable history – a kind of political trusteeship for Buddhism. But according to the Chinese, Tibet was a renegade province that was always under Chinese control."

"And which is true?"

"Neither and both," Lucky said. "The Tibetans are unique in language and culture, but at times, they were a province of China. It all depended on how strong the Chinese government was at the time. But then, Tibet itself was a poor, remote province, difficult to govern, and far from the concerns of most Chinese."

Coleman traced a line on the desk with his finger, "Do you think this is a political ploy?" he asked. "A way to draw attention to Tibet's plight?"

"I don't know," Lucky said. "But if there is something to this mushroom — and I have my doubts — but if there is, then it's more likely that the Chinese would want to suppress or control that knowledge than that Lobsang would use it to attract attention to a cause. So far as I can tell, he's done nothing in the past thirty years but avoid attracting attention. Why would he start now?"

Coleman looked at her blankly. "Didn't you read the file? He has drawn attention to himself before this — he's supposed to have written a book. By hand. Some sort of religious thing. People copy it by hand and pass it around. It must not be very long."

Coleman clicked off the video screen and went to the window. For a moment, he squinted and seemed preoccupied with something happening on the street below. He grunted then turned to Lucky. "I'm going to be the richest man in the world, you know. I told you that. This is my big opportunity. My moment. This thing, this possible outbreak, this incident. It could be my springboard. When people hear about it, they'll be panicking in the streets, searching for a cure. And guess who'll have it? It won't be suspicious. I'm a tireless worker. I've spent my life working for people's welfare. I've whipped

121

the Health Services into a fine-tuned machine. After all, I graduated *summa cum laude* from Georgetown. I have an MA with Distinction from Cornell and a PhD from Harvard. I'm a Fulbright Scholar. I have all the credentials. What's more, I care—or at least, the pollsters say that's the perception people have of me. Smart. Caring. But caring is not enough." He shook his finger at Lucky. "I'm missing the n-factor. Nasty. Jimmy Carter was universally praised as a nice man, but Reagan trounced him in the election of 1980. Do you know why? Because nice is not good enough to get what's yours. You want your neighbor to be nice. Your minister. Your doctor. Your schoolteachers and your bus drivers and your baristas and your what-have-yous. The world needs nice people, Lucky. You're nice. Your son is nice. Your house is nice. Your housekeeper is nice, even if she does have a shady background. Oh, yes, I know all about her. Maria. You're not the only one who can research. But what makes a visionary is something else, something that sets them quite apart from the rest of the species. A businessman, Boyce, has to be seen as *mean and efficient*. Especially in this day and age. A pit bull. Don't tread on me. I have not yet begun to fight. Nothing to fear but fear itself. Blood, sweat, and tears. That kind of thing. This — this Lobsang fellow — is my moment."

Coleman sighed and turned to face the image on the screen. "Reagan changed everything. He wasn't just a politician. He was an actor. He knew that appearances are more important than reality. Carter commanded a nuclear submarine. While he was playing Patriot Games shadowing Red October at Twenty Thousand Leagues Under the Sea, Reagan was making films like *Boy Meets Girl*, *Girls on Probation*, and *Naughty but Nice*. But Reagan, the actor, understood the importance of perception. Carter didn't. Remember what I said about people who follow the rules? And Reagan understood the presidency better. At least, the public perception of the presidency. Carter played by the rules. Reagan was a pure politician. He knew it was more important to look strong than to be strong. So what? Shrewd move, if you ask me. The man knew what he wanted, and he was smart enough to go out and get it. That's how the game is played. I learned that long ago. I want to be one of those people, Boyce, and I know how to get it, too. Find out what this Lobsang wants." Coleman crossed the room to the door. "And while you're at it, best make up your mind what you want, too. Ask yourself: Am I willing to do whatever it takes?"

A few minutes after Coleman left, Lucky realized she hadn't told him about the hard drive. But then she thought, *He has to know. Why didn't he mention it? But I suppose he knows. If he'd wanted to talk about it, he would. But does he know the hacking program is still on my computer?*

Lucky had no idea what to do about the situation. She was just thirty, with a good job and a good education, but nothing she'd ever learned or experienced had prepared her for this. Her ambitious and ruthless boss might be spying on her, but he also valued her, and was willing to treat her well if she delivered.

Could she deliver? Everything came back to the same question: what did Lobsang want? How could she know him? Lucky remembered a story Shanti had written in a letter before she died, a story that had stuck with Lucky. She closed her eyes, imagining Shanti, so tiny, wrapped in a green silk sari, narrating in that melodious, high-pitched voice. It was a story about a blind man who wanted to know the Buddha's teachings. Since the man could not read, the Buddha sent the man walking all over India. "If you want to know me," he'd said, "walk my path."

But it wasn't about *walking*, it was about *living*. Paths were *lived*, not walked. You could never truly duplicate someone else's experience. Oh, you could duplicate some facets of it, sure. If you walked across the desert, it would be hot and you would be thirsty. But who could say what unique experiences each traveler would encounter? The cry of a hawk and the smooth arc of the bird circling overhead…the colors of a sunset, or the way the light played off a particular rock formation…a cool blast of wind, perhaps, carrying the scent of a distant shower…the way the moonlight fell about you when you woke in the night. Lucky wondered what path this man,

Lobsang, was walking. She wished she knew. It would be easier to visualize a solution then. And which way did she want to go? She had had enemies before: enemies in her personal life, enemies in business, even enemies who meant her harm for reasons of their own. But she had never thought about getting inside the skin of one of her enemies before—getting to know them so well that it was like knowing herself. What did Lobsang want?

If you can never walk another's path, then can you ever truly know them? No, Lucky decided, not unless you understood life, yourself, and your relationship with the universe. It was not enough to walk. One had also to be aware of, to witness, one's own journey. Shanti used to ask Lucky why she liked coffee so much. Lucky tried to explain about the complexity of the taste, the aroma, the subtly stimulating effects of the caffeine, but Shanti always cut her off. "Enough with the psycho-babble already. All you want is to find a shortcut to staying awake. It's a full-time job separating reality from the illusion. That's why most people fail. They can't be honest, not with themselves, not with anybody else. They live in the illusion."

"But doesn't the illusion…"

"But but but," Shanti said. She laughed. "You sound like a tuk-tuk. There are no 'buts' on the path to enlightenment. Either you live in the present reality or you live in the illusion. Reality is hard work, but in the end, it is the only thing that is rewarding. The illusion is easy to carry, like a bag of feathers. But try eating feathers at the end of the day."

Lucky spent the remainder of the day in a self-imposed hell, researching the history of China and its tangled relationship with Tibet. According to legend, China began with the creator of the universe, Pangu, who slept 18,000 years in an egg. Upon awakening, Pangu broke the egg and separated the pieces, creating heaven and earth. After this came the age of heroes, myths, and legend, which gradually transitioned into written, verifiable history: more than two thousand years of conquest and rising and falling civilizations — intrigue that spanned five thousand kilometers from the Caspian Sea to the Bering, from Southeast Asia to the northern extremes of Manchuria.

It was like riding a barrel down a river—sometimes the Chinese were on top, but sometimes they seemed to drown in their problems. The Chinese had great strength to draw upon, but there were so many enemies, so many other people, and kingdoms to deal with. In 640, King Songtsan, of Tibet, married the niece of Emperor Taizong. Besides uniting the political fortunes of their kingdoms, King Songtsan might have inadvertently imported Buddhism to Tibet, because the niece, as well as another wife, were Buddhists. But after a few generations, the cooperation collapsed and the Chinese conquered Tibet, ceding independence later as their imperial power waned. When Genghis Khan subjugated China, the Tibetans negotiated a surrender with a much higher level of autonomy than the Chinese. After that…

Lucky rubbed her eyes. As much as she feared Coleman, she was beginning to resent him for pulling her away from her home. On the other hand, all this thinking made her blood flow fast. It was stimulating, perhaps even more stimulating than Amay.

Amay.

She focused on her research again.

The Mongols established the Yuan Dynasty, but in time, a revolution led by a peasant and a former Buddhist monk established a new regime: the Ming Dynasty. For nearly three hundred years, the Mings presided over a flowering Chinese civilization — an era so peaceful and skillfully managed that the Chinese felt they had achieved the apex of human civilization, and thus, neither needed nor wanted outside trade or interference. It was the beginning of the peculiar Chinese practice of isolationism that, to Western eyes, left it veiled in mystery.

After the Mings came the Manchus, from the north. Although not accepted as Chinese by the Han people, by the eighteenth century, the Manchus had conquered all of what later became modern China, including Taiwan—the last holdout against their power. Their borders and treaties were cited by modern China as proof of its territorial claims. And they included Tibet.

Lucky shut her eyes and envisioned Lobsang as a young boy growing up in a refugee camp. That would have been in or around Dharamshala. Hot in summer. Cold in winter. Probably hungry all the time.

Lucky was a Parsi. The Parsis were driven from northwestern Iran to India after being declared heretics by the Persian caliph. Depending on whom you asked, the emigration took place somewhere between 700 and 900 CE. She smiled as she remembered the story her father told her: that when the Parsis arrived in Gujarat they were met by an envoy from the king bearing a glass of milk. 'You cannot stay here,' the envoy said. 'The land is full, as the glass is full.' According to legend, the leader of the Parsis took out a spoonful of sugar and added it to the milk. 'But we are so few,' he said. 'Just as a little sugar makes the milk sweet, so also we shall make the land sweet.' The king was so impressed with the tactful and clever response that he granted the Parsi's request to settle—on certain conditions, of course.

Lucky frowned. Her ex-husband, Viki, was a descendant of the Raj who allowed the Parsis to settle in India. His Aunt Geeta—practically Lucky's mother-in-law (since Viki's real mother was dead)—had been adamantly opposed to their relationship. Opposed to the point of sabotaging their marriage.

I wonder how he is? she thought. She hadn't thought about him in ages.

She returned to her computer. The more she knew the less Lucky felt she really understood India, even though it was the land of her birth. What was it they used to say? It takes thirteen lifetimes to know India? But the more she read, the more one thing became clear. Like China, India had been for thousands of years a swirling mosaic of languages and religions and kingdoms and customs. No individual piece represented the whole, nor could India be understood without placing the minute pieces in perspective with the entirety.

A STAR CALLED LUCKY

At the end of the day, she felt she understood China, Lobsang, and Tibet even less than before. All she really knew about the man was that he refused to follow modern rules—but he was in a land with a million rules and a thousand conflicting interpretations of whatever rules there were. The Monty Hall problem. Dys-logic. Her head swarmed with ideas, none of which made any sense.

Finally, she started e-mailing her old friends in India. *Six degrees of separation.* Even if she didn't know the key, perhaps she might get lucky. Behind door number three: Lobsang. A prize. A job in Washington. More money than she could spend. Freedom from Amay. And then what?

She turned off the monitor, went to the window, looked out over the Capitol and the Mall. In the end, Shanti had said a good life was simple, but difficult. *How true*, Lucky thought, *how true.*

Amay was waiting for Lucky at the hotel. He had brought her a stunning new sky-blue dress from Urban Chic. As usual, he had forgotten to take off the tag, and when Lucky saw the price, she went through the roof. "Twelve hundred dollars for a freaking dress? Are you out of your mind? I could have flown to India and bought one just like it in the Crawford Market for less money!"

Amay looked down. "Sweetie, it's just money, and you're worth every cent. Do you remember when I was too poor to take you out for Chinese? If I want to buy you a dress, let me buy you a dress. The money doesn't matter."

In the end, Lucky wore the dress just to humor Amay. Then, of course, they had to go somewhere, and Lucky had to cut short her evening call to Sean so they could make the reservation. They followed up dinner with a long walk along the Mall, eventually coming to the Lincoln Memorial. It was late and it was still warm, but there were only a few tourists around. The white marble statue practically glowed in the light. On the south walls were murals depicting Freedom, Liberty, Immortality, Justice, and the Law. They walked to the north wall, where Lucky stared at Unity, Fraternity, and Charity.

Amay touched the small of her back, turning her toward him, then dipped his head in for a kiss, but Lucky pushed him away. "I'm not on vacation," she reminded him.

"But do you have to work tonight?"

Lucky shook her head. "I just can't get it out of my head. It's pretty intimidating stuff."

Amay took Lucky by the hand. "At least you could let me in?" he asked, "Maybe I could share the burden."

"I can't talk about it," Lucky said. "And besides, you wouldn't understand. How did the opening go?"

"Good," Amay said. "Good. I think I talked Berber into coming to New York."

"I thought you didn't like him."

"No, I like him very much. I don't like the gallery, but then, neither did he. He was excited about coming to New York. Perhaps you'll get to meet him."

"I'd like that," Lucky said, but her mind was far from artists and gallery openings. Lucky looked at the mural. It was dominated by a giant angel with outstretched wings. She held her hands high in a gesture of… of…*Hell*, Lucky thought, *it looks like she's signaling a touchdown*. The idea was so absurd that she burst out laughing.

Amay stared at her. There were other tourists around. Really, the place, all the heavy stone, the Greek temple architecture, it was all so solemn. And here Lucky was laughing so hard she had to sit down on the cold marble floor in her $1200 dress.

Amay bent down and held her hand. "Are you okay?" he asked.

Between peals of laughter Lucky managed to say, "Did you know that Abraham Lincoln was of Lebanese descent?"

"What has that got to do with anything?"

Lucky wiped a tear from her cheek. "What has *anything* got to do with anything?"

Later, at the hotel, they made love, more because Lucky knew Amay would never sleep if she didn't than because she felt amorous.

And fall asleep he did, in her arms. She gazed at him long after he had dozed off. He was sweet, but so clueless. Or was it Lucky who was so clueless? Why couldn't she be happy with a man like Amay? It wasn't like he didn't have options. She could tell at openings and concerts how other women looked at him. He wasn't handsome—not like Viki had been—but he took good care of himself. He dressed well. He was intelligent. He was nice. He was...he was... he was just like the mural at the Lincoln Memorial: Liberty, Immortality, Justice, Law, Unity, Fraternity, and Charity, and all that. He was a real Boy Scout. Touchdown.

But at the end of the day, Lucky wasn't sure she wanted rock steady. She let go of Amay and lay on her back, looking up at the little rainbows of reflected light playing across the ceiling, wondering vaguely what was acting as a prism. As she looked at the light, she realized two things. First, there was something not right about Coleman, and she didn't want him to be a world leader. There was nothing in Coleman that likened him to men like Lincoln. Second, the only man she'd met recently who made her tingle with excitement was that damn Buddhist monk. What was his name? Usko? *I'm such a fool*, she thought. *Why do I always want what is out of reach?* For a long time, she lay awake thinking about that.

CHAPTER 10

Lucky woke early, dressed quietly, kissed Amay while he was sleeping, then slipped into the hallway and made her way to her room, looking around carefully once inside. Nothing appeared disturbed, but she had the uncomfortable intuition that someone had been there. It wasn't a thing she could put her finger on. A scent, perhaps? The subconscious smell of a stranger or strangers? Does air smell different after somebody else breathes it?

She showered quickly and changed, then walked briskly to the office, stopping at Starbucks along the way for a latte. Upon checking her e-mail, she stared at the screen in disbelief. She got up, walked around the room, and then sat down and stared at her computer again. Before her coffee was cold, she was on the phone with Coleman. "You're not going to believe this," she said.

"What? Has Wonder Woman found him already?"

Lucky frowned and paused. If she could have told Coleman to 'piss off' right then and there, she would have. Instead she said, "Not quite, but I have a clue about where he is. That's a start." In the silence that followed, she could almost hear Coleman grin.

"I'll be there in half-an-hour," he said.

Twenty minutes later, Coleman walked through the door. He was wearing a white IZOD tee shirt and khaki pants. He looked like he was headed to the tennis club; Lucky half-expected him to be carrying a racket. "Tell me everything," he said, coming around the desk and looking over Lucky's shoulder.

Lucky looked at the e-mail. Six degrees of separation might be the average, but in the right circles, that number could be cut. In the end, that's what so many things came down to—*connections*. Whom you know. And in India, Lucky still knew a lot of people. She had sent e-mails to her friends, especially anyone connected to medicine. All she had asked was for was a contact in Dharamshala—the name of someone—anyone—who had practiced medicine there and might know somebody who knew somebody who knew somebody. And her mother's doctor, Dr. Vakil, had replied: "The man with a magic cure? I'm not 100% sure, but I believe I've met him." Of course, there were thousands of men in India and hundreds in Mumbai who claimed to have magic cures. But this reply was, well, just plain *lucky*. Dr Vakil had written, "I'm reasonably certain. He's not someone you meet and forget."

"Looks like he's in Dharavi," Lucky said. "That's a slum in the heart of Mumbai — perhaps the largest in the world. It is spread over 500 acres and houses about 400,000 people. He runs a few makeshift charitable clinics there. Makes sense, if you think about it. It gives him a job and makeshift covers too. It also gives him a wide network of people who can shelter him, as there's a huge refugee population in and around there."

"Is this information reliable?"

"I think it is."

"How reliable?"

"An old friend, nobody with any particular political agenda. I was asking for contacts to Dharamshala. Somebody who might know somebody who knows Lobsang."

"You're a genius."

"Thank you." Lucky blushed. "I think that's the first nice thing you've said about me."

"And it might be the last. So you say this friend met Lobsang? He knows him? As in he can give us an address?"

"I wouldn't say he *knows* him, but he met him—a long time ago, in London, actually, when Lobsang was in medical school. But he recognized him right away when he saw him in Mumbai. He knew him well enough to remember him but he thinks his name is no longer Lobsang. And, again, he said 'reasonably certain.' That doesn't mean 100%."

Coleman tapped his fingers on the desk. He seemed to be counting. "It's the first new intelligence we've had in months," he said. "If it's accurate. That's what we need to know next."

"He may know people who know where Lobsang is. I mean, if Lobsang is in Dharavi, it's a place to start."

Coleman was leaning over the desk now, knuckles down, looking at the e-mail. "How recent, Lucky, how recent? Is this current?"

"I didn't ask how long ago, but he says recently—look here, he's used the word, 'recently.' I take that to mean in the past few weeks. Months at the outside."

"Hmmmm," Coleman said. He walked to the window, looked outside. He seemed to be counting, adding numbers in his mind. He mouthed something soundlessly. "But he doesn't know where Lobsang is?"

"Not exactly."

"You said he did."

"I said he ran into him. They chatted. He thinks that Lobsang was in Dharavi."

"Thinks or knows?"

"Thinks."

"But he's in touch with him now?"

"They've had some correspondence."

"About what?"

"He helped Lobsang obtain some surgical supplies and such. I think it was charitable work. He made a donation. Not money, just some supplies."

"But no address? A home? The clinic?"

"No, he's checking on it." Lucky watched as Coleman stared at the computer.

"Look, he says Lobsang's working in the slums, so there might not be a proper address. But he says here," Lucky ran her finger again to the lines on her computer, "that he'll ask around."

"Why not?"

"Why not what?"

"An address?"

"Have you been to Mumbai? Did you visit the slums?"

"I've been, but I had no business in the slums."

"If you'd seen Dharavi, you'd understand."

Coleman seemed to be thinking about this. Lucky thought he might be trying to recall the slums. At the very least, he may have seen Dharavi from the overpasses while driving through the area.

"Okay," Coleman said. "I think we could have a general location. That narrows things down. One more thing — this friend's name?"

"Dr. Vakil, why?"

"Just curious. I wondered if perhaps he was someone we already made contact with."

"Have you?"

"Not that I know of. But you can bet we'll talk to him now." Coleman walked across the room and sat down at the edge of Lucky's desk. "You trust this man?"

"Implicitly. He was our family physician."

"Nice work, Lucky." Coleman paused and looked at Lucky with something like surprise. "I can't believe I said that. Don't repeat that to anyone, you'll ruin my reputation. And don't count on hearing anything like that again. Now, go back to your hotel and get packing."

"Packing?"

"Packing. As in your things."

"Why? Where are we going?"

"*We* aren't going anywhere. You're going to India to work with my team there. I can't be seen in India."

"Why am I going to India? I don't think I want to go to India."

Coleman stood up abruptly and shouted, "What is this, Twenty Questions? This isn't reality TV, we're hunting a miracle cure that might prevent the second coming of the Black Death! I recruited you to be on my team because you speak the lingo." He paused, looked around, then lowered his voice to almost a growl. "Look, Lucky, We've got people on the ground there—people I can trust. But you know the city, and you know this doctor—this Vakil man—and you might be the most intuitive person I've ever had in my employ."

"That's all well and good," Lucky said, "but this was always meant to be a test drive, right? What was it you said, 'Just for a little while'? Well, it's been a little while, and while I've enjoyed it, this isn't my field. What I know now is that I want to go home to my son. You can find this monk without my help."

"But —" Coleman sputtered, his face reddened. "I thought you liked it here?"

"Like it?" Now Lucky was taken aback.

"I mean immunology. Health Services."

"No. That's not what I mean," she said. She looked up at Coleman, staring down at her with the veins pulsing in his neck. "It's politics I don't like. Or maybe I do like it, but I don't believe in it. I'm a people-person, Mr. Coleman —"

"Clevis."

"Clevis. I teach yoga. I do some stuff with the Department of Corrections. Last night, I realized that I just work better with people one-on-one. I'm not saying politics isn't important—it is. And we need honest politicians who can play the game, get things done. I'm not putting you down or arguing with you. I just realized that I'm not what you want me to be, and I can't be what you want me to be. And if I tried, I'd only be letting us both down. I have a little boy waiting at home, and I don't intend to raise him the way some people I know raised their daughter. I made a promise to Sean's father and I have to keep it. I'm sure you have good people in India who can get done what you need to do. People better than me. Why, I haven't been to Mumbai in years, and from what my friends say, I'd hardly recognize the place."

Coleman eyed Lucky carefully, then nodded. "Okay," he said. "If that's how you feel about things."

"It's not about feelings," Lucky said. "It's about knowing what I can and can't do. You need to know that honestly from me, don't you?"

"Absolutely," Coleman said. "And thank you. I'll see that arrangements are made." He turned and left the office, the door shutting behind him with a soft click.

When he was gone, Lucky slumped in her chair and closed her eyes. "Wow," she said. "Wow." In the quiet, she could hear the air whirring in the ventilation system. She sat up and looked at her laptop, then drummed her fingers on the desk and looked around the room. She sat for almost five full minutes, just taking in the morning sun shining in the window, the cooing of pigeons on the ledge outside her windows, the sound of the traffic outside. Then she called Barkley. "I'll be back this afternoon," she said.

Barkley replied, "You sound cheerful. I assume this is good news?"

"It is — I suppose."

"Well?"

"Well what?"

"Did it work out?"

"Mission accomplished. Why? You sound concerned?"

"Concerned? I was wondering if perhaps you and Coleman weren't too… too much alike."

"Alike?" Lucky thought about this. "I couldn't imagine two people less alike."

"I mean you're strong people, both of you. I wondered if you might clash. No, not *if* you might. More like *when*."

"We got along okay," Lucky said. "But I get the feeling that his ambitions might lead me places I don't want to go. I'll be home this afternoon."

"And we'll be glad to have you back at your desk."

Lucky looked around at the office and sighed. *Her* desk. This office was nice. The Feds certainly had more money to squander on amenities than the State of New York. Maybe she'd still get an upgrade and a promotion with the Department of Corrections. After all, she still had that presentation pending — the one that had been sidelined when Coleman burst onto the scene.

The phone rang a few minutes later. It was Amay. "Why didn't you wake me?" he asked.

"You looked so peaceful. I'm the one who had to work today."

"I would have gotten up with you."

"I know."

Silence. Then, "I'm on my way to the airport. When will I see you again?"

Lucky sucked on her lip. "I'm going home today, too. I'm not sure exactly when, so please don't wait for me."

"I would have, but I have a lunch meeting. You'll pick Sean up when you get home?"

"Of course."

"Then how about dinner tonight when you pick him up?"

Lucky sighed. "I'd better take Sean home and have some time with him. I'm sure he's missed me. And I could use a little quiet time to de-stress."

"We could all go out—all of us. He'd like that, too. And what could be less stressful than dinner out?"

Lucky sighed. She didn't feel like arguing. "Okay then, tonight."

"Dinner?"

"Okay," Lucky said. "We can all go out."

"Great. I'll see you about…"

"I don't have my ticket yet. I'll call you."

She began packing her things. She finished packing her things. She checked her watch.

A tall, middle-aged woman in a strict blue business dress suit appeared at the door with a stack of documents in her hands. "I heard you were leaving. I'm sorry." She extended an envelope to Lucky. Inside was a first-class ticket back to New York, scheduled to leave at 12:00 PM.

"Thank you," Lucky said.

"You should sign these, too."

"Mr. Coleman doesn't waste any time, does he?"

"No, he doesn't."

Lucky took the papers and looked at the first one. A nondisclosure agreement. "What, did he type these up last week?" she asked. When the woman shrugged but did not answer, Lucky sat down and began to read and sign them, one by one.

When she was done, Lucky picked up her things at the hotel and caught a cab to the airport. She half-expected to run into Amay, although she knew that he had tickets on an earlier flight, and she wanted to be alone. She had just enough time to buy a coffee before she boarded her flight.

CHAPTER 11

In New York, Lucky waited for her luggage until all the other passengers were gone, watching one lonely little red bag make the circuit over and over again. Eventually the sign changed, indicating that luggage from another flight was about to disgorge, and she was forced to admit defeat. She found the lost items counter, filed a claim for the missing bag. It was annoying, but not the end of the world. The airline promised to call her as soon as the errant bag was located. The baggage agent, a nice young woman with a thick Italian accent, said that because of Lucky's late airport arrival, the bag was probably bumped to a later flight and the airline just couldn't get it through security in time. "We'll call you," she said. "Don't worry. It happens. These things almost never get lost. We'll have it delivered to your home."

Lucky sighed. She hated unfinished business. Even though there wasn't much in the bag that she was worried about losing, it would just be nice to go home, have a shower, and be done with it. *Some jobs*, she thought, *just won't go away, even when you want them to.*

As if on cue, her phone rang—Collette. Lucky ignored it, but the phone rang again, an annoying electronic beeping sound not at all like her friendly ring tone. Lucky dug the phone out and saw that Collette had sent her a text message—strange, since she knew Lucky usually ignored them. With some trial and error, Lucky managed to open the file instead of accidentally e-mailing it to all her friends, or—wait, could it be? It could. Gordon Bolton—the creep from the train. The message read, *Do you know this guy?*

Lucky called. "Where did you get that picture?"

"He's standing on my front porch," Collette said.

Lucky almost dropped the phone. "Get out of the house, NOW! Out the back door, run, and don't look back. Call 911, then call me when you're safe."

Lucky jumped the barricade to the front of the line and pushed a passenger out of the way to steal his cab. "Please! An emergency!" Then sitting inside the cab she shouted, "Connecticut," at the driver. "I need to be there *yesterday!* I don't care what it costs—just hit it! If you get a ticket, I'll pay it." Screeching down the access road and almost airborne with each speed bump, Lucky called 911 and identified herself as working with the Department of Corrections. "There's a violent felon at my neighbor's house," she said. "Gordon Bolton. He has outstanding warrants for robbery and assault. Six foot, one-eighty. White male, approximately fifty, with scarring on the right side of his face. There's a teenage girl in the house alone. She said she was going to call you. Did she call?"

There had been no call. Lucky shivered. She gave the address and asked that they rush a police cruiser to the house. She said she was on the way herself. She called Amay on his cell—voicemail. She called Alec. He promised to meet her at her house as soon as he could get there—in a half hour. Lucky checked her watch. She called Collette. Nothing. She called again. Still nothing. She called Amay— voicemail again. Should she tell him? She hesitated. "Call me," she said. "It's urgent."

It took thirty minutes to reach Collette's house. There was a single police cruiser parked in the driveway. Lucky threw a hundred at the cabbie and leaped out without asking for change. The lone officer, a woman of sixty or so, got out of the cruiser as Lucky rushed to the porch. "Sergeant Wessex," the cop said, following Lucky. "I take it you're the complainant."

"Lucky Boyce."

"Nobody's home," Wessex said. "The house is locked, we checked all over. Nothing."

"Did you go in?" Lucky tried the door.

"Locked up tight. Nothing broken, nothing disturbed. No teenager home alone. No probable cause. Just a big old empty house in the 'burbs."

"But she called me. She sent a picture of the guy. He was on the porch."

"So how'd she get the picture?"

"Security camera." Lucky pointed at the hanging plant. But even as she did she saw that the camera was nowhere to be seen.

Wessex looked at the plant and shrugged. "The alarm company says the house is secure."

"There was a camera," Lucky said. "It was there just a few days ago."

"The alarm company doesn't have a record of any such device."

Lucky looked around frantically, but it really did seem that everything was fine. The windows were dark, and the little green light by the door blinked that the alarm system was armed.

"Ma'am, may I ask what your relationship is with this child?"

"We're friends," explained Lucky. "Sometimes she babysits my son."

"And the mother knows you and the daughter are…*friends*?"

"She does."

"And does the mother know the child—" she consulted her notes—"Collette, was not in school?"

"I suppose," Lucky said. Struck by an idea, she went around to the side of the house to try the gate. It was locked from the backyard.

Wessex followed. "We climbed the fence already, Ms. Boyce. Nobody's home. Nothing looks wrong."

Lucky called Collette again. No answer.

"May I ask how you know this guy Bolton?"

"It's a long story."

Wessex pushed the blue hat up off her forehead. "I bet it is. Can you show me the photo the kid sent you?"

140

A STAR CALLED LUCKY

Lucky showed Wessex the photo. In the shade of the porch the photo was practically black and white, taken from an angle above and to Bolton's left. It looked just like the kind of grainy photo one would get from a security camera. He was wearing a sports coat, his hands thrust into his pockets, no hat, just looking straight ahead. There was nothing—besides it being Bolton—that was alarming about the photo. There was nothing, Lucky realized, that even proved conclusively that it was taken from the front porch.

Officer Wessex seemed to come to the same conclusion. She asked, "Could Collette have gotten the photo from somewhere else? A computer maybe? The Internet?"

Lucky thought about this. "Possible, but not likely."

Wessex nodded. "We get these kids sometimes —"

"Look!" Lucky said, turning suddenly. "This is not some *kid*. She's really smart, a little misunderstood, maybe —"

"A little punky, maybe? Likes computers? Likes games? Dresses weird?"

Lucky stood, open-mouthed.

"Ma'am." Wessex laid a large hand on Lucky's shoulder. "I know she's your friend. She'll turn up in a few hours, a few days at most." She smiled a tight (and not very friendly) smile. "We called Ms. Kennedy and she seemed more concerned about Collette spending time with *you*." She cocked her head. "Something about a little unauthorized trip to DC. Maybe you better cool your friendship with this kid for a while. We take missing person reports seriously, but we also investigate exploited minors."

Lucky's blood ran cold, but what could she say? *Excuse me, but I've been working for the government and I've got this secret program on my laptop, and I was just working on this secret project that I'm not supposed to talk about, and this kid might have sent a secret government program to the Bulgarians?* That would go over real well. *And after only thirty days in the loony bin, they might let me out.* "Can you come to my house with me?" she said. "I don't feel safe going there alone, and this guy, Bolton, may know where I live."

Wessex nodded. She called in that she was checking another house in the neighborhood and drove Lucky home. Alec was waiting on the porch.

Wessex looked at Lucky's expression of relief and failed to hold back a smirk. "I take it this is not the man you were worried about?"

Alec looked from Lucky to Wessex and back. "Everything looks okay," he said.

Lucky glared at Wessex, who tipped her hat and left.

"What's going on?" Alec asked.

Inside, Lucky told Alec the whole story—Bolton, Coleman, Washington, Collette, everything. It was only interrupted once, when she'd gotten up to going to Washington, by Amay calling Lucky back.

"Are you okay?" he asked. "You on your way over?"

Lucky hesitated. "I'm okay," she said. "Only I… I… I lost my bag at the airport. It was upsetting, that's all. And I had to run home for a little while."

"But you're coming, right?"

"I'll be there in a couple of hours. Let me catch my breath."

Lucky hung up and continued onward, explaining the most recent events. By the end, Alec was looking deeply skeptical.

"What?" asked Lucky.

"It's just…" He paused. "This is so much, and it's all happened so fast. One day you were doing your usual thing, then you were in Washington, then you quit, and now you're possibly being pursued by a felon."

Lucky was a bit disturbed. "Don't you believe me?"

"It's not that," said Alec. "When you got home, you fully expected to be seeing a dangerous criminal on your doorstep, and yet when your boyfriend called, you told him all that was wrong was a missing bag."

Lucky shrugged. "If I'd told him, he would have made too much of a fuss. He would have hired a security guard to stand in front of my door. He's done it before."

A STAR CALLED LUCKY

"It sounds like a security guard wouldn't be such a bad idea," Alec pointed out. "So why not just tell him?"

"I just don't want to deal with all that. Not after having to deal with everything else. It would just be too exhausting. Every time we talk about problems I have, I have to end up comforting him. I mean, I love him, but I just can't tell him everything right now."

Alec just kept looking at her, with a sobering, quiet frown.

His silence bothered Lucky more than what he might have said. "I'll tell him," she said, "later. You want some tea?"

"You've been under a lot of stress," Alec said. "Maybe you're working too hard."

"Right," Lucky said.

Alec checked his watch. "I'll pass on the tea," he said.

"You're not leaving, are you?"

"I have an appointment, unless you really need me."

Lucky shook her head. "No," she said. "I'm okay. Please keep your appointment."

Alec hesitated at the front door. "Call if you need me."

When he was gone Lucky changed into a T-shirt and loose cotton pants, then threw her yoga mat on the kitchen floor, sat down in lotus pose, and tried to clear her mind. *Breathe*, she thought, but her mind was racing and she couldn't get into a rhythm. First there was all the confusion about Coleman—and that happened so fast. And then there was the lost bag, and the call from Collette, and now she didn't know what to think. And the throbbing in her lower back got worse and not better until she finally shifted into child's pose, and then downward dog. From there she inched her way back until she was standing with her palms flat on the floor, and that helped. She wiggled her butt ever so slightly and felt the vertebrae align with a satisfying crack.

The doorbell rang. *Collette!* Lucky rushed to the front hall and threw the door open, ready to give the girl a well-earned tongue-lashing. Instead, she found the world's shortest cabbie, a rumpled little man in what must have been the world's oldest (and ugliest) suit—a lime-green herringbone tweed that might have dated from the 1940s. Lucky looked incredulously at the driver, and then at the cab idling in the driveway, just to make sure. It was a plain blue Toyota with white sign on top. Tip Top Taxi. The driver wore ridiculously oversized, black, plastic-framed glasses. On his head was a grey and white tweed wool golf cap. His hair was white and hung down over his ears. Lucky was about to ask what he was doing there, but finally spotted her suitcase standing on the ground by his right leg. "Thank you," Lucky said, "Do I owe you anything?"

"I no turn down tip," the cabbie said, "But truth is, airline fare pay." His accent was such a thick mixture of Bronx and Eastern Europe that Lucky barely understood him.

Lucky reached for the bag, but the cabbie held up a clipboard. "I need sign dis," he said.

Lucky reached for the clipboard but the cabbie pulled it away. "Firss I need open bag and make sure evree ting A-okay."

"You need me to look in the bag?"

The cabbie nodded. "It's so dey no t'ink I don' took nutt'in'."

Lucky took the bag and turned to the living room.

"I need you to open fronna me." He shrugged. "I no make rules, lady. Dey jus' wanna you make sure I no take."

Lucky looked at the cabbie. Then she laid the bag down and opened it. Her things were just as she had left them. Not neat, not messy, just packed in a hurry. The pictures and papers from her office were laid on top. *Glad I packed my undies underneath it all*, Lucky thought. Just as she was about to stand up, she noticed something about the cabbie. He wore a pair of cherry colored Doc Martens high boots. Then it struck her….. could this be the little woman on the train with Gordon Bolton? Could it be? Or was her head spinning?

She looked up at the cabbie, who was now pointing to the side of the bag.

Now what! She looked, and found a box in the bulging side zipper.

Lucky opened the box and was amazed to see a syringe filled with what looked like blood.

A STAR CALLED LUCKY

The note inside was typed with a part of a Sun Tzu quote, *"Supreme excellence consists of breaking the enemy's resistance without fighting."* Below that it read: *Remember your duty to mankind. Remember Bloodhound. You will never be free.*

The cabbie looked at Lucky and said, "Boss also says you to go India. Boss say get the job done. Boss say, you may get disease one day. Who know?"

Lucky stared at him, open-mouthed. "Are you threatening me?"

"Boss wants an answer. When you go?"

He then folded his hands and stood, refusing to budge.

Lucky shut her mouth and considered the man carefully. "Who is your boss?"

"And boss says you must do your job not only for yourself but for good of all."

"Tell your boss I will let him know."

"My boss says till he knows, I not to leave."

A black limo pulled up in the driveway behind the cabbie. In the front seat were two men in suits and dark glasses.

Lucky decided that now would be a good time to panic.

"Tell your boss —" She stopped abruptly.

"Okay, I will go… but on my own terms. I will make my own arrangements. Do you understand? "

"Boss make arrangements."

"No. Tell your boss I will go on my own terms. If and when I need help, I will let him know. Now leave."

The cabbie kicked at the ground and seemed to be mulling things over. Then he walked away and made a phone call, although he never took his eyes off Lucky.

He then walked back, picked out the syringe from the box, squirted the red liquid all over Lucky's face, and said, "Leave tomorrow, Boss says …you may be sick, you need the mushroom now. Boss says…get it fast. Nothing but the mushroom can help ya!" He laughed and picked up the box, put the syringe inside, turned and headed for his cab. As he opened the door, the black limo pulled out and drove away. The cabbie followed.

Lucky stood there for a long time in stunned silence, before getting a towel. The liquid looked and smelled like paint as she wiped herself clean.

And then Collette appeared, turning the corner from the side of the house. Lucky ran to her and threw her arms around her, which was how Amay found them when he pulled up in his Mercedez.

Amay got out and looked at Lucky. "Are you okay?"

"I'm okay!"

"This is not what okay looks like. You look like hell!"

"Can we just get out of here, *please,* before they come back?" Lucky said.

"Who are they?"

"The guys in the limo!"

"I didn't see a limo." Amay looked back, as though it might still be there. "What's going on?"

"I need to get out of here. Let's go," Lucky said. She rushed to Amay's car.

Collette jumped out of the way as Amay opened the door. Lucky climbed in the car. "Before who comes back?" he asked.

"The cab driver and the government guys."

"The cab driver?" Amay looked at the cab, now starting to move and then took out his cell phone. "I'll call the police," he said.

"NO!" Lucky and Collette shouted at the same time.

Amay let his hands fall to his side and asked, "Why not?"

"Just don't," Lucky said. "Let's GO. I'll explain!"

"They may be in on it," Collette said.

"The cab company?" Amay asked.

"The cops," Collette replied.

"Please let's get out of here." Lucky was near to tears.

Amay shut the door.

"Just a minute!" Collette shouted. She ran around the side of the house and returned a moment later with her My Little Pony backpack. She threw it in the back seat, then ran in the house for Lucky's suitcase, and threw in the back seat, too. She climbed in and they drove away. "Where are we going?" Amay asked.

146

"Anywhere," Lucky said. "No, wait. Someplace where nobody will find us for a while."

"I can take you to the gallery."

"No," Collette said.

Amay said, "I've got some friends upstate. They have a country house by Bear Mountain."

"Where's Maria and the kids?" Lucky asked.

"They just got home."

"You have to get them out of there," Lucky said.

Collette said, "I've got some friends in Waterbury. We can hole up there."

"Who is she?" Amay asked, turning to look at Collette.

"She's my babysitter," Lucky replied.

"This isn't making any sense."

"You're telling me!"

"Just drive north," Collette said. "Trust me."

Lucky dug into Amay's coat pocket for his phone, found it, and dialed. Maria answered. "Maria, it's me. Don't say anything. Take the kids, all the kids, *now*, and get out. Go to your uncle's house. Go to your uncle Juan's and stay there until I find you. Don't ask any questions. Turn off your cell phone and don't call anybody you know. Do it now. I'll get word to you somehow at your uncle's when it's safe." She hung up, then threw the phone out of the window.

Amay looked at the open window. "That was —"

"Good move!" Collette said.

"What did you do with Bolton?" Lucky asked Collette.

"I didn't do anything," Collette said. "Well, not with them. Not exactly. When you told me to run, I ran. I ran to your house. I was waiting for you, hiding over there, but then this older guy showed up, and he started poking around, trying the doors and such, and I didn't know who he was or anything."

"That was Alec," Lucky said.

"Okay. Anyway, he didn't look dangerous, but I wasn't taking any chances. So I just hid in the bushes until you came home with that psycho cop. I sure wasn't going to come out with her around — she hates me. So when she left, and that first guy left, I was just about to come up to your porch when that other car pulled up. I thought, *Uh-oh*. I went around the side of the house, but that tall dude was still there—the one whose photo I sent you."

"Bolton…," Lucky said. It came out almost like a question.

"How did you get mixed up with *that* guy?" Collette asked.

"It doesn't matter," Lucky said. "I saw him on a train and the little cabbie driver too when I was on my way to work."

"Anyway," Collette continued, "I almost walked right into him, but he didn't see me. He was looking around the front of the house. Then I heard you talking to somebody. I wanted to warn you, but what could I do? The back door was still locked."

"They had another car, a big black limo," Lucky said. She looked around anxiously. "I wonder if they're following us."

Amay cleared his throat. "What is this all about?" he asked. "Lucky, what have you got yourself into?"

"I'm not sure," Lucky said, "I don't know what's going on, but I'm sure as hell going to find out." She ran Amay through the events of the past few days, starting with Coleman hacking her computer to send her data to the mirror site, telling Coleman she could not work for him, the lost bag, Bolton being on the train and in Collette's backyard, the police officer, the cabbie, the syringe, the blood threat, and the message. She shivered.

Amay listened, then asked, "But why do we need to run?"

"I just want to be in a safe place, Amay. I need to sort this out. If I don't go to Mumbai, I'll wind up in the same prison where I teach. I see it clearly. You see, it is all so complicated. The train ride, Gordon Bolton the criminal, the computer, the programs, the magic mushroom, Dr. Vakil giving me Lobsang's whereabouts, and Coleman determined to get Lobsang. Maybe he feels I can do the job being from Mumbai, but I have to go on my own, not as Coleman's employee. That's my best chance to find out anything there. And then I can come out clean and clear up this whole computer mess. Besides, if I don't go, I guess Bolton will have me for dinner!"

Collette piped in, "I'm sure they're looking for your laptop now."

Lucky turned to Collette. "How far is it to your friends' house?"

"About an hour," Collette said, "if this guy doesn't drive like a wimp."

"I don't want to get a ticket," Amay said. "Or in an accident."

"You're already in an accident," Collette said, "and the cops are probably looking for you, anyway."

"Why would…I just don't get it….you both seem to be hallucinating!"

"Please just drive, Amay. Besides, she might be right," Lucky said. "We have to ditch the car."

Amay took a deep breath. "Why so dramatic, Lucky?"

"Can't you see? I don't want Coleman hounding me. I need to go on my own terms."

"Who is she again?" Amay said turning his head.

"My babysitter."

"That nutty kid you're always talking about?"

"Collette," Collette said, "Not that anybody'd care. After all, teenagers are to be seen and hot nerd."

"*What*?"

"Never mind." Lucky smiled.

www.*astarcalledlucky*.com

CHAPTER 12

They stopped at a little mom-and-pop store in Darien for some snacks. Amay ran inside and paid cash — at Lucky's insistence. "For God's sake, will you listen to me just once! Do *not* use a credit card! Just do what I say, will you? Please! Without arguing?"

"Look at him run," Collette said, as Amay looked left and right before ducking inside the store. "Does he look suspicious, or what?"

Lucky scanned the building and the street.

"Whatcha lookin' for?" Collette asked.

"Cameras."

"You're paranoid."

"A few days ago you said I wasn't paranoid enough."

"Well, don't take it too far."

"You know what Coleman put on my computer, but I know what was on my computer before he put anything on it."

"Are you talking about Bloodsucker?"

Lucky paled. "Bloodhound?" she said. It was almost a whisper. The words caught in her throat.

"Yeah, something like that." Collette squirmed in the back seat.

Lucky glared at her. "Tell me. You might as well tell it all."

"I didn't do anything. Yazma found it. He read your hard drive, remember?"

"Yes," Lucky sighed. *With time off for good behavior,* she thought, *I might make parole by the time I turn forty.*

150

"The thing is," Collette said, "Yazma told me you were in some deep shit."

Amay climbed into the car and dropped bags of Trail Mix in Lucky's lap. He peeled out in a cloud of burning rubber.

Still later, they found a pay phone, and Collette called her friends to come and get them at the gas station near the freeway. They munched on hamburgers at Denny's at the station while they waited.

Lucky looked at Collette. "What did Yazma say?" Lucky asked.

"He didn't say anything about you."

"You said he said I was in deep shit."

"Oh, that." Collette put down her hamburger. "He was talking about your boss—what's his name?"

"Coleman."

"Yeah, him." She took another bite of the burger and slurped her coke.

"But what did he say?" Lucky asked.

"He just said this guy was spying on you."

Lucky thought about this. "Well," she said, "it isn't right, but sometimes companies do that. Even governments. Especially if they're dealing with some sensitive information — if there's a security issue."

"This wasn't a background check, Lucky. And this guy wanted more than information. He wanted to know everything about you— who you talk to, what you say, where you shop, what you think, who you know, everything. That's not about information, it's about control. If he wanted, he could send e-mails from your account. Deposit money. Take money. Put up pictures of you. Anything."

"Well, he is in the government."

"And that makes it right?"

"No," Lucky said, "but it makes it plausible."

"That's just it," Collette said. "There's no reason for somebody to want that kind of control over you." Collette opened up her backpack and handed Lucky the little Netbook.

"You brought it!" Lucky exclaimed.

"I figured it was important," Collette replied.

Amay asked, "What's so special about it?"

"I took something I shouldn't have from the Department of Corrections, but then Coleman did something he shouldn't have done to my computer. He put a program on it—what was it?—a magic mirror. Maybe they know I have it."

"What's that–exactly how does it work?" Amay asked.

"Tell him, Collette."

Collette said, "It makes it look like you're online doing whatever you are doing, but it's actually exporting everything you do to another website. It records everything. Keystrokes, passwords, sites, e-mail, everything. It's a hacker's dream. And this one was good. I mean, the government made it."

"The GWC?" Amay asked. "That doesn't make any sense."

"I know," Lucky said.

When they reached the gas station, Collette's friends were waiting, and after they high fived, Lucky and Amay shook their hands, Derrick, Sunny, Cleo, and Kink. Derrick was middle aged, short, balding, with a salt-and-pepper goatee. He wore a black tee shirt under a brown sports jacket, Levis, and neon green Nike sneakers. Sunny was in his late teens or early twenties, also short, black, and wearing jeans and a black muscle shirt. Cleo was in her late teens, a blonde, and tall, nearly six feet. She wore pink pants and a fake-fur leopard print jacket. Kink was in her early twenties, very short, a honey blonde, and she wore a green tee shirt over black spandex tights.

"Nothing like traveling inconspicuously," Amay said.

"It's my mother's car," Cleo said.

"I was talking about you," Amay replied.

"What the f–k?" Collette asked. "How the hell are we all supposed to fit in that?"

"Three in the front, four in the back," Derrick replied.

"And you know what's really cool?" Cleo asked.

"What's that?" Collette replied.

A STAR CALLED LUCKY

Derrick held up his Blackberry. On the screen was a photo of
Collette. "There's an Amber Alert for you, girl."

They drove to Waterbury. It was past midnight when they arrived.
The house was a McMansion in a gated community just north of
town. They spread out on the floor of the living room. Lucky looked
at the little Netbook. Kink hovered over it. "So, can you show us that
cool program you were talking about? Bloodsucker?"

Collette winced as Lucky shot her a glare.

Kink reached for the On button but Lucky shouted, "No! If you
turn it on, they'll know right where we are."

"Too bad," Amay said. "I'd like to see that myself."

"We could change the computer's ID," Derrick suggested. "Of
course, we'd have to jerk the hard drive."

Collette looked sheepishly at Lucky. "If I told you something," she
said, "would you promise not to get mad at me?"

"I'm beyond getting mad right now," Lucky said.

"If all you wanted was to use Bloodhound, I sort of made a
copy, too."

"You 'sort of' made a copy. As in, accidentally?"

"Well, after what Yazma said, it kind of sounded interesting.
Maybe even useful. So he made a copy for me. I was thinking maybe
that was why they came to my house. Anyway, that might explain
how they found me."

Lucky arched her eyebrows. "But you have a copy? A copy of
Bloodhound! On your computer?"

Collette nodded.

Lucky held out her hands. "Give it to me."

Collette fetched her laptop from her backpack and they fired it up.
Lucky found Bolton in the state public records, and once she had the
photo she went to work. Ten minutes later they were all staring at
the screen at a photo from 1984. Two brothers, side-by-side. A
going-away party. One of the brothers was thin and wore glasses, a
button-down shirt and slacks. The other brother was tall and
muscular. He wore jeans, a blue ball cap, and a gray tee shirt that
read: UNIVERSITY OF MONTANA GRIZZLIES. The smaller of

153

the two was Coleman. The other, the records stated, was his half-brother—Gordon Bolton.

"So he's got his own little crew of home-grown plumbers," Amay said. "He's a politician. But if we were to sit and analyze, he just has two goons running around. It's not like the FBI you know."

"There's more to this than fixing leaks," Lucky said.

"What then?"

"I need to check my e-mail." Lucky opened her Hotmail account. It was entirely empty but for a single new e-mail marked SENDER UNKNOWN. "Here we go," Lucky said. She opened the e-mail. In it was a single blue hyperlink. The article led to an article on the website of an Indian news service. Lucky read out loud to the group. "Mumbai police are investigating the break in and robbery of a local physician's apartment, Dr. Eruch Vakil, in Madhuri building at Worli Sea Face…the robbery included cash and electronic items including a desktop computer." Lucky stopped. "For the love of God," she said. "What have I got myself into?" She closed out the browser.

Amay put his arm around her. "We'll go to the police," he said. "They can protect you."

Lucky shook her head. "This is the police, I mean the GWC. So they are not going to protect me. And anyway, it doesn't matter. It's not me I'm worried about."

He looked at her. "What, then?"

"I have to dodge Coleman. He'll follow my every move."

She looked at the Netbook, then turned to Collette. "It's working again?"

Collette nodded.

"And if I turn it on, they'll know?"

"They'll know," Collette said

Lucky opened the Netbook and turned it on. She went straight to a travel website and bought a ticket in her name for the next day from Boston to London, England.

Amay looked at her. Collette said, "But they'll know…"

"Of course they'll know," Lucky said. "I even used my credit card."

Lucky then bought another ticket from Hartford to Houston to Buenos Aires.

"But Lucky," Collette said. "They'll still know where you're going. You used your computer."

"That's right," she replied. "But I'm not going to Buenos Aires, either. We're going to use Derrick's computer and I'm buying a ticket from Montreal to Mumbai, with Amay's credit card. I need to go to Mumbai to find Lobsang. And if I don't, Coleman may kill him and then hang me. I have inadvertently told him where Lobsang could be. And I don't want to be hanged or live with his death on my conscience."

"But doesn't Coleman want you in India?"

"Of course he does, and that's why I have to convince him I'm somewhere else. I need to work on my own. Lobsang will run for miles if he thinks I am on Coleman's team!"

Amay shook his head. "Sounds thin."

"What else can I do?" Lucky asked. "Maybe I can find this guy first. Who knows? Maybe I can persuade him to give me the mushroom. And if he does, then Coleman will have what he wants and leave us all alone. If I stay, Coleman will hang me on charges of stealing Bloodhound. If I go alone and convince Lobsang, along with my Mumbai friends, he may listen and I may get back my life. Coleman knows I can find Lobsang. I've proved it with poor Dr. Vakil!" She shivered.

She turned to Amay and touched him on the cheek. "Amay, promise me you'll take care of Sean. Once I go, Coleman will be too busy tracking my whereabouts to worry about Sean and Collette."

"But Lucky, do you really need to go all the way to India? He is smart making you run around to get his job done. I mean, what are the chances of finding Lobsang? And why hide all this from Coleman? It's his job, why not get his support?"

"Like I keep saying, Amay, till I find Lobsang, I am not safe, and neither is Lobsang. Or you. Or Sean. Coleman will do anything to get what he wants. This is the only way. And again, I can only hope to get Lobsang if I go alone. I've studied the man and I know with Coleman's people around, I wouldn't even see his shadow."

Amay looked confused.

Lucky smiled and said, "Please, Amay, drive me up to Montreal tomorrow."

"But they're looking for you," Amay stammered.

Lucky smiled. "I work for the government," she said. "I work for the Department of Corrections. You think I don't know how they work?" She opened her suitcase and took out her travel wallet, then pulled out a dark blue-jacketed passport. "They're looking for Lucky Boyce," she said. "This is my old passport. From India. It is still current. They can look for Lucky Boyce till their eyes fall out. Tomorrow morning, I'm *Mizz* Leela Singh."

"Leela?" Amay quizzed.

"Yes, the Singhs changed my name when we got married to Leela Singh. I hated it then but I guess it works now. We never know the outcomes in this grand design called 'life'."

CHAPTER 13

Eighteen hours later, Ms. Leela Singh was gliding through traffic in an air-conditioned Benz, sipping a bottle of ice-cold Seven-Up and thinking, *I bet this isn't what Coleman had in mind.* She flew first class, on a $7,000 ticket from Montreal. And she stayed at the Taj. Sure, why not. Hiding in plain sight. All with Amay's credit card. They might be watching the airports in Boston and Hartford, London and Buenos Aires, but she was pretty sure they weren't looking for her in Mumbai and definitely not at the Taj Hotel.

She was alone and living as Ms. Singh. But that didn't mean they wouldn't find her accidentally. And this was what worried her. *They're looking for Lobsang. I'm looking for Lobsang. I have to find him before they do and hand him over and put this behind me. I need to buy my peace. We're going to cover some of the same ground, talk to some of the same people.* She would need help, but she couldn't risk seeing anyone who had been in her contact list. At least, not anyone important. Not anyone among her immediate family and friends. And not even Dr. Eruch Vakil. Coleman might not be looking for her, but he still might be watching them.

Lucky spent her first evening shopping—not for luxury, but dressing to fit in. The less she stood out, the less likely she was to be picked out and recognized. She thought about a burqa and veil, but decided that might create more problems than it solved—Muslim women didn't go to the places she'd be going, and she'd never be

157

able to pass as one if anyone tried to talk to her. No, a green silk sari with a matching necklace of fake emeralds was enough for today. And a small black bag. And now it was morning, and the car she'd hired was slowing for city traffic. She would start her search in one of the most unlikely places, turning back to old contacts from her jewelry business in Bombay. A good starting point, she told herself—after all, the *six degrees of separation* had to work.

Zaveri Bazaar was tucked in behind the cloth district at Mangaldas Market. The streets of the district were jammed: businessmen hurrying about their errands, laborers pushing two-wheeled wooden carts piled high with bolts of cloth, kids in uniforms plodding along reluctantly to school, beggars and policemen and vendors and idlers and God-only-knows who all else, the mind-numbing jostling crowds that swelled to overflowing on the streets of Mumbai every day. It was hot, but thanks to the monsoons, it wasn't the heat of May-June. Still, the first waves of heavy rain had already moved north to the Himalayas. Ever-damp Mumbai was drying out a bit, anyway. The feeling of home returned — Lucky loved Mumbai. They drove into the alley as far as they could and then she got out and elbowed her way through the crowd as if she had never been away.

Zaveri Bazaar itself was slightly less crowded and she took in her bearings over a cup of chai, then headed west and north, eyeing the little side alleys until she found the one she was after. Halfway down the lane, she turned into an unmarked doorway and climbed a set of gray wooden stairs that might have dated to the days of the maharajas. On the second floor, she turned down a dark hallway and opened an unmarked door.

The office was shabby and unadorned, with a narrow hall that led to two rooms adjacent to each other. Four men were seated in one of the rooms; the other was empty. One was behind a desk, one standing beside him, and two were seated in front of the desk. The man behind the desk was old, nearing seventy now, with closely trimmed white hair and a short, white beard, and standing beside him was much younger man, maybe twenty-five. The men at the desk were foreigners, Germans, perhaps, their suits Western, their hair white-blond. Their backs were to Lucky. Among them all, on the desk, was a balance beam scale, a small, open, paper envelope, and a pile of perhaps a hundred stones sorted into four piles: diamonds, rubies, blue sapphires, and emeralds. The older man looked up at her for a moment then practically leaped from his seat. "Miss Lucky!" he shouted.

"Karsan Kaka," she said. "How are you?"

Before he could answer, a shadow crossed Lucky's heart. At the sound of her name, one of the men at the desk tensed, straightened in his chair, and turned slowly to face her. It was her former partner's crooked accountant, John Steel. "Hello, Lucky," he said without smiling. Lucky had never been able to work out John's role at Lockwood Enterprises and if he was in any way involved in framing Lucky for the heroin smuggling. She had no doubt he knew, but there was no concrete evidence against him.

Karsan Kaka, understanding something was amiss, was already pushing Lucky toward the door. "Miss Singh," he said, "I mean Miss Boyce, I would do anything for you. May I have just a moment to complete this transaction? Please, wait for me in the hall, there is a chair. I will send for tea for you. Please do excuse me. I will be there in ten minutes."

Lucky looked at John, sideways in his chair, facing her. His hands were folded at his chest as if praying and then he stroked his chin absentmindedly with one finger. "Strange to see you, Lucky. I work for myself, now. They buy and sell diamonds in Brazil, too," he said. "Lots of them, actually."

"So you moved to Brazil," Lucky said.

Karsan was clearly agitated. "Please," he said, petitioning her toward the door.

Lucky turned and left. Behind her, John called again, "Nice seeing you."

As she waited, a young boy appeared from down the hall with parathas, a batada vada, and tea. Eventually, Karsan Kaka and the young man appeared. If John left, it had been through another door within the room.

She wondered how Karsan would be able to help but as Shanti said, all good deeds always return in equal measure.

Karsan approached Lucky slowly, head down. "He buys many stones, but I do not think he is connected to Lockwood," he said.

"I hope not. After Lockwood framed me, they might have parted company. Besides, Lockwood is still cooling his heels, thank God! But I hope this guy pays in cash."

"Always in cash." Karsan said and smiled. His limp had become more pronounced, but he no longer wore the rustic, worn-out clothes of the village trader she had first met five years ago. His white dhoti was of fine linen, immaculate, and pressed. His kurta was white, but richly embroidered about the neck in fine silver thread. His vest was of gray cotton and embroidered in a blood-colored brocade.

"My grandson," he said, gesturing to the tall youth beside him. "Ishan."

Ishan was tall and dark, with straight dark hair and eyebrows that cut across his forehead in a long, unbroken line. His face was scarred white in large patches and streaks on his right side, and on the right side of his mouth, he showed four gold teeth. He was dressed in a Western suit but without a tie. He extended a hand to Lucky. His grip was strong and warm. As he withdrew his hand, Lucky saw that the young man had only three fingers.

"Please," Karsan said, "won't you come with me?"

They returned to the little office. A servant brought more tea and they sat at the desk, now clear of the gemstones. "And how are things in New York?" Karsan asked.

"Good," Lucky replied. "And it looks like you are doing well, also."

Karsan nodded — a gesture, almost a bow. "With much thanks to you, Miss Lucky. We can never forget your goodness."

"And how is your family?"

"They are well."

"And little Reema?"

Karsan beamed. "She is in college now, as well, her first year. She studies economics."

Lucky smiled and nodded.

"Ahh, but the time passes like a river in the night, Miss Lucky. One day, you look around and you are old and your children grown. Now, my grandson will study to take over my business, and soon, I will be but a memory."

Lucky sighed. The formalities of India. "You are a healthy man, Karsan. I can't picture you retiring."

"Nor I you, Miss Lucky. Have you gone back into the business?"

"No," Lucky replied. "I've just come to visit for a little while."

"And always good to see you."

"Karsan, I need your help."

Karsan set down his tea and leaned forward. "I am forever in your debt, Miss Lucky. What can I do for you? You have only to ask and I shall do."

"I am here to meet a man. But he is very secretive."

Karsan sat back in his chair and touched his beard. Ishan stirred uneasily beside him. "And who is this man?" Karsan asked.

"His name is Lobsang Telok."

Karsan set down the cup. "And who is he that I should know him?"

"He is a doctor. A Tibetan. If you had met him I'm sure you would remember him. He speaks English well. He was trained in the UK. But he is…different. He may have changed his name and has renounced the world, so to speak."

"So he is a monk?"

"I don't think so. Just a doctor. But he has some different ways."

"But you, Miss Lucky, you are a Parsi. What would you want with a Tibetan doctor? You are not ill, are you?"

"He may be in danger. I don't know. I want to meet him. He does charity work for the poor and is known to cure many illnesses. He may have makeshift clinics somewhere in Dharavi, but I hear he meets only those whom he wishes. I don't know more…it doesn't matter. I'd like to meet him. And I have come alone."

Karsan and Ishan exchanged glances, then quietly spoke between themselves. Karsan slowly raised his right hand to his head and tapped his temple with his index finger. Ishan left the room and Lucky could hear him talk faintly on his cell phone.

"I am just a poor jeweler from the hills," Karsan said. "I say my prayers, I love my family, and I try to live a good, clean, honest life. I have little time for foreigners and their troubles. Tibetans or otherwise."

"But you might know someone who might know him, yes? You have many connections in the Dharavi slums. You had mentioned to me that you and your relatives once lived there, too."

Karsan shook his head. "I did live there many years back. But only for a short time. You have an excellent memory, Miss Lucky. But now, I have only business connections and friends here. My relatives have gone back to the hills, to my native village." Karsan put his cup on the tray and took Lucky's cup as well.

Ishan entered and whispered in his grandfather's ear.

"Okay," Lucky said. "Well, thank you for your time." She stood up to go.

Karsan smiled. "Don't be in such a hurry after such a long time. Wouldn't you like to stay for a little while? Perhaps have a bite of lunch? Surely, you have missed our cooking, or do they have Indian food in America? Besides, if you have just a moment, I would like to make a small present to you. You are dressed so well, but that fake emerald doesn't suit you." He reached into the desk drawers and, after some fumbling, produced a small sheet of folded paper. He held it out to Lucky. Inside was a pendant with an emerald on a fine gold chain.

Lucky unfolded the envelope and studied the stone, held it to the light where it glittered, flawless and deep green.

"I do not have time to wrap it properly, but I could never have you leave my shop in your *present* condition. May I?" He took the chain from Lucky and, standing behind her, removed the fake necklace and fastened the pendant around her neck.

Lucky looked at the paper in her hand.

Then Karsan picked up a box, which had a cell phone and a charger and handed it to Lucky. "I keep these for my foreign clients. They always need this when they come to India. You can use it and return it to me and do not worry, make all the calls you need." The cell number was handwritten and stuck on the back.

"Thank you, Karsan Kaka," Lucky said in gratitude. She accepted the cell phone with both hands but she knew she had to be careful about whom she called as the phones of Colette and Amay could be tapped.

"And thank you for this beautiful necklace. What was it you once said to me—may you have so many grandsons you cannot count them all on your fingers and toes?"

"Ah, yes," he smiled, "but God has even granted me three lovely granddaughters, and for that, I am forever grateful."

Karsan stood up and led Lucky back into the hall.

"Ishan will take you to a friend who can help, but first, please, visit the clothing store downstairs and choose some suitable clothes, A sari won't do, as Ishan will take you by motorbike. Is that all right?"

"But where will he take me?" Lucky asked.

"I cannot say now. But we owe our livelihood to you, so how can we not oblige you, Miss Lucky? Please let us help."

Karsan took her down another flight of stairs through a narrow passage that led to a different alley. Across the lane was a small lady's tailor shop.

In the shop's tiny fitting room, Lucky removed her sari and changed into a salwar kameez and simple shoes that the tailor provided. They were a little tight, but not too bad.

Ishan was waiting outside on a small motorbike. He wore a small blue helmet covered with stickers emblazoned with Sanskrit script. Lucky couldn't read them, but they seemed to be religious.

Karsan waved a silent goodbye to Lucky.

Lucky sat behind Ishan and they buzzed off, jetting through the alley and then turning east and south until they hit the main road.

"Do you know where to go?" Lucky shouted.

Ishan nodded, but did not reply.

"But where are we going?"

"You are looking for a doctor," he replied. "I can take you, but you must know you are being followed. Our chowkidar told us there are two men following you. In this business, we always know when someone is tailing us. This business has many risks. At first, Karsan Kaka thought it was something to do with John. But it was something else, as we were told that the two men were asking downstairs if they had seen a lady in a green sari. Maybe you had better buy a burqa, Miss Lucky."

He stopped at a corner shop, and Lucky bought a black burqa and veil.

CHAPTER 14

Lucky wondered if Coleman's men had traced her, but as long as they left her alone, she wasn't worried about being followed. What did worry her was the ride on the motorbike. She had ridden side-saddle on motorcycles before, as a young girl in high school, but she never had liked it even then. Now, dressed in all the layers, she liked it even less. She worried that the long robes would catch in the spokes. She worried that the wind would tear away her veil. She worried that she would fall off on a turn, although Ishan drove carefully, if quickly, darting in and out of traffic as he snaked north. They were just past the Chor Bazaar and it was mid-afternoon; things were shutting down so people could get out of the heat. They stopped outside a mosque, and Lucky tripped and almost fell while climbing off the motorbike. Ishan frowned, then pointed a finger to a row of women squatting in the sun on the opposite side of the road. "Wait there," he said.

"How would a Tibetan doctor be connected with a mosque?" Lucky wondered but she would just have to see where this would lead.

Lucky sweated profusely, the heat made worse by the heavy black cloth. Her thoughts went back to Coleman and her eyes now darted to and fro. Would Coleman's men find her? And then? Would they join her or deport her for stealing government secrets? Would Ishan think she was part of a conspiracy? Would she then be able to reach

Lobsang? She knew Lobsang would never agree to be part of a deal with governments or politics. Why couldn't Coleman understand this? Was it not obvious that Lobsang would never yield to money or political pressure?

If he would have, it would have happened already, and the magic mushroom would be available in every store. And Lobsang would be a very rich man.

Am I too paranoid, or am I not paranoid enough? Lucky asked herself.

Involuntarily, she raised a hand to her face and patted the veil against it, wiping away the stinging perspiration that kept dripping into her eyes. One of the women looked at her curiously. "It is hot, yes?" she said in Urdu.

Lucky stammered, trying to remember the words, the accent, then replied, "Yes, it is," in Hindi.

"You are not from here." The lady spoke back in Hindi.

Lucky didn't want to be rude, and she didn't want to enter into a long conversation, either — one she was sure would blow her cover. What if they asked her to go inside and pray? She looked down at the street and mumbled incoherently — something that made no sense, even if the woman had heard her. Her mind crept back to being watched. *Why can't Coleman leave me alone? I'm on the job!*

She wondered how he was tracking her. How did the men reach Karsan Kaka's office and search for a woman in a green sari? *Silly,* she chided herself. They would have had her photo, and it would take Coleman only seconds to have a team scouring Mumbai for her. Cover: *blown.*

The woman next to her would not stop talking. "I see. It is your first time, yes? Do not worry. Allah will provide. If the need is great, there is no dishonor in begging. In fact, it is said that we honor those whom Allah has honored with much by giving them the chance to practice Zakah."

Here it comes, Lucky thought. *She's going to ask me about Zakah.*

"You know about Zakah, don't you?" The woman took a little stick and began scratching in the dirt.

A STAR CALLED LUCKY

Lucky shook her head. *What is Ishan doing? Why is he taking so long?*

The woman patted Lucky on the arm. "It is okay," she said. "*Zakah* means purification. Giving up a portion of one's wealth is necessary. Allah gives to some in abundance, but to keep it they must give a portion away in alms. Thus, we beggars also serve Allah's will and purpose. It is an honor to give and to receive with gratitude is to honor the giver. When in need, it is even an honor to beg, for this gives the blessed the opportunity to repay the blessing."

So that's it, Lucky realized. *She thinks I'm a beggar.*

The old woman had drawn a circle in the dirt. Now she drew a triangle inside of it. "All things are connected," she said. "Why are you here?"

"I am here for my son," Lucky said.

"So are we all, my child, here for our families. Your son—he is ill?"

Lucky shook her head and got up and took a few steps. The woman got up behind her.

Suddenly, a three-wheeled delivery van veered toward them in the alley and the old woman flung her hand up and shoved Lucky out of the way. They lay dazed for a minute, sprawled in the dirt together. Then Lucky quickly righted herself and dusted off, adjusting the veil over her face. She looked down at the new platform shoes. Had the old woman seen them?

The old woman was looking at the van careening down the alley. "So reckless," she said.

Lucky nodded.

"My son," the old woman said, "he needs surgery on his heart. He is so small, the poor thing. We kept taking him to the doctors and they gave us this medicine and that medicine, told us to feed him milk, told us to feed him chocolate, told us to feed him only vegetables, told us to feed him only meat. Finally, one doctor told us, 'It is the boy's heart. He has a hole in his heart and the blood cannot flow properly, so he is always small and skinny. Soon he will die. There is a hospital where they can do this thing, but the cost—fifty thousand rupees! Where is a poor family to find that? Why, it is more than my husband makes in…in…in a very long time. I don't know if he will ever make that much money. So, for thirty days I have come here every day and prayed that Allah would make me a miracle. Thirty days I have eaten dust and insults and dodged traffic and let my tears wet this piece of ground. But you know what? I believe in miracles. Do you believe in miracles?"

Lucky looked at the old woman. "I don't believe in miracles," she said, "I *depend* on them." Ahead, she could see Ishan hurrying from the mosque in the company of a group of young students. They were talking excitedly and gesturing wildly with their hands. At length, Ishan kick-started the little motorcycle.

What the hell? Lucky thought. She checked for the cell phone in her inner pocket and pushed it down further so that it was safe. Carefully, she reached around her neck and found the necklace's clasp. She dropped the necklace and the stone into the old woman's hand before climbing onto the back of the motorcycle. *Sometimes,* she thought, *you need all the credit with the gods that you can muster.* Perhaps it would pay for the operation.

"Where now?" she asked Ishan.

"Were going to meet Mohammed."

"Mohammed?"

"Mohammed, the mattress maker. He may know this man you seek."

Six degrees, Lucky thought, as they zipped through traffic. She counted off the names: Karsan, Ishan, Mohammed. *Three down, three to go.*

CHAPTER 15

Mohammed was tall and thin, dressed in a clean white shirt and gray trousers with old, but neatly shined, black oxfords. He was in his early to mid-thirties, with black hair nicely trimmed, and his face was clean-shaven. His sole distinguishing feature was a thick pair of black plastic glasses. He was sitting in his shop, sewing a mattress by hand when Ishan and Lucky arrived. He looked up from his sewing and greeted Ishan like a long-lost friend.

"Please," he said. "Come in, come in. Sit down. Will you have tea?" There were three other men sewing in the shop, two bent over sewing machines, and one, like Mohammed, sewing with a needle and thread. Without waiting for an answer, Mohammed clapped his hands and the man put down his needle and went out of the shop, returning a few minutes later with a small black tray and porcelain cups of steaming chai.

Lucky looked around. She knew the neighborhood well — had passed it a thousand times. It was close to the Grant Road station and headed up toward Malabar Hill where her in-laws, Arun and Geeta had lived, and further west to Warden Road, where she and Viki had shared their marital home, back — *could it be*—five years ago? She might even have bought mattresses from Mohammed. Or, more precisely, when she sent her staff to buy mattresses, they might have bought them from him. She touched one. It was made of

169

blue-and-white striped coarse cotton. She made a sour face. *Not the same*, she thought.

"Our mattresses," Mohammed said noticing her expression, "come in a variety of thicknesses and qualities, but we use only the best materials." He looked and spoke to Ishan only. He would not, of course, say anything to Lucky: he would be expected to assume she was Ishan's wife's sister or some relative. He would never speak to her directly, nor would he expect her to speak to anyone — including Ishan — in his presence. "We can make them in any thickness. We have foam rubber and cotton padding. Our best mattress," he said, lightly stroking the cloth with his finger, "is a composite of two different kinds of foam with a layer of fine raw cotton stuffing both above and below the foam. It will never settle or form lumps."

"We are not here for a mattress," Ishan said. "I am looking for a doctor. I was led to understand he does charity work. Sayeed suggested that you might be able to help me. His name is, or used to be, Lobsang Telok."

Lucky took a cup of tea before realizing that she had no way to drink it through the veil. While the men chatted, she quickly set the cup back down on the tray and stepped outside to wait and watch. Looking up and down the street, she wondered if she had, in fact, eluded surveillance. If Coleman was watching Karsan Kaka, he would know by now where she was and why she was here. How much about Karsan and his habits would Coleman know? How fast could the computers make connections? She fingered her American cell phone, which had worldwide roaming, and then realized that it might be possible for them to track her via the cell phone towers, even in India. Would they? She doubted it, but what if they were eavesdropping? Electronic snooping? They might have detected her phone and the number. She switched it off.

Mohammed's shop was little more than a plywood shed in the middle of a u-shaped cluster of plywood sheds. There were men like Mohammed in each of them, all relatively well dressed, and more men, in workers' garb, bent over sewing machines, or stuffing

170

mattresses with cotton pulled from oversized burlap bales, or drinking tea, or lying down in the shade taking an afternoon nap. Traffic was building outside. Groups of schoolchildren in fives and tens walked by, swinging backpacks and bookbags and laughing. Every now and then, a child walked by alone. They all looked happy.

Ishan came outside and touched Lucky's arm. He leaned over and whispered in her ear, "He will take us himself. He thinks your man is still in Dharavi. However, the doctor only meets those who come through a proper connection."

"You're a miracle worker," Lucky said. "How did you get him to do it?" She half expected a story of a bribe—an envelope of gemstones or a bit of gold passed surreptitiously between them.

"I told him you were an American, that you were alone, and that you needed his help." Ishan replied.

Lucky almost swallowed the veil. "You WHAT?"

"He said he had heard the doctor has been expecting visitors."

What is that supposed to mean? Lucky wondered.

They crawled along in rush-hour traffic, riding in Mohammed's little black Maruti Zen. Mohammed drove, Ishan rode beside him, and Lucky sat in the back seat. The AC was broken, and even with the windows down, it was hot. The fumes from all the traffic only made things worse. *Some people*, Lucky thought, *do this day in and day out.*

They were approaching the Mithi River when they turned off and drove east into still more traffic — a narrow road that bordered Dharavi, Mumbai's most notorious slum. *If my mother could see me now*, Lucky thought. *In one day, from a Benz to a Maruti, from Malabar Hill to Dharavi.* She knew instinctively that this was where they were headed, that this was where Lobsang would be. Why not? What better place to hide? And where else would a doctor who served those in need be most needed? Hadn't she suggested as much to Coleman? If you wanted to renounce the world but still work where you were needed, there probably wasn't a more needful place. She had read all about Dharavi, that it housed 800 people per acre. Was that possible? She looked out over the rows of two-story mud and brick huts. Most were topped with sheets of tin. Some were made entirely of tin. *God, they must get hot in May*, she thought.

There was a road in, but it was impossible to drive. Mohammed parked and they walked into the human jungle. To her surprise, Lucky realized that most of the people here were Hindus. For some reason, she had thought of Dharavi as a Muslim slum but it was clearly not. But in a few hundred meters the nature of the stores and homes changed, and she knew that she had passed into another district. Here were leather workers—no Hindus among *them*. The ditches lining the road ran with a greasy, foamy chemical residue from the tanning process. The stench was all but unbearable. Lucky pressed the veil tightly to her face but it did not help. Beyond the tanneries they turned down an even narrower lane that zigged and zagged between huts so poorly constructed that Lucky was afraid they might collapse right on top of them. But even here children played. "There is laughter here," she thought, "despite the poverty." A soccer ball bounced toward them and, impulsively, Lucky kicked it back to the boys who chased it. Ishan and Mohammed stared at her. "Oops," she said.

And here, too, were women hurrying home from work with plastic bags of vegetables and rice and potatoes, and men with briefcases and toolboxes. These were not the homeless poor. They were working men and women, the wheels that made the industry of Mumbai turn, but to whom a better home was just a pipe dream. *What did they do?* Lucky wondered. She knew Dharavi was, in a way, a garbage recycling marvel. Segregating waste by human hands and then recycling and finishing it with very basic equipment. *How much did they earn? And what price did they pay for living here?* Not in rent but in the toll on the quality of life and the lack of sanitation, the almost inconceivable crowding. Wasn't Dharavi once a fishing village? Wasn't it once home to boats and nets drying in the sun? She had to hurry to keep up. Mohammed was walking faster now, practically speed walking.

They turned down yet another lane — a space between two chawls (slums) and barely wide enough for one person to pass, turned sideways. Ahead, Lucky saw lines of prayer flags strung across the narrow corridor. There was no breeze. The colorful flags hung limp, as if they had given up all hope. Mohammed pushed ahead, Ishan behind, Lucky stumbled along after them. She was so hot and dehydrated that she felt faint. She wanted to call out after them to stop, but she dared not. They stopped in front of a lone metal door cut into a wall on the back of a long brick chawl. Mohammed rapped on the door, and it opened an inch. There was a single shining eyeball set in a dark face, a dark room behind. There was an exchange of muffled voices, and then the door opened and they went inside.

The room was windowless, lit by a single bulb that dangled from a set of threadbare wires fixed to the ceiling with tape and clothespins. The floor was dirt, although it was covered with an old Kashmiri wool carpet. They left their shoes by the door. It was dim and cooler inside than outside, but it certainly didn't look like any clinic Lucky had ever seen. In the middle of the room was a single low table and on the table was a hookah, and in one corner was a clay pot with a cheap, plastic fern inside.

Two men faced them from the floor. They did not stand. They were young and broad-shouldered, with dark eyes and broad, square faces, wearing dark blue Indian-style shirts with embroidery around the neck that flowed down and under their arms, where the shirts fastened with brass buttons. One of them was on a cell phone and continued speaking as he gestured irritably for Mohammed and Ishan to sit. Lucky didn't want to risk sitting in her flowing robe and wasn't sure what the proper procedure for a woman here was, so she stood by the door behind them. A moment later, it opened and two more men came in. They wore Western slacks and white shirts. Then another man appeared from a door behind the two seated men. He brought water and tea. He served Mohammed and Ishan, then Lucky.

The two newcomers spoke between themselves in a language that was neither Hindi nor Urdu. Tibetan, perhaps? Lucky could not tell the language, but the men's features seemed Tibetan — flattened noses or slit eyes. One of them struck a match and torched a stick of incense, filling the room with the sweet scent of jasmine. The other, when he had finished talking on the phone, said to Lucky in perfect English, "My name is Sonam. I understand you want to meet the doctor," He eyed Lucky suspiciously.

"That's right."

"But you look neither poor nor sick."

Lucky hesitated. "I believe he may be in danger. I know why. I need to talk to him. I want to ask him to help us with his magical powers. That," she said, "and I want to help him."

"You can take off the veil."

Lucky hesitated; she did not quite like the tone of Sonam's voice. He appeared to be gruff.

Sonam waited while she had no option but to remove the veil.

"Don't worry. But we are still curious as to why you would seek out Lobsang. He has been in danger since the day he was born."

"In a way, I am in danger, too, but I would still like to talk with him. Maybe even write about his cure —"

"Yes, yes, a book. East meets West. Everybody is writing a book. We hear that three times a week Miss Boyce, we want to know the real reason why you have come."

Four little words came to Lucky's mind: *You are so busted.*

"Like I said," but she was interrupted by the ring tone of Sonam's phone, which he immediately answered, again in the strange language. He gestured for Lucky to sit and she did. A minute later, two other men appeared. They wore loose cotton pants and black, raw silk shirts with black embroidery around the collar. One of them said something quickly and Sonam nodded.

Sonam pointed at the man and said, "Gautam. Remover of darkness. That's what his name means. He will take us, but you alone. Your friends cannot come. Only you."

A STAR CALLED LUCKY

Lucky looked at Mohammed and Ishan. Mohammed nodded, but Ishan shook his head.

Go or not to go? She took a deep breath and said, "Okay." She wondered about the group of men now gathered in the room. Were they all connected with Lobsang?

They drove in a battered old black Skoda, with Sonam at the wheel, Lucky in the middle, and Gautam on Lucky's left side. The back was filled with cartons. It was cramped and crowded, but at least the air conditioning worked, although for some reason, it fogged the windshield.

I hope Tibetans are still nonviolent, Lucky thought. *Well, maybe times have changed. I hope not, even if desperate times call for desperate measures.* She wondered what Shanti would say about her predicament. "Well, of course you blew it. What did you expect, out doing Jane Bond, trying to rescue people again? You always overestimate your abilities, grasping for things beyond your reach." *But what the hell was I supposed to do?* Lucky said in an imaginary reply. *Call the police and let them deal with it?* Lucky thought about all the charges she might potentially face: theft of government secrets, interstate transportation of a minor for immigration violations. The US government took a dim view of immigration violators, and Lucky wondered if they would investigate further and find out more about Maria's family. Lucky was never sure if they were aliens.

The problem is, she imagined Shanti saying, *that you never stop to look at the big picture. You see a little bit of it and you think you've got the whole elephant! You know what the Chinese say about dragons?*

They had had this conversation many years ago. At the time, Lucky had answered, "No, I don't."

Shanti had explained, "Dragons aren't invisible—but you have to infer them. They are bigger than anything. Their heads and backs are the mountains, their hair is trees, their breath is the clouds. You have to see the whole picture to know the dragon."

175

Now Lucky thought, *It's kind of like yoga. There are all these muscles and bones working together. It's the big picture, not just a pose or a single muscle or bone.*

The car lurched to a sudden stop. *Well,* Lucky thought, *whatever my future is, I guess I'll find out now.* She looked at the men, studying their faces, trying to understand what they were saying, and then a curious scene flashed across her mind: the day she was almost murdered in prison. Mike Lockwood had paid these two creeps to kill her. Romero was one. What was the other's name? Lucky couldn't remember. She remembered the cinching pain of the belt around her throat. But what kept flashing through her mind that day was not that she was going to die, but rather, that everything was going to be okay. And it was. And it had changed her life, too. She had grown up that day. She'd stopped worrying about money or appearances or any of the other silly, vain things that had troubled her from her teens to her early twenties. She no longer had any place for hate in her heart. In the days following her divorce, Shanti had shown her that hate could never win; it destroyed only the bearer. "Only when you have love even for your enemies can you win. Your thoughts are more potent and then your actions are more prevailing," Shanti had advised. Even now, she didn't hate Coleman—if anything, he was a prisoner of his own ambition.

Reformation. Wasn't that her calling card with the prisoners? She knew she had done many things right. She knew. And she was not guessing—she *knew.* And she had done many things right since then, too, although maybe this charade wasn't one of them. She had been lying against the wall, the cafeteria erupting in flames, and this creep Romero with a knife was going to kill her. But he hadn't. Maybe killing wasn't as easy as they made it look in the movies. She hadn't paid a whole lot of attention at the time — she was pretty out of it, to tell the truth. But there had been a short fight, and then Steve was there, and he took the belt from around her neck and held her close. And then he kissed her hand. And there had been guards, and medics, and an ambulance, and that, as they say, was that.

176

Then the driver restarted the car, took a U-turn, and parked to the side.

And then the questioning began.

How did Lucky hear about Lobsang? Whom did she work for? What was her business?

Lucky tried to answer in a cool voice. But the questioning slowly grew unpleasant.

Suddenly Gautam raised his voice and said menacingly, "Look, we know a lot about you, and we know you are not telling the truth." He leaned forward, his face inches from her's and continued, "We may live in Dharavi, but we are not fools and we don't tolerate fools."

She knew she had to get out somehow. She saw a coffee shop a few yards in front and said she needed to go to use the restroom, but they didn't fall for that. So she raised her voice, hoping against hope that she would attract attention — and sure enough, two men passing by peeped into the car. When Gautam stepped out to talk to them, Lucky shouted in Hindi "Help!" Then, throwing caution to the wind, she opened the door, pushing Gautam to to the floor as she jumped out. Gautam's raised voice followed her as she rushed into the waiting taxi behind and slammed the door shut.

"Worli naka" she instructed the driver and then offered him double the fare if he sped. He looked at her closely in the mirror while he drove away. Her heart raced the whole way, and she couldn't stop herself from turning around every few minutes to make sure no one was following.

Once out of the taxi at Worli, Lucky went up the stairs to a restaurant on the first floor. She ordered curry and rice for takeout, trying unsuccessfully to keep her eyes from darting to the door. When the food arrived, she went to the bathroom and stuffed her burqa into the bag underneath the food.

She took another cab, this time to the Gateway of India, then walked back to the Taj Hotel. Crisscrossing the corridors of the hotel, she entered her room. Once safely behind the bolted door, she drew the curtains and sat on the chair near the window in darkness.

Her peace was interrupted a few minutes later by a call from Karsan Kaka, calling on the cell phone he had given her.

"Lucky, are you all right?"

"Yes, I'm fine."

"I am so sorry! We did not know Sonam or Gautam, you must believe this, but we trusted Mohammed. We were just trying to help, but these people were no good. They must have wanted to extract money from you. Mohammed now tells us they do work for money, but he did not expect that they would behave like this. They are his friends. Now they say they want Rs. 100,000 to find Lobsang."

Lucky listened, knowing Karsan Kaka was speaking from his heart and was genuinely worried. She also knew that she had been compromised and now, she couldn't give too much away.

"A bribe? No way," she almost said aloud. But she paused before saying,

"Karsan Kaka, I am fine. I will contact you again when I need to. Please forget about this. If anyone asks, say you do not know where I am."

"Yes, yes, I understand, Lucky, and no harm will come to you, not from Mohammed's people. It was a misunderstanding. They only wanted money to find the doctor for you. They will not harm you. Of that, I am sure. I will pray for you."

Lucky thanked him and ended the call.

"Now what?" she thought as she sat back in the darkness.

Rs. 100,000—well in dollar terms, it was around $1,600 but how would she arrange this? "No way," she chided herself again and then she remembered the other lead.

Dr Eruch Vakil. That would be too dangerous. Coleman's team could be watching him. But wasn't she in the thick of it already?

Then it struck her. She knew that there was a good chance he would be playing cards at 6 pm at The Willingdon Club near the race course. Surely, he wouldn't be followed there? And not within the club. She would have to take her chances; she knew the club well.

Lucky entered the Willingdon Club from the main entrance and turned right to the card rooms.

She summoned a waiter and asked him to call Dr. Vakil. "Tell him it is Hutoxi," she said, knowing that Dr Vakil would instantly remember her mother Hutoxi. And then she placed a Rs. 100 rupee note in the waiter's hands when she detected his reluctance.

It seemed like a long few moments before Dr. Eruch Vakil appeared. From his welcoming expression, she knew instantly that he had not linked her e-mails to the robbery in his house.

"Lucky, how nice to see you."

"I need your help. Please, can we talk? It won't take long."

"Take all the time you need! I am so happy to see you, my dear. After so long. Next time, though, you can use your own name."

Lucky explained her plight as best as she could without making it sound too bizarre. Dr. Vakil listened in silence. After a few moments of contemplation, he said, "Leave it to me. I will contact my friend and let you know if he can help."

"But Doctor, I need this to be done immediately, you can understand."

Without glancing at her, he pulled out his cell phone. Lucky stopped him.

"No, Doctor—use the landline in the corner."

He obliged, although he looked at her strangely. Lucky stood beside him and listened to every word — and couldn't believe what she was hearing: that he would contact Lobsang and get back to her as soon as possible. She asked to be contacted at the Taj Hotel, room number 363, and as she thanked him, he asked her to come over to his house for dinner.

"I will as soon as I finish this business. Give my love to Mehroo and the kids." She hesitated. "Is there any untraceable way that I can use to contact you?"

The doctor thought for a moment. "Maybe my emergency number? I don't use it for anything beside hospital emergencies, so it's unlikely that anyone would be tracking it." Lucky wrote the number down and thanked him again.

She had barely returned to her hotel room when there was a loud knock on her door—and she was sure she heard a voice she seemed to have heard before, but couldn't place. "Who could it be?"

She opened the door and framed against the white wall behind was the monk from the PETA protests in New York, Usko Tahti. "What are you doing here?" she managed to stutter, quite aghast.

CHAPTER 16

Usko silenced her with a finger on his lips. "You need to check out right now. Pack up, pay your bill, and meet me outside around the corner at the Starbucks." He then left as fast as he had appeared.

Lucky rushed to get her bags together and stop at the hotel front desk before running into Usko at the entrance of Starbucks. He gestured to follow him to a car parked across the street and as they drove off, Lucky started her barrage, "How did you... how did you..."

"Find you?" Usko got up, stuck his head out of the window, and looked left and right. Satisfied, he shut his eyes, looking suddenly exhausted. Then he became alert and smiled. "I've been on you from the day after you arrived, but there was no way to scoop you up, so we followed you all over town. We almost had you there, but you slipped out each time and we lost you for a while. You really blew it, you know. You should stick to teaching. They could have harmed you."

Lucky nodded. "Which 'they?' Coleman? Sonam? Gautam? Who?"

"I don't know. Who knows? Many have been looking for Lobsang for years, too. Does it matter? What I want to know is, why are you looking for him?"

"Does it matter?"

Usko frowned. "It does to me."

"At first, I wanted him because I believed Coleman and agreed to work for him. Now, I think Coleman will stop at nothing to get his mushroom. Even kill Lobsang. That wasn't part of the original bargain. Find a cure for disease? Sure. Kill a man to get it? No, thank you."

Usko smiled. "I hear Lobsang is very careful about whom he meets. Who knows? Maybe if he knew why you were here and what you risked for him, he might meet with you. But I doubt if he'd part with any samples."

Lucky shut her eyes. "All I ever wanted to do is to convince Lobsang to use his mushroom for the good of humanity and then get this mess behind me. That's all I want."

"I know, Lucky. And that's why I am here, as well. To help the good."

"I guess so, but stick to… well, whatever it was you said you did before you went to work for Coleman."

"I was a yoga teacher."

"That sounds good. So, how did you find me?"

"You know a kid named Collette?"

Lucky looked up.

"I'll take that as a yes. Where is the amber necklace she gave you?"

"Why?"

"It is near you somewhere, isn't it?"

"Yes, in my bag." Lucky pulled it out.

"A transmitter," he said smiling. He dug in his pocket and produced a small, black plastic device that looked like a cell phone or a remote control. He showed the screen to Lucky. It featured an electronic face that pointed toward the transmitter, with a readout below showing the distance in meters. He shrugged. "You can order this online from any spy store."

"Collette?"

"She's a real pain, isn't she?"

"She *called* you?"

"She wouldn't *stop* calling me. I had to cancel my speech at the Lions Club to come to Mumbai to save you."

"So she's okay?"

"Of course she's okay. Why wouldn't she be? She's pretty sure she'll be grounded for a long time."

"But she's safe?"

"Last I heard," Usko said. He looked at his watch. "An hour or so ago."

"And my son—Sean—is Sean okay? And Amay? And Maria?"

"They're okay. So far as I know, the only one in trouble right now is you."

Lucky looked away, tears brimming in her eyes. "So what happened? Tell me from the beginning."

"The beginning?" Usko repeated.

They were at Marine Drive now. Usko stopped the car and told the driver to take Lucky's luggage to a house. Then he strode away along the oceanfront, as Lucky followed.

"Yes, the beginning. How did you get here?" Lucky questioned.

"Collette and some of her punky friends called me. I guess they were snooping around in your computer and found this thing—Bloodhound. Somehow, they were worried about you, but then they found me, and they knew we had met from the e-mail you sent thanking John Black for the bail. They said now you needed a little help, so here I am returning the favor. And now I know how you found me. You had used this program to spy on me."

"I wasn't spying," Lucky said. "I was curious."

"Hmmm."

"It doesn't matter—I helped you. I bailed you out of jail, remember?"

"Out of the frying pan and into the fire, if you ask me. If this is what 'help' looks like, next time call NYPD."

"They wouldn't have helped me. Not here, anyway."

"Maybe not," Usko said. "Anyway. Collette got my number and started calling me, and she wouldn't quit until I agreed to help you. To tell you the truth, I didn't think a whole lot about you, but there was something sweet about you. Your story—I thought you were working for Coleman, but when Collette told me about him, his program, and what he could do to you—I knew this was my chance to nail him."

"But how did she know what was happening to me? I mean, here in Mumbai?"

"Don't you get it? Coleman used this program to create a mirror site to follow your every move. But that site is tied right back to Coleman. Collette and her Bulgarian friend—all they had to do was follow the program right back into Coleman's computer and create a mirror site of their own. Coleman doesn't know yet that we have the program. We're listening to every phone call, reading every e-mail, even watching video feed in real time."

"But Coleman is the head of the Global Wellness Council! He's a part of the *government*. You can't hack his site!"

"Two things, Lucky," Usko said. "Government sites get hacked every day. And this is not a government site. It's not even on government servers. It's not without firewalls, but it's not perfect, either."

Lucky stared at Usko hard. "If it's not a government site, then what it is it?"

Usko shrugged. "Coleman's a rogue. He's not in this for the government. Coleman works only for Coleman. He's got his own thing going on. He's just using his high position the same way he is using you. He set you up with the help of his few cronies. I've been trying to get to this guy for a year now — and then you come along. Look, I knew he was crooked, but I had no idea how crooked 'crooked' could be."

"And you figured this out?"

"Well, I had help. Collette and her friends."

"Great," Lucky said. "My future depends on a sixteen-year-old antisocial dropout."

Usko shrugged again and held up his hands in a gesture of helplessness. "Hey, you've got me."

Lucky looked at Usko.

"I mean, we're all on your team, you know. We managed to reach you in Mumbai."

Lucky laughed. "I suppose she couldn't do any worse than I've done."

"Lucky," Usko's face was tense and earnest. He leaned close to her, his voice lowering almost to a whisper. "We have enough on Coleman to nail him *forever*. Bank accounts, a black-ops testing lab in Latvia, e-mails, test results...it's a freakin' gold mine. And Collette keeps sending it on. I got a guy in San Francisco organizing it all, and he's sending encrypted copies to friends in Germany, Ireland, Sweden, Spain, and Indonesia. They can't shut us down or wipe us out if we come out with this. And when we do, Coleman is history."

"But how will you get it out? And even if you have the proof, I mean, who will believe it?"

"TV, blogs, you name it. Some people even still read newspapers. PETA activists are everywhere. We have thousands in the US alone. You've seen the demonstrations. We have some power. People power. But the real power is in politics. What Woodward and Bernstein wouldn't want to break this story? It'll be the biggest American political scandal since Nixon bit the dust."

"No, Usko, there's no time to run around playing politics," Lucky said. "My problem—our problem—is here and now. If Coleman finds Lobsang, there's no telling what he'll do. And if Coleman is as crooked as you say—well, even if he gets the mushroom..." she shrugged her shoulders, "who knows? Maybe he'll use it for good, and maybe he won't. I have some leads to Lobsang..."

"Not now. Let's hear it all when we reach the apartment. It's a long walk, but then we can have dinner and discuss how to proceed."

They headed south along Chowpatty Beach until they found a place where they could sit for a while and then they walked toward Worli. "You were in the army?" Lucky asked.

"Twelve years."

"Why? Why the army?"

"I wanted to make a career of it, ever since I was a boy. I guess it sounded like a shortcut to adventure. We have our heroes, too, even in Finland. And our enemies."

"I read about you."

"And what did you read?"

"You were a hero."

Usko shrugged. "What's a hero?"

"You served in Bosnia."

"Lots of people served in Bosnia."

"But you left under some kind of cloud."

"Let's just say I got out."

They were passing the building where she and Viki had lived all those years ago. She thought of how many fears had she faced since she was that young, foolish girl in love with a handsome playboy. It had started drizzling, Lucky started sneezing. She coughed. Her sinuses felt scratchy. She looked at Usko. "Why did you come to help me?"

Usko looked up to the sky. The drizzle lightened and stopped "I am obligated to help people," he said. "It's my penance. Besides, I misjudged you. Funny how you can see somebody once and then……" his voice trailed off.

"And then…what?" Lucky asked.

Usko looked out over the ocean. "Sometimes you just can't forget the look in their eyes." He looked back at Lucky, looking at him. "Anyway, when Collette called, I didn't believe her at first. It sounded like such a far-fetched story. But then, I know what governments are capable of. I've heard worse. I've seen worse." He looked at Lucky. "You read my story. You know where I was."

Lucky stopped and looked at him.

"The ethnic cleansing in the Balkans was planned fifteen years in advance. Can you imagine that?" He turned and walked on.

Lucky hurried after him, taking Usko's arm and stopping him on the sidewalk. "What happened? What happened to make you change, Usko Tahti? Why did the soldier lay down his gun?"

Usko looked Lucky in the eye, held her gaze and then looked away. "You've heard of Srebrenica?"

"I have."

"And what have you heard?"

A STAR CALLED LUCKY

"There was a massacre."

"Massacre is too nice a word."

They had reached the Haji Ali Mosque.

He continued. "I was at Srebrenica in June and July of '95. It was near the end of the war. I was with the UN. The Dutch were in charge. Colonel Karremans. He wasn't a bad man, but he didn't have much to work with, and he wasn't sure what to do with what he had. We were outgunned and unsupported. We knew what was going on. But Karremans had no tanks, no artillery, only about six hundred men with sidearms and not much ammunition. And there hadn't been food delivered since May. The Bosnian Army, under the terms of the deal that made Srebrenica a 'safe haven,' had surrendered their weapons. The Dutch held them under lock and key.

"The Serbs made no secret that they wanted all the Muslims out. They encircled the town. When they captured the first Dutch outpost, they took thirty hostages. The Dutch never fired a shot. Karremans called for air support but when the allies finally sent bombers, the Serbs threatened to kill the Dutch hostages, so he called them off. There were 30,000 people in Srebrenica, mostly women and children and old men. The Bosnians didn't want to let go of their homes. So Karremans cut a deal. The women and children were bussed out to Tuzla, but the men stayed behind. It was all very confusing. The men were trying to get their arms but Karremans wouldn't allow it. We all knew what was going to happen. It had been going on for years in the little villages surrounding Srebrenica."

They stopped to enjoy a view of the beach, the sea link and the lights of Bandra and beyond. There were hordes of people out, taking advantage of the cooler air.

Usko hung his head. "Do you know what bullets sound like when they shatter skulls?" he asked.

Lucky shook her head.

"It is enough to make you wish you were deaf." He turned to Lucky. "I shot two Dutch soldiers. I killed them to get the keys to the armory. They call it mutiny, and they hang people for that. I was passing out weapons to the Bosnians so they could defend themselves, but it was no use. There was me and a few Bosnians against 600 Dutch and 2,000 Serbs. The Dutch took me down, killed two of my men. It's one of those dirty little secrets of war — like all the men who rat on their officers. I was held for a while in a military prison in Amsterdam, then deported to Helsinki. I expected to be tried, but things were hushed up. Nobody wanted any more bad publicity about the debacle. *Especially* the Dutch. I was told that if I kept my mouth shut, the charges would go away. In the end, it all came to nothing — except for the 9,000 Bosnians buried in mass graves. That's how government works, Lucky. Backroom deals. So when Collette told me this crazy story about some guy in the GWC—"

"GWC is the US Global Wellness Council. They have *real* powers!"

"Whatever. When Collette told me the story, something about it rang true. I never liked this guy Coleman. So I decided to check it out. I guess I'll flunk out at Columbia this semester, but maybe I'll get something out of the deal. A paper." He turned to watch the children playing on the beach. "It looks like back home," he said, "only it's colder over there."

Lucky touched Usko's back, let her hand remain while she looked earnestly into his face. "I'd have done the same thing," she said.

"Would you?"

"I would. I couldn't stand there and let innocent people be killed."

"That doesn't make what I did right."

"You tried to save them."

"But I did not do the right thing."

"You chose the lesser of two evils."

"There is no lesser between two evils. Only evil."

Lucky shook her head. "How can one know what's right? It's the oldest question in the world."

"And the easiest to answer. What's right never changes. People can rationalize to the end of time, but the truth stands: Life is the most sacred gift and we are here to respect it, to promote it. What other people do, what they believe, is no justification for my doing what I know to be wrong. Gandhi said, 'An eye for an eye leaves the whole world blind.' He said, 'Victory attained by violence is tantamount to a defeat, for it is momentary.'"

"He also said, 'It is better to be violent, if there is violence in our hearts, than to put on the cloak of nonviolence to cover impotence.'"

Usko looked at Lucky. "What he meant was that a false dedication to nonviolence as a mask to cowardice was no better than violence. Nonviolence does not mean impotence—the inability to act, or the fear of acting. Quite the opposite. A commitment to nonviolence takes the highest level of courage. Peace is not for the faint of heart. Even Sun Tzu said that 'supreme' excellence consists of breaking the enemy's resistance without fighting."

"You've read Sun Tzu?"

"But of course. I was an officer, remember?"

"So what else could you have done?"

"I should have stood my ground and died there with all the men and boys shot down in the pits they dug. I should have dug with them. I should have died with them. It might have made a difference if a Finn went missing. If people didn't care about Bosnians — about Muslims — being massacred, maybe they would have cared if I had died with them. But I didn't have the courage."

Lucky shrugged. "What good would another needless death have done?"

"Who can judge what's needless? Maybe the death of a Finnish soldier would have made a difference."

"And maybe not…"

"But I have to live with it. And what's worse, it wasn't because I didn't know what was right. I knew — but I was afraid."

"But today —"

"But today *what*?"

"You weren't afraid."

"Of course I was afraid! What are you — crazy? Courage does not mean the absence of fear. It means the willingness to do what is necessary in spite of one's fear. Only fools disregard fear."

"But you did it. You faced your fear."

"I did what I had to do. I guess you could say I've mastered my fear. But it doesn't mean I don't feel it."

Lucky looked at Usko.

"Wait a minute," she said.

"What?"

"You said you renounced violence — you left the army."

"I did."

"But would you disarm a man to save me."

"Perhaps…..A little."

"How do you disarm someone *a little*?"

Now it was Usko's turn to laugh. "It would depend on the situation…..Are you testing me?" his voice trailed off. "Okay, so I'm not perfect. I'll work on it."

They walked on. "Tell me," Lucky said, "why did you give it up — the army, violence, all that. What made you become a monk?"

"I was in Afghanistan in '03. We were moving on Kabul. Our camp came under sniper fire. I led a team up into the hills. We found the snipers. Oh, the Afghans are brave, and skillful in some ways, but in tactics, not so well-trained. They were easy to find. I had one in my sights. It was my job to kill him, and it was a job I did well. It was morning. We'd gone out at night and slipped through their lines just to get behind them. The sun was to the sniper's back; he was a perfect silhouette. Just black. No features. That's what they teach you — don't think of the man. Think of the silhouette. It's easier to kill that way. But there was a hawk in the sky above me, and he cried out, and the sniper turned and I saw that he was a boy of ten or twelve, and he was no different from the boys whom I had seen laying on their backs in ditches in Srebrenica with their heads blown apart. I had him in my sights. I couldn't pull the trigger. At that moment, I knew two things: I could never kill again, and I was going to have to make up for all the killing that I did.

"I knew it when I was a boy, too, when I made my first killing, a deer. The scream of that deer never left my ears, but somehow, I never heeded the warning. I still joined the army. In a way it was my destiny. You know the rest, don't you?"

Lucky shook her head.

"I went to The Hague and blew the lid off the massacre. Not just the Muslims — everybody knew about them. I'm talking about the Dutch. I went into court and I confessed everything."

Lucky gasped.

Usko looked her in the eye. "They didn't court-martial me for deserting in Afghanistan. They court-martialed me for *murdering* those two Dutch soldiers. The only reason I am free is that my lawyer claimed I was mentally ill. He argued — over my objection — that I suffer from post-traumatic stress disorder. All I can say was that if God wanted me in prison, I would be in prison. Since I'm free, there must be some purpose for my life."

"But everybody knows about Srebrenica now. How can they prosecute you?"

"How can they not prosecute the *Serbs* responsible? Deals were made. Reputations are at stake. There are people in power now who had a stake in things then. And they don't want to be held responsible for their actions. They prosecuted me to make sure that anybody who knows anything keeps their mouth shut. The official story has to stand. What they did to me is called *retaliation*."

Usko showed Lucky the building where they were headed. As they crossed the road they held hands. The clouds had rolled in again and the wind had picked up, but for just a moment, the full moon broke through a tear in the sky and flooded the whole beach with white light. They stopped and faced each other, and Lucky wondered exactly when her hand had found Usko's. Just as quickly, it was dark again and to the west, they saw a curtain of rain sweep over the lights of the mosque.

They ran for the apartment, but were too late. The rain drenched them, and by the time they reached the apartment, they were soaked.

Lucky was shivering even though it was still warm outside. Her teeth chattered.

And then after a long silence she hesitatingly glanced sideways at Usko and said, "I don't know how to put this but Coleman's guy sprayed me with a red liquid back in New York. Do you think I could be infected? I mean, he did threaten me, saying I would need the mushroom."

Lucky thought that for an instant Usko looked startled, but his voice was firm as he said, "That seems highly unlikely, Lucky, I mean it's not easy to infect people, and besides, if you were infected, flu symptoms would have shown up by now, enough time has elapsed."

"About now," Lucky said thinking back, it's been haunting me ever since that day. And now I'm shivering to death."

"I think you are just cold and exhausted, let's see if you don't feel better when you've changed out of your wet clothes and had a warm drink."

"Okay, I suppose so," Lucky replied, trying to brush the thought away from her mind. At last, they climbed up the entrance to the small building, which had 'North View' written over the rusted wrought iron gate. Lucky smiled. The gate and building were south facing! *Perception!*

It was an old structure, at least four floors high, with no elevator. They climbed the stairs to the first floor and entered an apartment. The door wasn't locked when they came in, but Usko latched it behind them. Inside the apartment was a large living room, with three shut doors and an open-plan kitchen, along with sofas and a dining table for six. The gray stone floor contrasted with the bare white walls. The table and chairs were of rugged design, in dark teak wood.

Usko showed Lucky her bedroom where her luggage was placed on a stool. Lucky entered the room, which had a single bed and a side table. There was an old, heavy desk and a chair in one corner near the bathroom. She went to the bathroom, locked the door, and slipped out of her wet clothes. She rubbed herself vigorously in the shower, trying to scuff some warmth into her skin, but it was no use—she was still cold. So she changed, draped the sheet over her shoulders for some extra warmth, and lay on the bed, not knowing what else to do. She finally got up when she heard voices outside her door. But by the time she went into the large living room, no one was there, so she sank into the sofa.

A man walked past and went straight to the stove without saying a word, and Lucky looked on as he boiled water in a stainless steel pan.

"Who are you? Where is Usko?" Lucky asked. He didn't answer.

He then offered Lucky a small, heavy, brown, ceramic mug of almost clear tea. She hadn't seen him put any herbs into the water, but there was a light, delicate fragrance to the drink. She drank it greedily, letting it warm her. Cinnamon? Cardamom? Ginger? It seemed to have subtle hints of all of them, but there was something else, too.

Lucky felt a strange calm descend upon her. She wanted to soak in the silence, but she chided herself, *Wake up and think ahead.* When she drew a blank, she remembered Shanti's words, "learn to accept the present." The man was puttering around in the kitchen, oblivious to her presence. Sipping tea, she walked across the hall onto the open balcony. The rain had subsided, and the sky was a dull continual stretch of blue-gray. She could just make out the Haji Ali Mosque perched on its rock, the famous causeway almost submerged at high tide, breakers crashing against it. Nearer, she could see the waves of the rising tide closer and closer, occasionally showering the sidewalk with salt spray. Far out in the bay; the tankers and freighters lining the horizon vanished into the gray gloom.

After a short time, two monks entered and introduced themselves as Yeshe and Kamala. Kamala looked like a meek middle-aged gentleman, but he was texting on his cell, which Lucky thought might mean he was really in command. He spoke to Yeshe — Lucky couldn't quite comprehend the dialect.

"Where is Usko?" Lucky asked.

"Coming," was all Yeshe said.

Yeshe silently fetched another teapot and poured Lucky a cup of hot tea, this time made with sour milk. He also handed her a plate of vegetable dumplings, which Lucky tried hesitantly. The little balls were tasty, hot with peppers and garlic. There was a flash and a crack of thunder, and they all turned and looked out through the balcony at the rain as it came pouring down again. Lucky thought it was nice to listen to the storm without being outdoors. After a few minutes, Yeshe began chanting in an impossibly low, resonant voice, absentmindedly thumbing his prayer beads. Lucky got up and went back to her bedroom, perplexed.

It was after dark and her body ached, so she started to stretch in downward dog, then went into triangle pose—then stood up with feet apart, bent forward, arms stretched, palms upward facing the walls, and placed her head far between and beyond her knees –a *lucky pose*. She felt the stretch running up her side and her hip adjusted with a crunching crack. As if in answer, she saw shoes and a pair of jeans approaching through the bedroom door.

An upside down Usko appeared in front of Lucky.

She straightened up, meaning to sit on the bed, but she missed and sat awkwardly on the rough carpet.

Usko laughed, offered Lucky his hand, helped her to her feet and led her to the hall.

"Are you hurt?" he asked.

"No, I was just stretching."

Usko wore a long gray kurta over jeans and carried, slung over one shoulder, a long, wet, black cotton bag. It turned out to hold several bottles of water and a plastic package of plain white dinner rolls. "Best I could do," he said. He handed Lucky a bottle of water.

Lucky could see Kamala and the other monk in the kitchen; a mild aroma of frying onions wafted toward her.

A monk appeared with a steaming pot from the kitchen. He said something and handed the pot to Yeshe, who set it on the dining table and opened it. Instantly, the air was filled with an intense mix of onions, garlic, and cilantro.

Usko smiled. "Do you like momos?"

"Right now," Lucky said, "I could eat fried yak."

"Careful what you ask for," Usko said. "Somebody's probably got some *tsamba* around."

Kamala piled momos on a plate and pressed the plate into Lucky's hand. They were hot but not spicy. Chicken, not yak.

After they ate, Usko told Lucky that they could talk in her bedroom. Usko lit the candle on the bedside table and sat on the chair near the table. Lucky sat on the bed and told him about her plight with Karsan Kaka Ishan, Mohammed, and Sonam. Then she told him about Dr. Vakil.

"He sounds most sincere, Lucky, and I hope he has news for you." Usko said.

"What should we do now?" Lucky asked.

"Let's wait for tomorrow."

"But we need to plan now and we need a backup plan too."

Usko moved toward her and placed his hand comfortingly on her shoulder, as if he were in control. He said nothing. Lucky placed her hand on top of his.

He looked lean and rugged in the candlelight Lucky got up and faced him.

"I am grateful to you Usko…" but he shook his head and pulled her closer. They hugged and he slipped her kameez over her shoulders, running his hands over her. His hands slipped to her back and his mouth found hers and then—she sneezed.

"Oh, God," she said. "I can't. I can't do this with you."

Usko looked at her. He was holding his breath, and then he closed his eyes and let his arms fall to his sides. "I know," he said. "I'll forever make a poor monk."

"It's not that," Lucky said, taking him in her arms and pressing her face to his chest. "I have a boyfriend, too. And…well, yes, you're a monk. And I have been through hell for many hours…..a few days more likely. The last thing in the world I want is to make you break your vows."

Usko gazed into her eyes and took a long breath. Then he turned and left the room.

Lucky came out and watched Usko walk to the balcony. But instead of seeking shelter inside, he sat down and began to meditate in the rain.

CHAPTER 17

In her dreams, Lucky found a nail in the side of her head. It didn't hurt much, and she pulled it out, but she was following her father through her old house in Calcutta and asking if she shouldn't go see a doctor. When her father turned around, he had Richard Nixon's face. An audience began to clap. She bolted up in bed, wondering where she was. Usko was kneeling bedside her on the floor, and she could hear the steady thrum of rain outside. She laid down again, and Usko bent over and kissed her cheek.

"Are you okay?" he asked.

"How long have you been here?" Lucky replied.

"All night." She looked at him quizzically and he added, "Thinking."

"About what?"

"How to get you out of this mess."

"And?"

He smiled and produced a straight razor.

Lucky caught her breath. "What's that? You're not going all Freddie Kruger on me, are you?"

"I'm going to shave your head."

"You're kidding, right?"

"Do I look like the kind of man who kids with a straight razor? We're going to try a different disguise. Didn't you ever want to be a nun?"

197

Lucky rubbed the sleep from her eyes. "I don't think so," she said, but even as she said this she knew that, in a way, it wasn't true. She was twelve when her father, Soli, took her to the priest to perform the *Navjote*—the purification and coming of age ceremony for young Parsis. She had recited her prayers, drunk the sacred *nirang*, and the priest had tied around her waist the sacred cord woven of lamb's wool. It was a kind of dedication that all young Parsis underwent, and yet, when it was finished, she was still hungry for more. But Parsis do not encourage fasting or renunciation of worldly possessions. According to the priest, the soul was already liberated, born into this physical world for a purpose — to practice good and to renounce evil. No special calling required. And yet, even then, Lucky had wondered if there was, indeed, something more. "Maybe," Soli had said, when Lucky asked him about this, "it is just that what people today consider special is just the way things are supposed to be all the time." Soli also wore the *sudra*, the vest denoting the "sacred armor" of the Parsis. There was a single pocket over his heart, which was to remind Soli to collect good thoughts, words, and deeds throughout the day.

So now she was getting her head shaved in the manner of a novice nun. She smiled. Shanti had once said that one didn't choose the path of enlightenment — that the path chose you. Why not shave one's head and put on a maroon robe? Surely, there was a relationship between form and function, and just to walk around like that for a day must have its own lessons and insights, right?

Lucky sat cross-legged while Usko worked carefully with the razor.

When he was done he wrapped his arms around her. "You're shivering," he said.

"I am," she replied. "I think I'm coming down with the flu. I might have a day before I feel…"

"Feel what?"

"Really sick."

And then the words of the cab driver suddenly played back in her head yet again, "Leave tomorrow, Boss says. You may be sick, you need the mushroom. Boss says…get it fast." She had been determined to brush it away and now wondered if Usko had been right in passing it off as an empty threat. She'd had no time to dwell on anything; it was all happening so quickly. *Could she really be infected?*

Usko interrupted her thoughts. "There is an old Buddhist saying that a day is the only thing we have."

"I'm no old Buddhist." She covered Usko's hands with her own, closed her eyes, and tried to breathe in his scent so that she would remember this morning. "I haven't been with a lot of men," she said. "But having my head shaved by you somehow feels quite erotic."

"Perhaps, it is the intersection of pain and pleasure or of having and not having."

"If I held my breath, would you make love to me?"

"I don't think you can hold your breath for that long."

"If I'm going to go to prison, then would it matter?"

Usko kissed her neck.

"It's not me I'm thinking of, though," she said. She pushed him away, stood up, and faced him. "It's you."

"I already told you I'm a lousy monk." He caressed Lucky.

"Is that a chance you want to take?"

"If I'm going to fall, I'd like it to be with you."

Usko had brought two dry, red monk's robes. Lucky laughed when she pulled on hers.

"What's so funny?"

"The day I first saw you, in New York, I wondered what a monk wears under his robe. Now I know."

"Careful what you wish for."

Usko handed Lucky a roll of Indian bills bound with an elastic band. She looked at him for a long moment and thanked him. As she placed it in her pocket, she remembered the cell phone. She checked the charge — low, but still functional — and placed it in her right robe pocket. And she wore Collette's amber necklace, for luck.

They sat at the dining table and Kamala appeared, carrying a tray with potatoes and tea and chapattis. Lucky had the feeling that Kamala knew everything but wasn't going to say anything. They ate in silence.

When they were done, Lucky went to the balcony. The rain had subsided, and the ocean was a listless gray, the sky streaked white and blue. She stretched on her toes in Sun Salute. "It's not far," she said.

"To where?"

"Mohammed, the mattress dealer. We'll have to go back and ask again."

"I don't think that's a good idea."

"Why not? He was taking me to meet Lobsang."

"He was taking you *somewhere*. But probably not to meet Lobsang. Just because somebody said they knew where Lobsang was doesn't make it true. It was probably just a ruse."

"I don't believe that," Lucky said. "I think he knew."

"Why is that?"

"Six degrees of separation. If Lobsang is here—in Dharavi—doing social service, word gets around and people like Mohammed would know."

Usko looked away.

Lucky cocked her head. "Do you know where he is?"

"Not yet, but we're working on it."

"We? What we would that be?"

"Let's visit our headquarters and you'll see."

"Headquarters?"

"You'll see," Usko said. "The nerve center of this operation."

"Operation? We have an operation?"

Usko looked at Lucky. "I told you I was in the military. Did you think I would do this all on my own with no command center? If Coleman wants a war—I am a soldier. Even a monk is a kind of warrior. We just use different weapons."

"I believe Dr. Vakil but not Mohammed," Usko said as they headed out.

"I think you should call him now."

"I will wait till noon, give him time."

They caught a cab to Jacob Circle and doubled back south on Azad Road. Opposite Jhula Park, they turned east, passing through an unmarked entry, and finally climbing a set of antique stairs to the fifth floor of an old building. At the end of a long hall, Usko opened a door to an apartment, and they walked through the hall into a passage and entered the room at the end.

In one corner of the room was a pile of bed sheets; in the other, a desk and a computer. Usko sat down and opened a program, typed in an address. *Skype?* Lucky wondered. A moment later, a face appeared on the screen. *Collette.*

"What's up, squirt?" Usko said.

"Is she there?" Collette shouted.

"Is she ever!" Lucky shouted back. "You little...you are the...when I get my hands..."

"Cool hair!" Collette said. "I'd shave mine, but Mom would kill me. But I did get this gnarly tattoo. Wanna see?"

"Not right now," Usko said. "What's the word on Coleman?"

"If anger was uranium we could power the world."

"No kidding?"

"Really."

"So what does he know?"

"He still thinks Lucky is searching for Lobsang. But he's not sure where she is!"

"Well, that's good."

"Not if you're Lobsang it isn't. They've got people looking for him all over Mumbai right now. I mean, even more people. Even the Mumbai police are in on it now. They're watching everywhere. Hospitals, train stations, you name it. It's gonna get hot."

"Great," Lucky said.

"But he doesn't know about us? Does he know what we have on him?" Usko asked.

"Not yet. But they're working the Bulgarians pretty hard right now, too. Yazma had to shut down for a couple of days. I think he skipped town."

"Damn!" Usko said. "That guy was good."

"Yeah, well, this is turning out to be some cool shit. But I wouldn't want the CIA after me. I might shut down for a while, too. I'm still reading Coleman's e-mails, but if he gets wind of me…"

"Colette, hold it, the CIA *is not* after you," Usko said.

"Yeah, but even if they were, they wouldn't harm a kid, would they?"

"I think not," Usko said. He clicked out and looked at Lucky. "I wouldn't go to see this Mohammed guy either. They'll be watching Lobsang now. My guess is he'll know it."

"So what will he do? Lobsang, I mean. What will he do?"

"What do you think he'll do?"

"If I were him, I'd have run last night. I'd be in Pakistan by now."

Usko shook his head. "Courage is not the absence of fear," he said. "Lobsang won't run."

Lucky nodded. "If we can't bring the mountain to Mohammed, maybe we can get Mohammed to come to us."

"And how do you propose to do that?"

She looked around the apartment. "Whose place is this, anyway?"

"Kamala's. When we join the monastery, I mean take monk's vows, we donate our assets to the order."

"Looks like it could use a mattress. Let's send him to see Mohammed, the mattress maker."

Usko smiled. "But first, can we get him there without being spotted and second, I feel you're chasing the wrong shadow?"

Lucky backed off. "Plan B?" she asked.

"Wait till I hear from a monastery I have contacted in Tibet. Maybe they will know."

"There's one more problem, though. If we can reach Lobsang, where should we meet him?"

"We'll cross that bridge when we come to it."

Lucky called Dr. Vakil. He said he needed more time. He asked where she was now and she said she was staying at Worli with a friend and not at the Taj.

202

"I'll call when I have news, give me a number."

Lucky gave him Usko's cell number.

"Lets take a walk," Usko suggested but Lucky refused.

Kamala brought them lunch and after eating, Lucky grew more restless.

"We can't sit here waiting. Let's check out the leads we do have. I mean, let's check out Mohammed, the mattress maker. Karsan said his contact Gautam would be willing to find out if we paid Rs. 100,000. Bribing is common here. In any case, it is better than just waiting."

Usko breathed heavily and said, "I know it is hard for you. Okay, I will ask Kamala to talk to him. Maybe we can bribe them."

Usko took Kamala aside and briefed him while Lucky looked on. He instructed the monk not to mention Lucky's name and gave him some money to use, if appropriate. With that, Kamala left.

Lucky went to her room and lay down, staring at the ceiling.

A thousand thoughts crossed her mind. Should she return to the US? Could she return to the US? Could they hang Coleman on all the information they had? Could they barter with him and buy her freedom? How long could she just wait and hope?

About an hour had passed when Usko interrupted her reverie.

"Now what?"

Out of breath, he exclaimed, "Dr. Vakil wants you to call him right now."

Lucky gasped and stood up. She called the number, with tears in her eyes. The words surged straight out of her mouth, "What? Where? When?"

"Tomorrow," said Dr. Vakil. "The 'where' is still tricky, though. It's got to be somewhere accessible…" Lucky held the phone away from her ear so that the voice at the other end reached Usko and then she responded.

"And crowded."

"But some place where you can still talk."

"And somewhere there are enough people to protect us…"

"And where we can't be watched from up above." Lucky pointed up.

"A busy intersection?"

"No, they could easily spot us from the air."

"An underpass — one of those pedestrian under crossings?"

"Too easy to block off."

"A movie theater?"

"What's showing?"

Usko looked at Lucky in disbelief and whispered, "Does it matter?"

"He doesn't trust theaters anyway. Too dark. And not enough people," Dr. Vakil said. He sighed. "Too bad this all has to happen tomorrow. I have tickets to see the Indians."

"The Indians?" Lucky asked.

"You know, the Mumbai Indians. Cricket."

"Where do they play?" Lucky asked.

"The Cricket Club."

Lucky looked at Usko and arched her eyebrows.

"Don't they play at night?"

"Not tomorrow they don't. The game is at four." Dr. Vakil paused. "I have good seats, if you want them."

"But what if he won't come?"

"Then I guess you can watch the match. Collect the tickets from my clinic anytime tomorrow." And with that, Dr. Vakil hung up.

Lucky sat down and stared at the phone in her hand. Just like that, everything had changed. Hopefully, for the better…

Usko went to the window and looked out, although it was so grimy that Lucky wondered if he could see anything. He studied the street for a minute, then looked at his watch and said, "Make sure you are not being followed. Like you said, Lobsang is likely to meet you only if you are alone. Now, you should stay indoors till tomorrow. I will get Kamala to pick up the tickets. Where is Dr. Vakil's clinic?"

"But you must come, too," Lucky said.

"Oh, I'm sure Lobsang will have heard about us already, I mean, through Gautam and the Tibetan connection…six degrees, right? I am sure he knows!" Usko smiled wryly.

"One more thing," Lucky said. "Anything I should know about being a nun?"

Usko smiled again. "Keep your head down and your mouth shut. And good night!"

CHAPTER 18

Usko and Kamala set out on a little motorbike to pick up the tickets. When they returned, Lucky took the tickets and held them up and, turning to Usko, said, "You must come, too."

"Now don't be too paranoid. It's only a man with a mushroom after all!" Usko said jokingly as he took a ticket but made no commitment. Lucky wondered what she was missing. He looked in control — completely calm.

Lucky caught a cab alone to the Cricket Club. Her mind was racing. Would it finally turn out to be the day she had been chasing across the continents? The clouds had passed, and as the sun burned through the haze, the heat seemed to rise up from nowhere, a choking, sweating, humid blanket that bled energy from everyone. And it was Friday. Lucky knew that people would quit work early, take long lunches, that on a day like this, the match would be crowded with absent businessmen and truant college students.

The robe she wore was a rich maroon robe of soft wool, but hot — hotter even than the burqa she had worn the day before. The cab driver was an old man with coke-bottle glasses, who seemed only a little older than the cab he drove. There was a hole in the floor, and when Lucky looked down, she could see the road moving slowly underneath her. The seat rocked up and down with every bump.

206

They crawled along slowly, the driver hunched over the steering wheel. Dozens of cars and motorbikes whizzed past, horns blaring. "People are in such a hurry these days," he said.

But Lucky wasn't listening. She was, instead, watching the dark-skinned boy in the white kurta who seemed to be carefully following them on a motorbike, always two cars behind. She tapped the seat to get the driver's attention. "Take me to the Trident Oberoi instead," she said.

She got out and paid the driver. The bike passed and went around the corner. There was nothing to distinguish the rider. He was short and thin, a teenager, perhaps, but in India, there were plenty of short, thin people. His face was swathed in a black and white checkered scarf, but that was not unusual, either. Lots of riders in India wrapped their faces, to shield themselves from insects and from the pollution. She checked her watch. Almost noon. There was plenty of time, and the Cricket Club was only a few blocks away.

She went inside, ignoring the uniformed concierge's icy stare. Surely, she wasn't the first robed Buddhist nun to walk inside the Oberoi. But then again, judging by the awkward glares as she crossed the lobby and walked down to the coffee shop, she was sure they had never seen a nun there before. *This is a minor issue*, she told herself, bowing her head to order a latte and a fat slice of Death by Chocolate pie.

She had just lifted a slice of the white, milk, and dark chocolate layers to her mouth when an incredulous voice called out, "Lucky?"

She looked up. *Viki!* It was her ex-husband. *Please, God, not now.*

He was standing in front of her, flanked by a very tall, beautiful woman wearing an exquisitely embroidered royal blue sari. Behind them, in an equally elegant pink sari, was Aunt Geeta, arms folded, looking like she'd just bitten into a sour mango. Except for a touch of gray on Viki's temples, and the tiniest hint of a paunch pressing against the vest of his Brooks Brothers suit, he hadn't changed a bit.

"Lucky…what on earth…" Viki gasped. Lucky stifled a groan.

"I'm on my way to a costume party."

"But your *hair*?"

Lucky touched her head self-consciously. "Well, I…"

"You don't have *cancer*, do you?" Geeta asked.

Lucky's throat hardened as she recalled the visits to Dr. Dasgupta and the myriad of excuses Geeta sought for Lucky's "infertility." She turned to Viki instead. "This must be your new wife." She smiled at the tall young woman in the blue sari. "You're even more beautiful than I had heard." She extended her hand, but Geeta shot between them and caught it, then shook it half-heartedly. She stood her ground between Lucky and the young woman.

"No cancer," Lucky said. "I've been attending a yoga retreat. No cancer, really. The hair—it was a matter of convenience. And dedication."

Geeta wiped her hand on her sari, and not subtly. "A ritual?"

"Exactly. A ritual."

"I'm Mina," the woman said, reaching around Geeta to offer Lucky her hand. She had a sweet smile. "I've heard about you, too. All good things," she added, hastily. Her eyes darted from Geeta to Viki.

"But Lucky," Viki said, "When did you come to Mumbai? How long are you staying? You staying here at the hotel? You should have called us. We would have booked you a room at our guest house."

Lucky shrugged. "Won't you sit down?"

"We were just leaving," Geeta said.

Lucky raised her eyebrows. "I won't bite. We've had our differences, but that was a long time ago. What's done is done and we can be civil about it. We are in the new age. Come, let me buy you coffees."

Geeta excused herself to go to the toilet instead, while Viki and Mina sat.

Viki shrugged and smiled weakly. "She's old-fashioned."

"I know," Lucky said sardonically.

"You're looking well in spite of your costume, Lucky," Viki said. "How are you?"

"I'm coming down with a cold," Lucky said. But she told Viki about her job in New York, about Sean. "I'm only here for a few days. I've been in Pune. Just a quick refresher course. I only had ten days' vacation time. I leave tomorrow. I would have called if I had had longer—and if I had known that I would be welcome."

"Of course you're welcome," Mina said. "Why wouldn't you be?" Her left hand rested on Viki's right. She wore a diamond of at least ten carats on her ring finger, set in a circle of ice blue topaz.

Synthetic, Lucky thought. *I wonder if she knows?*

Viki talked about Singh Enterprises. They were, as always, losing money. To hear the Singhs talk, Lucky thought, no business had ever lost more money for so long and managed to stay afloat. They had been bleeding money since the days of the maharajas, and every change in government only made things worse. Taxes were high, expenses kept rising, and competition was merciless. In the meantime, the Singhs soldiered bravely on. Shivram had died of a heart attack at his desk. A half-dozen equally-toady parasites had sprung from the ranks to take his place. Lucky had been right about him. Viki sighed.

While Viki was talking, Lucky looked over at Mina. She was drumming the fingers of her right hand. *She wants a cigarette*, Lucky thought. Mina's hair was long and black, luxurious and shiny. Her face was powdered and rouged, her eyes lined with kohl. There was something tired about her, even though she couldn't be more than twenty-three. *She must spend hours in front of a mirror every day*, Lucky thought.

She pictured Mina sitting in a dressing room with a servant or two. She would be smoking. The window would be open, with a fan on, to keep the smell out of the house. Geeta would know, of course, as she knew everything, but she would *pretend* not to know, all the while dropping not-so-subtle hints about the dangers of second-hand smoke and the potential harm to fetuses. There would be a party that night, or the next, and endless, meaningless conversations. Mina looked like a minor movie star, and Lucky wondered how she and Viki had met. Already, her face was showing the tension lines that would become the wrinkles of middle age. *This could have been my life*, Lucky thought. *No regrets here.*

They finished their coffee and pastries long before Geeta returned. When she did, she was putting a cell phone away and concocting some story about a problem at home between a cook and a repairman. On this pretext, Viki got up to go — but not before paying for the coffees.

"Here is my business card — it has my mobile number if you need anything," he said, as Geeta walked on ahead and Mina held on to his arm.

When they were gone, Lucky wandered in and around the hotel and stopped in one of the boutiques inside. She still had a few hundred rupees, but it was not enough to buy a dress and a wig at any of the boutiques. She wondered if she should have asked Viki — he would have given her the money — but she didn't want to involve them in her troubles. They were, after all, divorced. Still, it was odd seeing him. Then, with a shiver, she realized that, no doubt, Coleman could be following Viki. She wondered about the boy on the motorcycle — could that have been a coincidence?

She considered her options. If the boy on the motorcycle was Coleman's spy, then they already knew where she was, and the best thing she could do was to get away. If the boy was not Coleman's spy, then Coleman might still know where Lucky was. But he also might not, and he certainly wouldn't know what she was up to. So, it might be possible to bluff — but she didn't want to take any chances. She had to be alone, without Coleman's men around. *Am I being paranoid, or I am not being paranoid enough?* She debated with herself then called Kamala from a courtesy phone.

"I need you to round up all the nuns you can and send them in cabs to the Trident Oberoi Hotel," she said.

"Right now?" he asked. "I think maybe I can only find six or seven."

"That'll have to do," Lucky said. "Tell them to come in separate taxis. I need them here in an hour. Have each one bring a salwar kameez and a scarf with them and to make their way to the women's bathroom."

She had another coffee. If Coleman knew, his people would have to be in the hotel. They would have checked out the guests by now. But would they watch a place like the Oberoi for Lobsang? They hadn't considered this option. Wouldn't it be ironic if he had been living there all along? Lucky headed to the bathroom to wait for the nuns, trying to look casual. They came sooner than she had expected, crowding the bathroom and each holding a bag as they filed into the stalls. She looked them over, decided on which one most resembled her in size and form, and tapped the woman on the shoulder before heading into the adjacent stall. The nun slid her bag underneath the divider, and Lucky changed quickly and then came out and dropped her robe into the bag along with the other nuns' robes. She left the hotel with them through the shopping center entrance, all now wearing a salwar kameez and a scarf covering their heads. The nun who looked like Lucky, and still wore a robe, took another entrance and caught a cab.

Outside, a growing stream of fans made their way to the stadium. Lucky looked neither left nor right. She blended in, following the crowd down the street and around the corner.

www.astarcalledlucky.com

CHAPTER 19

Soli, Lucky's father, had been a both a player and a fan of cricket. Lucky hated cricket, but she still had fond memories of playing it with her father in the street, along with the rest of the neighborhood children. Well, mostly fond memories, with the exception of one high, bouncing ball that had chipped a front tooth. It was an incident she hadn't thought about in years, but it came back to her as she stood at the top of the steps and looked out over the pitch. Fortunately, she had been only eight when she broke the tooth, and the permanent tooth that replaced the broken one was fine, but Lucky had never lost her anxiety around playing sports. Alec had played too and had not been too bad in the field, although he never mastered the art of fast-bowling. Like most Americans, he tried to throw overhand with a bent elbow, baseball-style. Still, he was great with the bat. What Lucky had liked about those days was sitting on the benches with Susan and Hutoxi, back in the days when Lucky imitated Susan's every nuance. She had not been to a cricket game since she had left India, although she had run across matches at Marine Park, in Brooklyn.

As Lucky came back to herself, she thought she saw Shanti in the crowd. Shanti. Wouldn't that be a hoot? And what would Shanti tell Lucky right now? Funny, Lucky thought, I know what she'd say.

"That's your problem, Lucky — you never see things from the other side."

212

But what side?

And then it came to her. She understood Coleman's ambition, her own quest for reformation and redemption, and even Lobsang's responsibility. But she hadn't once thought about the mushroom — if it existed — what would it want? What was its relation to all this? For that matter, to people in general? In the eyes of a mushroom, were people even worth saving?

Lucky bought a bag of curry-flavored popcorn and found her seat. The afternoon was hot and humid, hotter than New York, but not so hot as Mumbai could be in, say, May. The rains of the day before had cooled things a bit and cleaned the air, although it was still sticky. The crowd filed in, slowly filling the benches to near-capacity. The teams warmed up, the game began, and Lucky stood for the Indian national anthem. She looked around anxiously for Usko, but he was not there. Surely, they were on the way. It would take time for Kamala to find Mohammed, to pass along his message, but he would get the job done.

The opposing Rajasthan Royals batted first. The game was slow. Lucky, who wouldn't have watched much anyway, grew nervous. The fans tried to get a "wave" going around the stadium, which brought to her mind Yankee Stadium — what would Mumbai fans think of a Jets or Giants game, or the Yankees or Mets, for that matter, on a night when sixty or seventy thousand fanatics stood up and cheered as the wave raced around the stadium?

She checked her watch. Four thirty. Not a good sign, she thought. She hoped Usko would come and hadn't gotten himself into something awful. She brushed away the thought. He'd be all right. Any man who could stand up under the fire of combat had to be all right. She felt a stone in the pit of her stomach and realized that the game going on down in the field hadn't registered at all in her mind. Her eyes kept scanning the stadium, trying to pick out faces from the crowd. At home, it would be night. Sean might be sleeping. She wondered where he and Maria were.

A man in a neat gray business suit came down the aisle and then edged along the bench toward Lucky. She made room for him to pass but instead he sat down beside her. He was nearing sixty, with short white hair and a trim white beard. He wore little round glasses and had a newspaper tucked under his arm. He unfolded it and began to read. Lucky cleared her throat. "Excuse me," she said, "but I have a friend who is coming. He's late for the match, but this is his seat."

The man ruffled the pages and said nothing. He was looking at a picture in the paper, and then at Lucky.

"Excuse me…" Lucky said.

The man looked at Lucky and smiled. "Allow me to introduce myself. My name is Lobsang Telok. I believe you wanted a word with me."

LOBSANG! Lucky almost tumbled off the bleacher. In shock, she looked left and right. Nothing around her had heralded the coming of Lobsang. There was no phalanx of special forces lugging machine guns. No intimidating men in dark suits and sunglasses. She was sitting on a bench in a cricket match surrounded by ten or twenty thousand fairly ordinary people cheering for their team. "What is this, a joke?" she finally stammered out.

"Since yesterday, I've been looking for a safe place to meet you," Lobsang said. "When the monks contacted me this morning, I was delighted."

"You were looking to meet me?"

"You've become a bit of a celebrity, really."

"A celebrity?"

Lobsang opened his paper and pointed to an article on the second page.

MIRACLE AT THE MASJID. Lucky leaned closer and read. According to the article, a woman had gone to the mosque to beg for money for surgery for her child. She needed an impossible amount of money, but having no options, had promised Allah to dedicate her child to Him if only He would save the boy's life. Before she left for the mosque, her husband had berated her. "It would take a miracle to find that kind of money," he said. The woman, according to the reporter, had replied, "If you're going to ask for miracles, you have to act like you expect them to happen," and as she sat in the heat outside of the mosque, a stranger — another beggar — had given her expensive jewelry, enough to pay for the surgery. When the woman told her story to the Imam, he declared the event a miracle. The police were skeptical. They thought the woman had stolen the jewels or that some domestic servant somewhere had purloined the gems and then had a change of heart. They were waiting for a householder to come forward and claim the stones. In the meantime, the woman was pressing forward with the surgery.

"How did you know it was me?"

"The stone went back to Karsan Kaka for sale and he tried to contact you. But a monk called Usko took the call and confirmed that the necklace was yours. Usko told me that it was you who gave her the jewelry. Simple really."

"What, Usko contacted you… I mean….."

"Why yes, he made contact with me so we could meet. Why is that strange?"

"I guess you can just never tell," Lucky said.

"Why did he hide this from me?" she thought. "So he made it look like Dr. Vakil was arranging the meeting? Just like him to underplay his role," and then she thought how Karsan's necklace that she had gifted had helped her. She remembered Shanti saying that just like no bad deed went unpunished, no good deed went unrewarded. It was just a matter of perception, though. The how and when and where of the reward or punishment — that was the thing that nobody knew. Sometimes, a person didn't even know if they had done good or bad. The best anyone could say was, *What were my intentions?*

She looked at Lobsang. He looked scholarly, grandfatherly. He looked like he could well be bouncing a toddler on his knee. Similar to how she had envisioned him, maybe the round head, or the glasses? She wondered if he limped. But all she could say was, "You don't look at all like I imagined."

Lobsang looked at Lucky and smiled. "Neither do you, my dear. But you're not the only one who can wear a disguise." Lobsang ran his finger through the collar of his shirt and loosened his necktie. "These things are *very* uncomfortable. Who on earth invented them? And why? I'd much rather wear a kurta." He sighed.

"They come from Croatia," Lucky said.

"Beg pardon?"

"Neckties. They come from Croatia, sort of, via France. It was back during the Thirty Years' War. Some Croat mercenaries were honored in Paris and Louis the Fourteenth thought the Croatian version of the tie was cute so he adapted the style. He called them *cravats*, from *Hrvati*, the French word for Croatian. But they were altered over time. The modern necktie, like yours, was designed by Jesse Langsdorf in New York. In 1920. Since you asked."

"I didn't know," Lobsang said.

"I am a fountain of useless trivia," Lucky said. "Never mind me."

"If they came from Croatia," Lobsang said, "they were probably derived from the traditional Arab *keffiyeh*, don't you think?"

"Perhaps," Lucky said. "Things go around and come around."

"Did you know the word Balkan comes from the Turkish words for *blood* and *honey*? Bal and kan. "

"I did not know that," Lucky said.

"Alas," Lobsang sighed, "I share your love for trivial details. I never quite understood why. But even when the British ran things, people in this part of the world never took to neckties. Perhaps it was the heat, do you think?"

"Perhaps," Lucky said. "That, and they're not very practical."

"Frank Lloyd Wright once said that 'Form follows function.' He despised ties."

Lucky offered Lobsang some popcorn, which he politely declined.

"One good turn deserves another, don't you agree? You saved the life of a child. The least I could do was to save yours."

"Save mine? I came to try to save yours."

"Did you think my life is in danger, and why?"

"Well," she hesitated, "I suppose I did."

"Who put that idea into your head?"

"What idea?"

216

"Of saving my life?"

"I did. Sort of. I mean, there are some people who are looking for you. They say you have this thing…" Lucky looked at Lobsang. He was holding his right hand out, palm up. On it lay a small, dried, mushroom. "Yes, I grant people are looking for this but I wonder if anyone will kill for it. How can one know another's intent. My guess is Coleman has just used you to run his errand." Lobsang looked down at his palm.

She thought for a moment. So could all this only be her imagination? Maybe she was not being followed…maybe……"I don't believe the stories I've heard about this," Lucky spoke confusedly, picking up the small bit of the mushroom.

"Then you wouldn't be afraid to take a nibble, would you?"

Lucky took the mushroom and looked it over. There was nothing remarkable about it. "It's not psychedelic, is it?" she asked.

Lobsang laughed. "No, I'm a doctor. And a Buddhist doctor at that. I wouldn't hurt a fly."

"The Spanish scoured the New World for the Fountain of Youth," Lucky said.

"But this won't keep you young."

"But it slows aging, right?"

"Yes. It does that. But only as an unintended side effect. I've been presuming that its main effect is to somehow boost the immune system."

"But you don't know for sure."

"I don't know," Lobsang said, "and I don't need to know. All I know is that this was given to me as a sacred trust. It is my family's heritage."

"So why are you offering it to me?"

"Because you did not ask for it and because you do not believe." He took the mushroom and dropped it carelessly into his coat pocket. Around them, the fans roared as one of the Indian bowlers took a wicket.

"Faith is a funny thing," Lobsang continued. "People look all around for miracles so that they have a reason to believe. And they choose the most unreasonable things on which to base their belief. Paintings that weep. Images that appear on tortillas. Ghost stories. And yet, the everyday wonders, the earth revolves around the sun at precisely the right distance to support life, there is water, and gravity to keep the planet in balance, and perfect order in the universe, and yet, people miss the very reasonable proof of the Giver of life, but still, they demand the unreasonable."

"I didn't think Buddhists believed in God," Lucky said.

"Oh, no," Lobsang replied. "Buddha himself said the question was irrelevant if asked for the wrong reason. But the proof of something larger than ourselves is everywhere. And we are part of that proof. We have only to see it and appreciate it."

"Then why the mushroom thing?" Lucky asked.

"Oh, that. It's part of the proof, as well." Lobsang stared out across the stadium.

"You mean it actually works?" Lucky asked.

"Of course it does. Just like penicillin, only better."

Lucky looked Lobsang over. "Then why not share it with the world?"

"What good would it do?"

"What good?" Lucky was incredulous. "Think of all the lives it would save!"

"Lives? What lives?"

"Why, everybody! Imagine a world with no more sickness. No more death."

"The mushroom only slows the process, my dear. There is no cure. And besides, who really wants to live forever on this planet?" Lucky stared at him, opening her mouth to continue arguing. Lobsang glanced at her as he handed a piece of the mushroom back to her. Lucky turned it over and over in her palm, breaking off a bit of the cap. "I don't believe it," she said, still in a daze.

Lobsang shrugged. "What you believe or do not believe does not change the facts."

She touched the mushroom in her pocket, and then, on impulse, took it out, broke it, and swallowed the little pieces on her hand.

218

Lobsang arched his eyebrows. "Are you afraid of dying, young lady?"

"No," Lucky said. "I just don't believe you."

"And if you came to believe me, what would you do then?"

"I don't know."

"I guess you'll find out, won't you?"

"I came to tell you that I think some people in the West are going to great lengths to get this mushroom; they want to know the source and everything about it."

"You mean Clevis Coleman?"

"Yes, but you didn't hear that from me."

"I've known about Clevis for some time. And the Chinese. And the British. And the Israelis. And the Russians. And the Finns."

"The Finns?" Lucky looked at Lobsang, her eyes wide.

"And probably half a dozen other nations would like to be 'the one.'"

"The one *what*?"

Lobsang looked at Lucky with the saddest eyes she had ever seen. "The ones with the immunity."

"I don't believe you," Lucky said.

"You said that already. And, as I said, your belief or disbelief won't change the facts. The mushroom boosts immunity and; therefore, prolongs life."

"Then why not share it with the world?"

"Two things," Lobsang said. "First, what makes you think this is the only life or that prolonging it unnaturally is a good idea? All men die. Not all will truly live even while they are alive. The wheel turns and we return and try again. This is the order of things. The seasons, the years, the clouds, the rain, and the ocean all tell us this. And, second, what makes you think having this power will save lives anyway?"

"Well," Lucky said, "scientists could…"

"Yes yes yes, they could synthesize the ingredients and make the elixir of immortality — your Fountain of Youth. But they're not ready for that."

"Of course they're ready."

"No," Lobsang said, standing. "They're not. They wouldn't share. Your nations are busy making and stockpiling biological weapons. They don't want the elixir of life. They want immunity so they can take life and survive the war."

There was a loud smack and the crowd rose as a majestic "six" floated into the bleachers, the ball landing only a few rows behind Lucky.

"Quite a shot, that," Lobsang said.

"Do you play?"

"What, cricket? No. That's a British game, and Indian. As a boy, I flew kites and played chess."

"What about in England?"

"I didn't have time to play games in college. I wanted to be a doctor, remember?" He turned to go but Lucky caught his arm.

"Do you really believe Coleman is running a weapons lab?" "Back to that again. What better place to hide?"

Lucky stirred in her seat.

"I know a little about biology and chemistry," Lobsang said. "I am a doctor. I have been to medical school. What is the one place in all the world where you could bring all of this necessary equipment together and not raise eyebrows?"

"I don't believe it," Lucky said.

"That's the third time you've said that."

"I know. And you're going to say that belief or disbelief won't change the facts."

"Funny," Lobsang said. "People will depend on gravity day in and day out, on photosynthesis, on the oxygen/carbon dioxide cycle, on rain, on the power of the sun, but when confronted with something natural, they will claim it cannot work. And in turn, when confronted with logical evidence, they would rather believe that statues weep, and that ghosts cure paralysis, and that politicians are good and pure and have our best interests at heart."

He pulled away.

"Where are you going?" Lucky asked.

"I'm going to confront the people who are looking for me," Lobsang said. "They'll find me anyway, eventually. It might as well be on my terms. Usko must have told you that. We met thanks to you, my dear, and we have found our common purpose."

"Wait!" Lucky said. She followed him into the aisle, toward the exit. "You know, I came to find you to free myself, but something in me has changed. I now want to see you safe, even if it means jail for me. Why did you agree to see me?"

"Because I want to confront them, and, as I said and say again, only on my terms."

"But this could be the end."

"There you go," Lobsang said, "talking about death in this life as if it mattered, as if it were the only life that counted."

"But if you want to stop them," Lucky said, "I think I know a better way."

Lobsang turned. "Just how do you propose to do that?" he asked, "if you don't mind my asking."

"I have an idea," Lucky said, pulling her cell phone out of her pocket. She dialed the number she knew by heart.

They left the stadium, cutting back to the hotel the way that Lucky had gone earlier in the day. From the lobby she dialed the number. "I'd like to speak to Clevis Coleman," she said. "Tell him it is Lucky Boyce and that I have something he's looking for."

CHAPTER 20

The meeting was fixed for the Taj Hotel, in Mumbai for the next day at 6 p.m. Coleman was to come with two associates and nobody else. The American Consul General and his legal team were to be there, as well. Nobody else.

They were back in the apartment, the headquarters —Usko, Karsan Kaka, Kamala, and Lobsang. They sat on the dhurries on the floor, drinking tea, Lucky close by Usko's side. "I can't thank you enough," she said to him.

Usko shook his head. "It's fate," he said. "We have no choice but to follow our destiny."

"But isn't the whole thing about choice?" she replied. "I mean, aren't we supposed to learn as we go — to gain enlightenment, so to speak."

"It's our fate," Usko said, "and it's inevitable. It's only a matter of when, not if."

"Even Coleman?" Lobsang asked.

Usko hesitated. "Even Coleman, in his own time. Is that a leading question? I mean, after all, you're the doctor. I'm just a poor follower."

"A poor follower? Are you sure? I think there's something that you're not telling us."

All eyes were on Usko.

222

Lobsang continued. "If you were a poor follower, you would have come to rescue the young woman. If you were not a follower at all, you would have come to see Coleman stopped. Don't you think I could have done that a long time ago? Don't you think, had I wanted, that I could have walked into one of his traps and been executed? I could have even reversed the trap, to his detriment. Do you think that I fear death?" Lobsang shook his head. "No, there is much more to you, my young monk, than meets the eye."

"I don't…I mean…what…" Usko went to set his mug down and spilled it on the floor. "I don't know what you mean."

"I believe there are some files you would like to discuss? Something that has come up unexpectedly in the past few days?"

Usko paled. Then he stood up and crossed the room, took up a black backpack from the corner, took out an envelope, and returned to the circle of friends. He held the envelope up head-high and looked from face to face. "Who read this?" He stared long at Kamala, but they all shook their heads.

Lucky was watching Lobsang intently. His expression never changed, but she had the sense that he was suppressing a smile.

Usko sat down and opened the envelope.

"Here it is, in black and white," he said. He grinned. "I don't know how you know, and it doesn't matter. What we were after for years, Collette and Yazma found in hours. E-mails, bank accounts, details on a lab in Latvia that's funded with black money to research disease. I thought, for a while, that Coleman just wanted to be president of the WHO. God knows what his real aims are. If I wanted, I could make a case that Coleman wanted to blackmail the world. Who knows? Maybe that's his way of ruling the world. He introduces diseases and holds everybody hostage for the cure. Maybe he wants to sell immortality, or maybe he just wants to make certain it stays a secret."

He looked at Lucky. "That's how the mushroom fits into the puzzle. The pieces are now in place. Coleman gets a sample of the ice mushroom, synthesizes it in his lab in Latvia, perhaps even chemically increases its potency, then mass produces it!

Abracadabra! He holds the golden key that humanity quests after — in his own little hands. He fulfills his deepest desires and he is the King of the World! And Lucky, the little courier," Usko continued, winking at her, "he has blackmailed or silenced you with Bloodhound! Quite easily done!"

Then turning to Lobsang, Usko's tone was somber now, "You know, meeting him may be the end of you."

Lobsang chuckled. "Maybe it's my time to die," he said. "And what is death, anyway? Does Coleman really think he can kill me or preserve anyone else's life? His perception is skewed. We neither create nor destroy life. We try to help, but in reality, we only shift from one location to another. It is all an illusion. Besides, the source of this mushroom has dried up. Blame the environment, blame climate change, blame pollution. Coleman knows this, hence the urgency to get his hands on the remaining few. Maybe he can research its properties and reproduce it and maybe he cannot. This is the only chance the world has to benefit from this *ice mushroom*. Like I said before, I meet Coleman now on my terms." With a hint of a smile, Lobsang added, "So I don't think he would have any more interest in the life of a poor doctor."

Usko began to pass around documents, as Lucky looked on in astonishment. "This came from Yazma?" she asked.

"It did," Usko replied. "The software goes both ways. He's mirroring you, but we injected the same software into his system. We have it all. And I can't wait to see his face when he finds out."

Abruptly, Lobsang got up and walked to the window. Kamala stood, and then Lucky stood up to. "What's the matter?" she asked.

"If only it were so simple not to want not to die," he replied. He turned from the window, knelt, and bent his head in concentration. "It's not even me I'm worried about. I should leave—for your safety."

Usko came to stand by Lucky. "The documents are out there now. If something happens to us, our friends will spill the beans. If

224

not," he shrugged, "the problem goes away. Coleman might hurt me, but I'll hurt him worse." Turning to Lucky, Usko said, "But you — I think we had better send you home. Lobsang and I can do the meeting."

Lucky shook her head and grinned. "I wouldn't miss this for the world," she said. "I've come this far. And besides, I owe him."

Usko looked at Lobsang, then Kamala, then Lucky. "Maybe I can e-mail him a teaser. Maybe that will hold him up just enough…"

The meeting, Lucky later thought, was as nondescript as brushing your teeth in the morning. As Lobsang had said, there was no killing, for it was just the opposite of what Lucky expected. Again, her imagination had led her away! No black-suited men. No Navy SEALs. No nothing. Just a quiet room where Lobsang handed over a box of mushrooms.

Coleman's team was matter-of-fact. There were only three of them, but no sign of Coleman. The man in charge looked around at each of them and then took the box with the mushroom. The bulky aides put the box in a briefcase and handed it to the chief, who chained it to his wrist like a jeweler. And then they left. No hello. No goodbye. No nothing.

When he was gone, Lucky turned to Usko and asked, "Why didn't Coleman come? What did you send him?"

"I sent him a copy of his mirror software. Now he knows we have the mirror software, but this won't bother him. What he doesn't know is we have wrecked his firewalls and used the same mirror to mirror him. Well, that's enough for today."

"And now?"

Usko looked her. "And now we go back to Washington to finish the job."

www.astarcalledlucky.com

EPILOGUE

A bank account at Lloyds. Another with Banca del Gottardo in Switzerland. Another in Vanuatu. A chop account in Hong Kong. A bank in Nauru holding 5,000 shares of Captain Cook stock obtained as part of a finance deal for export licenses for cryogenic equipment for a hospital in Kenya. A shell company incorporated in Aruba with real-estate investments from Austria to Zimbabwe — most made under fictitious names and financed by similarly fictitious companies, with transactions filtered through more banks in more countries with more corporations. An 8,000-square-foot riverfront property in Leesburg and a 25th floor flat in Manhattan. A $25,000 Persian rug in his living room and another in his bedroom. He had a Tibetan mastiff in the back yard that cost almost that much. He had a wife who was devoted to him and a mistress who was addicted to him. He was about to be sworn in as the new Secretary of Health and Human Services, and his name was being tossed out in articles coast-to-coast as the next sure-thing for the president of the World Health Organization.

Clevis Coleman, Coleman thought, as he adjusted his tie in the mirror, *you are one smart son-of-a-bitch*.

Take his suit: Tussar silk, gathered in the wild in India and dyed with natural indigo to a deep, perfect navy blue, hand-tailored by a seventh-generation Hong Kong tailor, and adorned with gold-plated

226

buttons. Only a week ago, he had ordered the suit — from Punjab House — and here it was, delivered last night to Washington on a Navy transport flight. He smiled at the mirror. His hair was perfectly trimmed, just a touch of gray showing on the temples at just the right place. A distinguished look. Military, yet not ignorant, not violent. He had even traded in his trademark black plastic-framed glasses for a new pair of "memory metal" nickel/titanium alloy glasses, with self-tinting glass. The only flaw was the little red line on his chin. He had cut himself shaving. A little styptic had stopped the bleeding. His makeup men would cover it up before his acceptance speech.

He was just putting on his cufflinks when he noticed the right sleeve of his coat. The buttons on it were *not* gold-plated. They were plain old silver-colored, probably tin. He looked at the buttons on his left sleeve. They were gold. He looked at the buttons on the front. They were all gold. How had this happened? He looked on the inside of his coat — the place where all good tailors sew on extra buttons — just in case. Sure enough, there was an extra gold-plated button. But the sleeves had three. Three on each side. No matter. Coleman smiled. There were tailors in Washington, too. Not as good as Hong Kong, maybe, and pricier, but they could fix a couple of buttons. He would call one. He would have his suit repaired. They could cut one button off the left and add it with the extra button on the right. His sleeve would be perfect, his suit would be perfect, his speech would be perfect, and his day was going to be… "perfect," he said out loud.

He kissed his wife goodbye at the door and went outside to his limo. The driver was waiting. But not his regular driver — that other one, the tall annoying one. What was his name? Irving? "Good morning, Irving," Coleman said. "Where's Carl?"

"Evan, sir. And Carl came down with the flu, sir. He called in this morning. Where to?"

"White House, Evan. We're meeting the President this morning."

They took the Leesburg Pike onto McLean and then caught 267 down to Arlington. Traffic was slow and they inched along. "I should have asked for an escort," Coleman said.

Evan ignored him, turning off 267 and cutting down 120 like they were going to Reagan International. "Where are you going, Evan?"

"Sorry, sir. There's a blockage up ahead. We'll take the circle around."

"Just don't make me late, boy. I've got a speech to give."

"Oh, I wouldn't worry about that, sir."

Worry? Coleman thought. *What, me worry?* "Just get me there on time."

"Just relax," Evan said. "Would you like the morning paper, sir?" He extended the *Post* back to Coleman without waiting for a response, and Coleman took it, more out of annoyance than anything else. He folded it on his lap and stared out of the window. His phone rang. It was the tailor. He was waiting with scissors and thread to make the repair. Two minutes, at most. Coleman smiled.

And then he looked down at the headline: BLACK OPS OR HOAX? *What the hell?* he thought. *What kind of shit is this? Wait till I get a hold of Steuver.* He bent closer to read. The article was claiming that someone in the government housed a top-secret and highly illegal lab, funded with black-op money and housed in a former Soviet military base in Latvia. They had informants. Photos. Agents in the field. Lists of equipment. Disbelieving, Coleman checked the top of the page again — no, it really was the *Washington Post* — and the date — no, it really was today. *How the hell did they get all this?* He wondered. They even had air and water and ground samples! Someone had told them everything!

Reading on, Coleman saw that the top brass of the HHS could be interrogated. He bristled at the suggestion. What could they prove? Nothing. He'd counter that it was a smear campaign. A sham. He'd find a way to spin the publicity into something good — something the voting public would remember.

"I'll have this guy's ass," Coleman said out loud. He lit a cigarette.

The car slowed and Coleman looked up, annoyed. They had turned down a side street. They were nowhere near the capital. They hadn't even crossed the Potomac yet. "What the hell?" Coleman asked. They had driven into the middle of a crowd.

A STAR CALLED LUCKY

There must have been a hundred men and women. They were at the Marine Corps War Memorial — the famous statue of Ira Hayes and his friends mounting the flag on top of Iwo Jima. Evan shut off the car.

"What's this?" Coleman demanded.

Evan turned around and smiled. "End of the line, sir," he said.

"We'll see about that," Coleman said, reaching for his cell. But even as he did, the doors opened. On one side stood Usko Tahti. On the other, Lucky Boyce.

"Hello, Clevis," Lucky said. "Or should I call you Mr. Coleman now?"

Colcman rose from the car, as if pulled by unseen strings. Usko came around and stood beside Lucky. The crowd began to gather in a tight circle around them.

Coleman looked at Usko. "What the hell is this about?"

Usko's face was tight, expressionless. "I said I was going to get you one day."

Coleman stared at him, then at Lucky. Finally, comprehension dawned.

"You haven't got anything," Coleman said. "Oh, that story in the press that nobody in their right mind will believe? Ha! Nothing! And if you hang me, I'll hang her! If anybody hangs, it'll be her. She'll be tried for treason. Something about some stolen government software, I believe. And some money I slipped into a bank account in your name, Lucky, in the Cayman Islands." He turned to Lucky. "I cover my tracks, I still have you. But the lab, how did you…the last we heard…"

"All it took was a program and a few hackers."

"A few hackers? I had that lab locked down with top-secret government technology! There's no way you did this by yourselves. Someone must have talked. Who talked?"

"No one talked," said Lucky calmly. "I found some new friends in Bulgaria. You're not the only one who can hack an account, Clevis."

Usko handed Coleman a sheet of paper. Without taking his eyes off Lucky, Coleman asked, "What is this?"

229

"A resignation speech," Usko said. "And an apology. What better place to give it than here, in a place where you can honor real heroes? Go on," he said, gesturing toward the statue. "There's a podium. The press is waiting. Resign now, and there's a good chance you might avoid felony charges."

Coleman stared at that. His eyes narrowed. "Felony charges? So you really are playing hardball, huh? You've chosen a strange way to go about it. Why not just remove me completely? Apparently, it would have been easy for you, especially with these new friends of yours."

"Did you ever get around to reading that Sun Tsu?" Lucky asked. "I mean, all of it?"

Coleman stared at her again. "I assume you're about to tell me what Sun Tzu has to do with this?"

"*The consummate leader cultivates moral law.* I would have taken you out all the way. It was Lobsang who said that maybe this was your chance to turn your life around. He believes in cultivating morality — especially in the immoral. Reformation is what I work for, but this wasn't my idea. It was Lobsang's."

Coleman's face reddened. "That blasted doctor? *He's* in on this too? I knew I should have killed him!"

"Killing is wrong," Usko said. "You may not think so, but you haven't held a dying man in your arms. I have."

"You got what you said you wanted," Lucky said. "And you have the resources to use it right if you want. I mean, the whole of the pharmaceutical industry, if you like. Or you can resign and do what you think is best. You should use this power for the benefit of society. The choice is yours. You can go on your way as you were and make your speech, or you can think about making the lies you said become true."

"I see," said Coleman. "You want me to be reformed, eh? Well, it seems to me that if I'm going to go down anyway, I might as well see one of you down for it, too. I haven't seen a shred of evidence suggesting I'm involved with any of this story, and it won't erase any of the things you've done — or that people will think you've done. My career's already ruined, so I see no reason why I should let you intimidate me into reading this." He twitched the paper in his hand derisively.

Usko and Lucky exchanged a glance. Finally, Lucky sighed. "We wanted to give you a chance at true reform, Clevis. But I suppose it's not to be. The Bulgarians have two programs that come from you. Whatever money you shipped into the trust account we transferred to the PETA charity accounts. And whatever you have done through computers and e-mails will come back. The circle is complete. And those accounts, although held in trust, can be traced. The Administration is going to be very interested in that. As will the IRS. If you want to run for public office, you'll never vet. You know that now."

Coleman stood stock-still, his mouth gaping. For once, he seemed to have no response ready.

"So," Usko continued, "You go up there and read this speech. Or we can leak the story. Newspapers, TV, you name it. You know what we know, and we know what we know, and you're going to leave Lucky alone. And as long as you do that, we might just leave out some of the details. But if I ever hear a word from her — or about her — that implicates you, well, let's just say there are two ways to end that game."

Coleman shook his head. "This can't be happening. I feel like…like…I feel like someone has poisoned my experiment."

"Come again?" Lucky said.

Coleman shook his head, refusing to answer. He turned to Evan.

"Ah ahhhh," said Evan. "I ain't your man no more, Boss. You goin' home, you takin' a cab."

Coleman stared at him, seemingly on the verge of responding, then suddenly turned and bolted through the crowd. A roar went up.

Lucky winced. "He hates PETA activists."

"They don't think much of him, either," Usko replied.

The crowd parted and Maria appeared, walking with Sean. He ran to Lucky and threw his arms around her legs. She had been home for a week, but he still cried whenever she left his sight. She knelt beside him and held him tight. She took his hand and walked through the park.

"Wouldn't it be nice," Usko said, "if someday there was no more war, or hate, or killing? If people shared, and they took care of one another, instead of gouging each others' eyes out to grab all they could?"

"It would," Lucky said, "but I don't think it will ever happen."

"Only one way to find out — make it happen." Usko was looking at the statue of the Marines and the podium where Coleman was not going to deliver his speech. "A shame to waste all that television coverage," he said.

Lucky looked up and held out a hand. "Are you coming back when you're done?"

"For a little while," he said. "For a little while." And then he turned and crossed the park to where the microphones waited.

"Perception, position, possession," Lucky said.

"What's that?" Maria replied. "I can't hear you."

"The three illusions. Goodbye, Usko Tahti. May you find the peace you seek."

And with that, she took Sean's hand and led him out of the park and into the city. But what she was thinking about was that better world, the one John Lennon sang about in "Imagine." Why not? Lucky thought. Wasn't it our obligation to leave the world in better shape than how we found it? And she stopped for a minute and closed her eyes, breathed in deep, thinking how nice it was to breathe through healthy lungs. It would be nighttime in India — but people went out late there. They would be walking in parks, too, whole families, breathing the same air, and dreaming the same dreams. And today, or tomorrow, or the next day, there would be a delivery to a little pharmaceutical firm in Delhi. A startup, but staffed with some good scientists. Scientists who hadn't yet abandoned their morals and sense of social obligation. There wasn't much in the box. A note, and the fragment of a mushroom. And what they did with it then, well, maybe that would depend on the mushroom's view of things.

Her cell phone beeped. Lucky smiled as she read and reread the text aloud to Sean,

"Let's make it happen."

xxxxxxxxxxxx

GLOSSARY

PETA—People for the Ethical Treatment of Animals

GWC—Global Wellness Council

H&HS—Health and Human Services

FDA—Federal Drug Administration

NRA—Natural Rights of Animals

The legendary ice mushroom is similar to the mushroom now known as *Yarsagumba* but is significantly morepotent. In the ancient Indian epic Ramayana, the ice mushroom is depicted as the powerful herb *Sanjivani* found in the Himalayan mountains. Here Hanuman, the monkey god, lifts the Dronagiri Mountain and carries it to Lakshmana who was severely wounded in battle and Lakshmana is then healed by the mushroom. The herb is nearly extinct today.

BAPSY JAIN is a best-selling mystery author, wife, educator and entrepreneur noted for the international success of her debut novel, *Lucky Everyday*, published by Penguin in 2009. *A Star Called Lucky* is the sequel novel to her bestselling debut and returns the reader to the exotic world of the spirited Lucky, whose new adventures are sure to captivate audiences around the world. Originally from Calcutta, India, Bapsy attended the Sydenham College of Commerce and Economics in Mumbai. After graduating, she left for the UK to qualify as a Member of the Institute of Chartered Accountant England and Wales. She divides her time between Mumbai and Singapore.

Visit her books' web sites:

<u>www.*astarcalledlucky.com*</u>

<u>*http://luckyeveryday.net/*</u>